Atlantis the Stones

Atlantis Series - Book One

Douglas Hoover

DWHOO Studios

Free Gift

Learn the story of the stone lost onboard the Titanic with my free novella - *Atlantis: the Titanic Stone* - by visiting www.dwhoover.com

Dedication

This book, this series and this career is dedicated to my wife, Cheryl, who not only tolerated my obsessiveness, but sparked and fueled my efforts. Without her fervent inspiration and encouragement this may have never come to pass.

Prelude

Daniel Knocks didn't find a treasure. What he did find was a small item that would change the world . . . at the cost of thousands of innocent lives.

Now, pay attention. We're going to share something with you. You need to accept and understand this information. It is not something you can dismiss as a good story. After you've heard it, you will still have trouble believing it. After you've been exposed to it, you will question everything you've ever known. The lives of everyone you know depends upon your accepting the truth and throwing away what you've come to believe as fact. Open your mind and you will see the world the way it really is.

1

The Find

"**G**ood morning, Leecie. It's 6:37 a.m., and day nineteen in Puerto Rico has begun. It's a beautiful morning, with the temperature hovering around twenty-two degrees Celsius, or seventy-two back home."

Daniel Knocks was alone. To the casual observer, it might look as if his mind, if it hadn't already left the building, was at the least, at the door and ready to make a run for it. But this wasn't the case. Although Daniel was alone, in the baggy breast pocket of his tan button-down shirt was his iPhone, which he was using to make a voice recording for his best friend, Aleecia Donnelly.

"We've moved again. We're now in the southwestern part of the island, and I think I'm going to enjoy my upcoming assignments here much more than the ones I've had so far. The three of us have checked into the Copamarina Beach Resort in Guánica. It's a luxury resort and, compared to some of the other places we've stayed, is like a palace. I know I'm not on vacation, although it kind of feels like I am. I mean, I'm on a tropical beach flying my drone around, I'm staying in a nice place, and the government is footing the bill. I can't believe I'm getting paid for this!"

Dan's three-person team was part of a larger inspection and study program requested by the Puerto Rican government. The team's had been sent to evaluate the island's conditions and the problems facing its people. Although most of the project members and resources went to cities and infrastructure, Dan's small team was tasked with gathering data and images of the assigned shoreline to try to identify existing and potential problems that might further weaken necessary public services.

Although the contract had been awarded to the U.S. Army Corps of Engineers, it was determined that the project would be outsourced, and the Environment, Great Lakes, and Energy department (EGLE), should consider it because they understand the importance of a healthy shoreline and the significance it plays in agriculture, ecosystems, and protecting infrastructures near the coasts. Alex Mayer, an EGLE department manager, had requested the assignment, viewing it as an opportunity to get away from his desk in Lansing, Michigan for six weeks.

Alex was Dan's cousin, so he'd naturally thought of Dan, who had captured some amazing video of the Great Lakes shoreline with his drone and, accidentally, helped locate a ship that had been missing for 150 years. Alex had seen the images and video clips Dan had posted on social media, shared his cousin's work with his bosses, and convinced them that using a drone was the least expensive way to evaluate the shoreline. When the project was approved, Alex offered Dan the assignment as an independent service provider.

Now on the beach, Dan paused for a few seconds and lifted his face—with slightly oversized nose and square chin, which Aleecia refers to as his hero's chin because of its small dimple—toward the sea and the sunrise. The warm morning sun on his skin, which was already sporting a deep tan, and the breeze blowing through his short brown hair felt good, even if the feeling was somewhat tainted.

"To tell you the truth, Leecie, I'm feeling a little shame. Part of me thinks I have no right to enjoy myself. I'm seeing a lot of misery. The earthquakes and hurricanes have spared no part of the country, and it's the same down here as it is farther north. A lot of people don't have some of the basics. The infrastructure has been severely weakened, and they're having trouble fixing things because the damage has devastated the economy. A lot of people don't have reliable electricity or even clean water. The whole country is suffering. I only hope what I'm doing here can inspire the committee to send aid and help these people."

Dan stopped speaking for a few minutes, and he continued to walk in silence as he reflected on some of the things he had witnessed. It was something he'd done a lot during his assignments, but being twenty-six and in good shape also meant he could handle the long, lonely walks.

"Leecie, I know it's not your thing, but I admit that I wish you were here. You always know what to say to lift me when I'm down, and I'm finding myself needing that. I keep finding myself emotionally torn. Recording video while walking a tropical beach and seeing new sights is a recipe for a vacation, but the significance of what I'm recording really contaminates the situation. It's like finding a strangers hair in your favorite cookie dough."

Dan's shoulders slumped and he paused to catch the breeze and feel the warm sun trying to regain his encouragement. After a few minutes he straightened and continued.

"I got to visit the Ruinas del Faro de Guánica, or the Guánica lighthouse ruins. I know you're probably not familiar, but it was significant in 1898 during the Spanish-American War. You know me, Leecie, so you know I got a thrill standing at another piece of history. I can't believe my hobby got me here and I'll be a little bummed when I have to go back to doing landscaping when I get home."

Dan enjoyed traveling, but beyond his home state of Michigan and the Great Lakes region, he'd never ventured too far. He'd often thought about broadening his horizons and seeing more of the historical places he'd heard about, so when this opportunity arose, he wrongly believed the experience would be good for him.

"I can't wait for you to see this video. I'm inspecting part of the Bosque Estatal Guánica, or the Guánica State Forest, this morning and I'll probably be here for the next day or two. I'm told it's a popular tourist attraction, but so far, I've only seen one couple. It's a subtropical dry forest and it's beautiful, Leecie. I've recognized a few of the plants because you have the same ones in your windows, but there's a lot I've never seen. I'll try to snag a few smaller ones and bring them home for you. Here, I'll go up so you can see better."

When he adjusted the controls, the drone soared higher in the air. The images were sent directly to the video file on the onboard memory card and were also broadcast to a video monitor that was a part of the drone's control unit.

"I'll try to edit the video and my ever-so-exciting commentary this evening and send you the file tonight, but a good Internet connection is hard to find, so I don't know if I can get it through. Even if I can't, we'll have fun putting it all together when I come home in a few more weeks."

Dan had the drone hover for a few minutes as he circled the camera.

"Okay, back to work," he said as he brought the drone back down so he could continue his inspection of the craggy shoreline.

It was only a short time later that something caught Dan's attention. In one stretch of the shoreline, the ground rose above the seawater a few feet. Although it appeared as if it were a small hill, the waves didn't crash against this part of the shore—the waves disappeared. Dan recognized this was one of the erosion patterns he had been told to look for. The waves would wash out the soil and create a cavern, but it was only a matter of time before the cavern collapsed and formed a sinkhole. Some could jeopardize acres of land and swallow everything above it.

"Hang on, Leecie," he said. "I may have just found another anomaly."

Dan brought the drone back, lowered to a few feet above the waves and positioned it at the front of the deformity. Just as he had suspected, there was an opening in the ground at the waterline. He carefully lowered the drone even closer to the water to try to get a better look inside the opening. It was too dark for him to see much, but the incoming waves reflected bright sunrays under the ledge and illuminated soil hidden from the light for hundreds if not thousands of years.

With the camera's tight zoom engaged, Dan could get a good first-person view on his monitor and an inconsistency caught his attention. He adjusted the camera controls until he could better see the unconformity, which brought a grin to his face.

"Well, what is this?" he said. "Hey, Leecie, check that out, it looks like the end of a small wooden box."

Dan had always been a closeted treasure hunter and it was one of the reasons he had bought the drone in the first place. People would often bury something important and, with the drone, he could get a bird's-eye view of the land and look for anomalies that might suggest man-made depressions or mounds. The downside was those anomalies could represent anything from riches to a mass grave. This box wasn't a huge treasure, as it could only be a few inches wide, but nevertheless, a treasure is a treasure, regardless of its size, and the image triggered the same rush Dan had experienced when he unexpectedly found a sunken Civil War–era schooner carrying a cargo of corn that was lost in 1878 in the clear water between Beaver and Fox islands in Lake Michigan.

Dan maneuvered the drone as he attempted to get a better look at what he had found this day, but he was hesitant to take the drone any lower. The waves had fallen into a semi-steady pattern and were similarly sized, but every now and then a bigger wave came in and disrupted the rhythm and he was concerned he might lose the drone in the surf.

He sighed, knowing his curiosity wouldn't let him walk away without at least trying to find out more about this little treasure and if he wanted a better look, Dan knew, he would have to get wet.

"Sorry, Leecie, I need to stop recording for a little while so I can check this out."

He brought the drone back to him and landed it on a small patch of dry grass. After sitting down in the sand and placing the controls next to the drone, he removed his sandals so they wouldn't squish when he walked. He also removed the back pouch he wore to carry necessities, took out his water bottle for a quick drink, and then stowed it with his other gear. When he pulled his iPhone from his breast pocket, he touched the screen to pause the voice recording. He removed his iWatch and placed it, along with the phone, on his sandals.

Dan walked around and found a safe place to step down from the land before walking into the Caribbean Sea. The water was cool but not cold and felt good on his feet. As he side-stepped to the opening, the shore sloped downward and gradually became knee-deep. He wasn't happy with the idea of getting drenched with seawater, but he could easily justify it if he found something good. If he found junk, which could be the case, he could say he fell in or, better yet, say he had to jump in to rescue a puppy. The thought made Dan waggle his eyebrows. Saving a puppy was noble.

He squatted down and peered inside. The cave, if you could call it that, was only about five feet long, about four feet wide by three feet high. This freaked Dan out a little, as it brought to his mind an earthly grave or pit just large enough to slide a coffin into or perhaps the back of a sandcastle hearse that some goth sculptor had fashioned. The cave bottom was at a slight incline, with the back a foot or two higher than the opening. While the water covered some of the entrance, it ended halfway up the cave walls.

The dim light eliminated smaller visual details, but Dan could make out the undeniable shape of a box inside. Getting to it, however, made him think twice, as it would require him to drop to his chest to squirm his way inside. Weighing the risk versus the potential reward and knowing that he would probably be disappointed with what he found, Dan determined trying was not worth the risk.

He was just about to walk away when a wave came in and did several things. First, it soaked his shorts clean through eliminating any reservations about getting wet. Second, it reflected enough sunlight under the ledge that he got a better look at the box. Third, it washed all the way to the back of the void and removed more sand, which exposed more of the box and only increased his curiosity. Finally, it gave him somewhat of a plan.

With the side of the box now a little more exposed, Dan could see that this treasure—whatever it was—was clearly not something he could walk away from. There was a small handle on the side of the box, which said a lot; it said that the box was special. The handle was probably made of brass, and Dan knew there was no reason to put a handle on a box of this size except as a decorative element, and no one would bother to put a decorative handle on a box like this unless it was important to them. There was no doubt, now—he was going in.

He took off his shirt and flung it in the direction of his gear, took two steps back, and proceeded to lie down. He paused when the cool water found his chest, but the chill soon faded, and he planted his hands in the sand below him and allowed his buoyancy to support his weight. The back of the cavern was free of water, but the bigger waves flooded it almost to the cave roof. One of those waves would be Dan's ride.

While he waited for the next swelling wave, he looked up and considered the ceiling. It too was made of sand and this stirred the uncomfortable thought of the roof caving in on him. His life could be at risk, he realized. Though he weighed up whether he really wanted to go inside, Dan was still young enough that the Monty Python's Black Knight attitude still whispered, "I am invincible!" in his ear.

He therefore decided that if he made a quick reach for it, he could be in and out of the cave before anything major happened. That major thing being his death by drowning.

"You're a looney," he said softly, adding the English accent and inflection à la Gram Chapman's Arthur, King of the Britons. When he got back to his knees and looked around again and saw that he was alone, he made the hasty decision to try and retrieve the box.

He looked back over his shoulder at the sea and noticed a bigger wave coming in. Determined to ride the wave in, grab the box, and then allow the water washing out to pull him back to safety, he once again laid down with his hands on the sand beneath him. Dan resisted the push of the next few waves and felt the water drop beneath him as it retreated toward the base of the incoming larger wave. After taking a deep breath, he let the wave carry him into the opening. But the wave pushed him harder than he'd expected it would, and he soon found himself going into the cave headfirst faster than he would have liked. It felt almost immediately as if the cavern were swallowing him, and he threw up his hands out in front to keep from hitting his head. Soon, he felt the back of the cavern and he quickly started feeling for the shape of the box. When his fingers sank into the wall, he sensed a rising swell of fear. It, too, was made of sand and could collapse at any second and seal his fate.

Knowing it would only make his situation worse, Dan fought the urge to fight against the force of the water to get out. Instead, he moved his hand up in front of his head in preparation for pushing off as soon as the water began to recede, when he felt the side of the box. It was right in front of him and he could close his fingers around the edges. The box was too large to fit in the palm of his hand, but Dan believed he could get a good enough grip with his fingertips that he could hang on and pull the box free. When the wave receded and started to pull him back out, he tightened his grip. When his body slid backward toward the sea, he tugged on the box, but his fingers began to slip. He reached forward with his other hand, and held onto the box as tightly as he could. The receding water pulled as it left, but Dan's grip was true. A few seconds later, however, he realized his plan was flawed.

He found himself lying in the cave, face down in the wet sand, with every finger clinging to the small box. When he raised his head and spat sand from his mouth, Dan looked around the cave as best he could. For a second, the image of Wile E. Coyote flashed in his mind and he realized his Acme "box retrieval plan" had failed in an unexpected way.

"Way. To. Go. Dumb. Ass," he pronounced slowly and sarcastically.

He knew he would have to squirm back out, like a fish on land trying to find water again. Doing so would increase the risk of a cave-in, but lying on the edge of the Caribbean Sea in a sand cave up to his knees already had him feeling like a complete fool, so why not take it to the next level?

Dan pulled on the box with little effect, so he began to dig around it with his fingers. His feet and legs were still in the water, and although the waves were gently pushing and pulling in a rhythm that caused him no real fear, Dan knew the next big wave was coming and he needed to be out of there by then. So, he dug, he pulled, and he wiggled the box until he felt a sense of relief as the sand released its grip and freed his prize. He held it in his hands to get a better look, but it didn't take long for the 'survival guys' working in the back of his mind to throw up a red flag. He felt a breeze on his calves because the water was gone. That could only mean one thing, the next big wave was here.

He took a deep breath of the musty air, positioned his left hand over his head, and with his right hand he clutched the box to his chest. The incoming water shoved him roughly, forcing him headfirst into the cave's back wall. After the push of water pinned him there for a few long seconds, it began hauling him out as if someone were yanking on his feet. His natural reaction was to slow himself, but when he grabbed at the sand on his left side, he accidentally pushed himself to the right. He crashed into the opposite right-side wall and the elbow at his side dug into the sand and twisted him sideways. His head and shoulder collided with the opposite wall on the left, and the soft sand began to give way.

Clumps of sand began dropping from the ceiling and crashing onto Dan's head. When panic set in, he released his grip on the box and, with all the strength and speed he could gather, started pushing his way out of the cave. The outgoing wave helped, as did his pushing and shoving with both hands and wiggling to stay on top of any falling sand. Dan came clear of the cave just as the soft walls failed and the sand from up top collapsed into the empty space below.

He got to his knees and sucked in huge gulps of air while he stared at the sand in front of him. The opening was no more, and he recognized he had just cheated death.

"You stupid fool!" he shouted at himself, as he dipped his hands in the water and washed the sand from his face. The adrenaline that was coursing through his body caused him to smack his forehead with the palm of his hand. "All for a stupid box?"

He remained on his knees for a few moments to gather himself, and when he did stand up, he realized how much sticky wet sand was covering him. He furiously threw himself into the waves, so the seawater could rinse him off. It was when he started to climb out of the water that he spotted the inspiration for his foolishness. When he'd released his grip on the box, the retreating water must have pulled it out of the cavern to where it now lurched back and forth in the waves just down the shoreline. Dan walked over, snatched the box from the water, and waded ashore.

After he reached his gear, he sat down heavily on the sand. When he set the box down next to him, he purposely ignored it as he tried to calm himself. He sat looking out at the water, rocking back and forth and simply staring at nothing as he sipped from his water bottle, waiting for the adrenaline to subside and the moment to pass.

After a full two minutes, he set down his water bottle, and wiped the sand off his feet with his bare hands and replaced his sandals. He retrieved his shirt, snapped it in the breeze, and used it as a towel before putting it back on. He shoved his phone back into his top pocket and fastened the watch around his wrist. When he had calmed to the point that he could think again, he picked up the box and began to examine it. It was approximately eight inches long and six inches wide and was just a little taller because of a semi-rounded top. It reminded Dan of a miniature pirate treasure chest, and he couldn't help but grin.

"You better be worth the risk I just took," he said to the box as if scolding a puppy, his words harsh but his tone without any real resolve.

The box was indeed something rare. Shaped slats of wood provided the length and sides and were fitted tightly together all of the way around. Metal, which Dan mistook for brass, had been fashioned into two bands and placed an inch from each end to hold the wooden slats in place. Two hinges and a latch held the box securely closed. The sides were in fact embellished with two small metal handles, which served no purpose except to make the box pretty. And it was pretty. Dan used the bottom of his shirt to wipe sand from the baseplate of the decorative handles, where he could see fancy scrollwork. He turned the box over in his hands and gave it a gentle shake to see if he could detect the sound of anything inside. He felt, more than heard, that there was indeed something contained inside the box.

He decided he wanted to share this moment with Aleecia, so he pulled out his phone and started a new video recording.

"Look what we got, Leecie. I had to do something foolish to get it, but I'll tell you about that later," he said while adjusting the phone so he could get a good shot of the box. He turned the box to examine the small latch that held it closed which comprised of two parts. The top part, on the lid, contained a small flat bolt with a knob handle. The bottom part, on the body of the box, contained a band where the bolt slid into place. A crude example of a modern slide bolt turned to work vertically.

Dan tried to slide the bolt up, but it refused to budge. Sand and time presumably held it tightly, but as he started to work on removing the sand, he stopped as a thought occurred to him; the metal was clean. There was no rust, no corrosion, no tarnish of any significant amount and the only metal Dan knew of with similar properties was gold. He now proceeded to look more carefully at what he was working with. It wasn't gold. No, it was something else. Something he didn't recognize.

"Hang on, Leecie. I have to put this down for a second," he said, placing the phone in his lap. After he had worked the sand out of the latch, he worked the small bolt back and forth. It gave a little more each time, and soon the bolt slid up to release the hold. Slowly and carefully, he applied pressure and pulled back on the lid, holding the box away from his face as if he were afraid something would jump out at him. There was a small creak when the hinges on the back rotated and daylight illuminated the contents. Dan identified a small container inside the box as a vase, and he again picked up his phone.

"Check this out, Leecie! It looks like some sort of pottery. What color would you call that? A blackish orange, maybe."

The vase fit securely in the wooden box, which had been lined with a thick layer, or layers, of leather. The leather not only provided cushion for the piece of pottery, it also protected the inside of the box from the damaging effects of moisture. The leather had worked so well that the interior of the box was completely dry. The vase was clearly something special. Ornate design with images resembling a bird with spread wings, spiral patterns, a serpent with a head that appeared human, and stars and the moon graced the surface.

"Hey, Leecie, I think we found something important. This reminds me of that Aztec art we saw at the Dennos Museum."

The neck of the vase was slightly tapered at the top, which provided just enough room for Dan to slide his fingers around its upper portion. He was afraid he might drop something, so he shoved the phone back in his breast pocket and continued to speak.

"Sorry, Leecie. You're going to get just audio for a little while. I need to be careful, and I need both hands."

With the little pressure caused by Dan's gentle tugging, the vase came free. It was symmetrical in shape and had a circumference of approximately four inches and was fitted with a lid. When Dan turned it over, he felt something inside the vase move.

"Yeah, buddy!" he said in response to the jewelry or old coins that he imagined were trapped inside.

Dan sat the box down in a safe out-of-the-way place under the branches of a little mangrove tree and took a few steps to get more sunlight, so he could investigate the pottery. The vase was sealed with a lid that matched the vase and fit so precisely it was hard to find the seam connecting the two pieces. Curiosity wouldn't allow Dan to *not* try the lid, which fit tightly but came free with a resolute pull. When he looked inside, he noticed a reddish tint that seemed to line the inside oft he vase.

"There's a large red stone inside, Leecie. Maybe a big ruby."

When he turned to allow the sunlight into the vase, the red tint was even more obvious in the direct light.

"Nope, not a ruby," he said. "It's not completely red, it looks kind of gray. But that's not right, either. It looks both clear and black at the same time, if that's possible. The center looks as if it's filled with thin clouds of solidified red smoke, which is what's giving it the reddish tint. It looks smooth, round, and about the size of a golf ball."

He moved back to the young mangrove tree and sat the vase lid down beside the box, then turned so the sun would shine into his hands. When Dan carefully tipped the vase, the stone rolled toward the open end and dropped into the center of his palm. His mind had the time to register that he'd expected it would weigh more.

Then came the light.

An overpowering bright white light appeared in front of Dan. He wasn't sure whether he saw this light with his eyes, or only with his mind, but the light removed everything else from his sight. When the integration began his body was forced to surrender control of all senses. The vase slipped from his fingers as his hands convulsed, snapping open before quickly closing around the stone again and catching it before it could fall. When his knees folded, he was pitched forward into the sand. His bladder let loose, pain engulfed his head and his mouth opened in a silent scream. When his empty hand reached up in defense, it snatched a tuft of his hair from his scalp.

Then everything went black.

2

The Bound

I t was from years of practice that Zack Lewis was able to open the bedroom door and enter with barely a sound. He stood still for a few seconds before uttering a name.

"Koltz."

There was no sound or movement in the room which was lit only by the dim early morning sunlight that streamed through the single set of half-closed curtains. Zack removed a partially chewed toothpick from the corner of his mouth and sighed. The sour, sweet scent of sweat and cologne filled the bedroom and coalesced as the musky odor of his boss Everett Koltz.

"Mr. Koltz?" Zack said. Louder this time with his Australian accent more prominent.

"What is it?" Everett Koltz sat up in his bed so quickly it caused Zack to jump.

"Sorry to have to wake you, especially since we were up so late, but I think you'd better come downstairs."

"Why? What's going on?" Koltz asked while getting out of bed with the kind of deficient coordination caused by being half asleep.

"We just received . . ." Zack stopped in mid sentence, his posture hardened, and he slipped a hand inside his sports coat. "You should probably put that thing away, mate."

It took Koltz a few seconds to rouse his mind, but when things did start to click, he realized he had unconsciously pulled a handgun from under his pillow and was now holding it firmly in his right hand and pointing it at the floor.

Koltz looked at the weapon for a few seconds, surprised a little to see it there, then shrugged and slid the gun back under the pillow.

"Sorry, Zack," he said, but both men knew that he wasn't. That sort of thing was just part of the life they were forced to live. Koltz turned on the bedside light, then pulled on his robe over his undershorts.

It would be clear to any observer that the two men were on opposite slopes of the physical fitness scale. Zack, though nearing the scale's apex, still worked at improving his strength and stamina. He stood at 6'1", weighed slightly over a lean, solid, and dexterous 200 pounds, and was thirty-one years old. His thick brown hair, cut short, displayed no signs of gray. His brown eyes were clear and alert, and his clean-shaven, sharp-featured face was tanned and featured a chin that sported a battle memento on the left side in the form of a thin scar.

Everett Koltz's apex had passed years ago, and every year thereafter had only watched his midsection continue to spread. He was now forty-five years old, weighed 185 pounds, and possessed features that hinted at his Dutch heritage. His shadow of a beard was spotted with gray that, because he had fallen into the habit of shaving every other day, was evident most of the time. Though he kept his grayish hair cut at a reasonably short length, it was thinning and only half as dense as it used to be.

Koltz lit a cigarette and took a long pull, before retrieving a bottle of bourbon from the nightstand next to his bed.

"You still take bourbon in your coffee?" he asked as he poured himself a shot.

"No." Zack said, relaxing his posture.

Koltz downed the whiskey, placed his wire-rimmed glasses over his blue-gray eyes, and glanced at his clock. It was 7:08 a.m., Chicago time. He ran his fingers through his hair and looked back at Zack, who was dressed as if it was already midday.

"Don't you ever sleep?" Koltz asked with a slight grin. The two had been up late performing monthly security assessments, and Koltz knew Zack could only have gotten a few hours of sleep. But it was a question he didn't expect to have answered and was only asked in an attempt at camaraderie. After all, it was important to have at least a basic friendship with a man like Zack, and Koltz knew it didn't matter whether it was 3:00p.m. or 3:00a.m., Zack was always dressed and ready to perform the job. Attired in belted black slacks and a button-down gray shirt, that Koltz found ironic, and a black sport coat worn unbuttoned, Zack's appearance represented a continuous state of readiness, and that demanded respect or, at least, fear. Koltz remembered the days when he could do the same thing, but age and the extra pounds he was carrying had hemorrhaged his energy. When it became obvious Zack didn't appreciate the humor, Koltz stopped his grinning.

"What's so important that you needed to invade my room?"

A little put off by his bosses nonchalant attitude, Zack couldn't prevent himself from feeling smug, knowing the news he was about to deliver would ruin his bosses day.

"We've gotten a new blip."

"What? When?" Koltz asked, a rush of adrenaline responsible for the sharpness in his tone.

"A short time ago, I should think."

Koltz paused and then looked hard at the man who had awakened him.

Although Zack was not intimidated by Everett Koltz's physical attributes, his position in the hierarchy outranked Zack's own, so it was still a struggle to meet Koltz's gaze.

"What do you mean you 'should think,' and why the hell was it a short time ago, Zack?"

"It's not exactly clear yet. It was Talbert's watch, and it appears he wasn't paying much attention."

"Why the hell not?" Koltz asked, giving the belt of his robe a yank as he tied it shut.

"We don't know yet. John's gone ahead and is holding the watch room until we get the situation sorted out."

"Oh great, send John," Koltz said as he crushed out his cigarette. "That guy couldn't manage a competent sentence, let alone an important situation. Good thinking, Zack."

Koltz crossed the room and tramped to the door. Zack purposely hesitated long enough to make Koltz break his stride, before stepping aside to let his boss pass. It was his way of telling Koltz he didn't appreciate the attitude.

As the pair headed down the hall, Zack reached into his sport jacket's inside pocket, deposited the old toothpick, and brought out a box of new ones. He pulled a fresh pick from the box and whispered into a tiny microphone clamped to the collar of his shirt as he slid the new toothpick into his mouth. "Boss is on his way."

Koltz, hearing Zack murmur, addressed him over his shoulder as they walked. "Why are you still using that outdated technology?"

"It amuses me," Zack said.

Koltz nodded. "It used to amuse me too. I'd once thought it was so CIA, but then I came to realize the truth."

"And what truth would that be?"

"That the CIA is only a small fish in a gigantic tank. Most people think the Agency operates in secret, but how can they do that when everybody knows they exist?"

"Good question," Zack said plainly.

In Zack and Koltz's world, there were only three groups of people who knew they existed. Group one included the people who worked within the same organization and who were, fittingly and unflattering, known as the Bound. Called so because they were bound to their duties by threats, not only to themselves, but by threats made against the people they loved the most. Group two included those people who they competed with and fought against, and whom they typically referred to as that crew of whatever phrase was most insulting and relevant at the time, usually shortened to the Crew. And group three were those who learned of the other two groups' existence shortly before they died. Group three, the dead, was by far the largest group.

"Is the boss angry?" asked a voice from the tiny speaker jammed in Zack's left ear.

"Worse," Zack said softly, "he's completely pissed off."

Koltz heard this, grinned, drew up his body to its full height, and quickened his pace. He felt in charge now; it was, in fact, the only time he felt alive.

Zack followed his boss down the main stairway of the building that had been home to their group long before either of them arrived there, and was referred to as The Den. To the outside world, the building was one of mystery and caused immense trepidation. First built in 1868 as a sanatorium for the mentally insane, the building was constructed on the outer edge of Chicago at a comfortable distance from the good, normal city folk. In 1908, a few escaped patients provided testimony as to just how easily they could pose a problem to everyone else, and the hospital was relocated to an increased safer distance from the city.

When the building became vacant, it was transformed into an orphanage and operated for several years until it suffered a tragedy. The milk given to the children contained too much formaldehyde, and ninety percent of the orphans housed there died. It was therefore determined that the children shouldn't be housed together in large numbers. The orphanage was shut down, and the children were spread among smaller homes.

The building's reputation had hampered business, sales, and rentals, and had sat empty, on and off, for years. In 1957, the building was scheduled for destruction when a predecessor of Everett Koltz purchased it and set up shop inside. The building's reputation for causing death as well as its rumored hauntings, were a part of its draw. Although people were encouraged to stay away, a false front office had been constructed for the curious.

The fake office front, complete with a receptionist, had only been necessary on a few occasions when someone had wandered in to inquire about the "consulting firm." Each visit would end with a pleasant *Thanks for visiting*, as people like Zack and John stood by ready to remove the interloper if necessary. The rest of the building was converted into living spaces, recreation rooms, meeting rooms, and work areas. Because too many questions were asked at hospitals, the medical area was revamped with up-to-date equipment. The basement, which was complete with interrogation rooms, a shooting range, and a dōjō, constituted the domain of people like Zack.

When Koltz reached the closed double doors at the end of the long hall, he slammed them open, which stirred the cigarette smoke inside into miniature white curly cue tornadoes. Koltz loathed the watch room. The air inside was musty with the aroma of a pungent mix of human odor, cigarettes, sweat, perfume, cologne, and the well-used carpet that had absorbed and now hid a great number of spills of unknown origin. The watch room had once been a patient ward, so the windows didn't open and the reinforced glass was covered in a dull beige film. The once-white walls were now yellowed by their continuous exposure to tar and nicotine, and the room was sparsely furnished with a few metal desks, a matching stained sofa and chair, and a small refrigerator and trashcan, both of which seemed to be perpetually full. But this room wasn't intended to be comfortable, this was a room intended to ensure that people paid attention.

"Why wasn't I notified sooner?" Koltz shouted. "I'm to be notified as soon as there's a change, *any* change. It's been a standing order from the start. What's so hard about that?" He proceeded to eye the seven people in the room, who mostly looked as if they had just gotten out of bed and unquestionably wanted to be anywhere else.

The only exception was John Bowen, Zack's partner. John stood at parade rest near the door with his hands clasped loosely behind his back, he was making sure no one left without permission. John was dressed in the same fashion as Zack, their attire the unofficial uniform. His dark blond hair was cut high and tight, and his German features and no-nonsense expression made clear that he was not to be trifled with. He and Zack had worked together for more than two years, which in their line of work, was considered a long time. Zack may have been physically imposing, but it was John who provided the strength. At 5'7", John was six inches shorter than Zack, but he outweighed his partner by at least twenty pounds of pure muscle.

Among the others in the room, which consisted of a range of eclectic backgrounds was Mary Reyes, a fit twenty something, who was sitting at a desk still wearing her silky nightclothes and anxiously rubbing her hands. Her collar-length black hair was still flat from her pillow, but her big brown eyes were alert, and her youthful skin showed worry lines of stress.

Also present was a middle-aged, round-in-the-middle man, by the name of Jim Talbert, who was dressed in blue sweatpants and a T-shirt that read *F. . . this.* He was shorter than most of the others in the room, and looked beyond tired: worn out, like a tire that had seen too much road. His shaved head gleamed with beads of sweat that dotted his crown and forehead.

When nobody answered his question, Koltz asked again. "What in the hell's going on, and why wasn't I informed sooner?"

"Sorry, chief," Talbert said after some obvious hesitation. "I had to use the can. I was only gone for a few minutes."

"So, you did what, left the station unattended? What were you thinking? You should've waited until you were relieved."

"Relax, chief," Talbert said. "I just stepped out for a few minutes. No harm done."

"Oh, how would you know?" Koltz asked hotly. "When did we get the blip?"

As Talbert shifted his eyes away from his boss, most of the other pairs of eyes shifted away from Talbert.

"A few minutes ago, I guess. I checked for messages when I came back."

"A few minutes is long enough to make a difference. Did you track the blip?"

"Of course I did."

"And?"

Jim hesitated again. "I saw a hand . . ."

"A hand?"

"Yeah, it was just an ordinary human hand."

"Just an ordinary human hand? And you don't think that's worth much? What else?"

"I don't know, sand and shrubs, like a beach somewhere."

"Somewhere?" Koltz shook his head in disgust, then took a breath to calm himself and raked his thinning hair. "Don't you people realize we are being watched?" he asked everyone in the room. "We are always being watched, and our lives, hell, our lives and the lives of those we care about, hang on our actions."

"We all know that, chief," Jim said, his mouth running off without his brain, "but nothing has happened in a long time, and sitting here holding that stupid stone all through the night is ridiculous."

There was a sudden uneasy shifting by most of the onlookers.

"Maybe it is, Jim, but those are our orders."

"Listen, chief, I think . . ."

"It doesn't matter what you think, I'm the one held responsible for what happens around here, and I'm not going to let your foul ups get me or anyone else killed. Zack, is the duplicator charged?" Koltz asked, without taking his eyes off Jim Talbert.

"Full and ready."

"Good. You and John take Jim downstairs and make me a copy of his recent memories. I want to know what he was doing while he was supposed to be on watch."

Talbert's eyes flew open. "Oh, come on, Koltz! I already told you where I was. You don't need to do that!"

"Oh, I think I do. Things are getting lax around here, and this is no game we're playing. You all seem to need reminding of that," Koltz said, glaring around the room.

When no one looked back, most seemingly interested in a stain stretched across the carpet, Koltz flipped his head in Talbert's direction.

With Zack and John stepping in, the resistance from Jim Talbert never got a chance to flourish. Talbert backed off and tried to put a desk between himself and the two men now quickly approaching, but John pulled a small cylinder from his inside breast pocket and pointed it at Talbert. Were it not for the word *Eradicator* being etched on the side, it could have easily been mistaken for a large gold ink pen. John pushed the button on the side and the weapon instantly harnessed the energy within the electromagnetic spectrum and a small yellow ball of light formed at the tip and jumped to Jim's midsection. The force hit him like a solid punch, knocking the air from his lungs and sending him to the floor in a heap. John then replaced the eradicator in his pocket.

"Probe his memory," Koltz said while looking down on Jim. "Get everything you can."

"Yes, sir." Zack replied as John bent down, scooped Talbert off the floor and tossed him over his shoulder. Zack closed the door behind them as they left.

There were a few seconds of silence before Mary Reyes spoke. Still sitting at the desk, she asked, "Do you want to see?"

Koltz took in a deep breath and let it out in a long release. "I think I'd better," he said, holding his hand out flat.

Mary nodded to a woman sitting to her left and the woman reached out, and happily placed a small clear, but blackish transparent stone that featured thin wavy red lines into his hand.

When Koltz closed his fist around the grape size stone, his eyes began to rapidly twitch beneath the lids. After a few seconds, he opened his eyes and nodded at Mary.

"Okay, wake everybody else up and get them to work. I want this solved as soon as humanly possible."

The others in the room headed for the door, suddenly anxious to get on with the task.

"You think they know?" Mary asked.

"If you're talking about the Reti, I guess if they don't know already they will soon enough. If you're talking about the Crew, I'd bet on it. And you know every time the Crew wins, some of us end up dead."

Mary nodded in understanding and then, looking around the room, her eyes went wide with the realization she was the last one there, and she closed her fists tight.

Koltz noticed the action and smiled at her weakly. "Sorry, but you know we need somebody in contact at all times," he said as he grabbed Mary by the wrist and squeezed. When she opened her hand, he transferred the stone into her empty palm.

"What about a watch rotation?" Mary asked while staring at the stone as if it were a poisonous snake. "Please tell me I don't have to keep watch."

"What's the matter, Mary, scared?"

"You know damned well I am. You know what kind of conversations we've had. If I get searched, you and I are both dead."

Koltz grinned. "You're probably right. But that's too bad because you're up," he said, now closing Mary's fingers around the stone. "Stay on the stone, but only until you can pass it off to somebody else. I want you to start organizing the search."

"And the watch rotation?"

"Draw straws to establish an order, and then switch off every fifteen minutes. Everybody will know we're going to get a call, and I'm sure nobody wants to be the one answering the phone."

Almost afraid to move, Mary stared at her closed fist.

"Relax, Mary," Koltz said. "They won't call right away. They don't stay on the stone continuously, that's what they have us for. It might take them a while to find out. You should be able to pass it off before they transmit. But tell Doc to be ready, we're going to need him."

Mary nodded, then stood and followed Koltz out the door, though she turned in a different direction. Whereas Koltz left to dress and start what he was sure was going to be a long day, Mary's intention was to get everybody else up to speed and working and, most importantly, to pass the stone.

3

Mental Reboot

D an regained consciousness, slowly. It felt worse to him than waking from a major drunken stupor. If today's medical experts could comprehend what had happened, they might say his neural system had just experienced some sort of regenerative phenomenon. The modern-day techie might more accurately suggest he'd gone through a total mental reboot.

It was the cackling cry of Puerto Rican lizard cuckoos that finally stirred his senses, the high-pitched crowing an assault on his reawakening system. Dan's biological defenses began to pull him from his murky state, so he could try to defend against or escape the damned shrieking that was hurting his ears and increasing the intensity of his headache. His coffee-brown eyes flickered open.

It took a few seconds for his brain to process into a coherent image the signals his eyes were sending, and a few more seconds for him to realize he was staring into a mound of sand. There was a time lag between when he tried to turn his head to when it happened, but when his muscles did respond his head moved slowly. The reward was bright sunlight that stung his eyes. Demanding better working conditions, Dan's eyes slammed shut.

This inspired a groan.

He drew a deep breath and inhaled the musty smell of fishy saltwater and wet earth and when he tested his muscles his fists jerked opened, his feet twitched and then moved, and his knees bent his legs toward the bright blue sky, but the effort was halfhearted, the movement more out of obligation than real enthusiasm. After a few more successful experiments with his arms and midriff, he gathered his strength and, with an infant's coordination and an unexpected blast of flatulence, he managed to force his body to roll over. His system demanded he lie still for a short time so his senses could catch up to the new orientation. Even through his eyelids, Dan could tell the day was bright. He could also feel a breeze ruffle his hair and move across his skin.

As he lay still, breathing deeply, his mind cleared, and his headache lessened.

"I am lying on the beach . . . somewhere. . . .and I am here because . . ."

Just as he began to make progress, the thought faded, and his understanding of his current situation was interrupted by a sudden vivid reminiscence that took center stage. But it wasn't just a memory. It was more a reproduction of an experience as his senses relived the event at a speed that condensed hours into seconds.

Dan was with Aleecia and reexperiencing their single passionate interlude. It had been a fantastic physical and emotional episode: more than sex, it was affectionate and poignant lovemaking. This was the most pure, sensitive, and vulnerable event Dan had ever experienced, and its manifestation came back to him so precisely his systems reacted as if it were happening all over again. If he'd had the time to reach orgasm, he would have considered this a wet dream; though his entire body responded with a short but intense shudder, the event was gone as quickly as it had arrived.

"Whoa!" he whispered in astonishment. "I remember that."

The sound of his own voice seemed real and normal and provided him a small measure of comfort, but that sense of familiarity faded quickly as more memories streamed back. These ones, though, were confusing and disorganized and made it seem to Dan as if the entirety of his life experiences were jumbled in time. Places, events, and people seemed randomly situated in a swirl of disjointed retention. It was as if memories had been spliced together by an editor who never bothered to read the script and Dan was simply a spectator to his own life story.

"Just stop it," he muttered. "Slow down."

Hoping to clear his mind, he drew a deep breath. When he slowly opened his eyes, he did so as if to check for a situation improvement. He worked his eyeballs from side to side and the lids up and down. Success! This time finding it more tolerable, Dan's eyes went back to work.

When he reached with a shaking hand to rub his clean-shaven face, he almost stuck a finger in his eye and barely avoided another visual work strike. He paused and quickly drew more deep breaths.

"Now where am I? I am on the shore of the Caribbean Sea, near . . ." The thought again faded and was replaced with other images. These were images more like nightmares, which were both horrifying and disturbing. Thoughts and visions so fast and upsetting that Dan felt his stomach clench to force them away and keep himself from vomiting. He released a small cry borne of fear and frustration and shook his head roughly.

"Focus! Dan, focus!" he said aloud while forcing himself to sit up. His body now responded out of fear and the will to survive, and he forced his thoughts to clear once again. When he looked around, pieces of information began to fall into place.

"I'm on the shoreline of the Caribbean Sea, in Puerto Rico, and, and I'm here to . . . capture images and video to look for, for shore erosion?"

He spotted a water bottle nearby and asked himself, "Mine?"

Focusing. "Yes, mine."

When he reached out to pick the bottle up, he noticed that a small ridge of sand had piled up against its bottom edge. He felt a slight sensation of anxiety.

"How long have I been here?" he muttered as he looked at the blank screen of his iWatch. When he pushed the digital crown to activate his home screen nothing happened. He tapped the face and tried again, but the screen remained suspiciously dark.

When he tentatively picked up the water bottle, unscrewed the cap, and drank, he suddenly realized how dry his throat felt, as if he'd had nothing to drink for some time. As he stretched his neck from side to side, his mental haze further dissipated. He poured water into his palm and splashed it on his face and neck, trying to remember what had happened before he . . .

Before he what?

Passed out?

"Must have," he murmured as he considered the heavy dusting of sand in the folds of his clothing and the small drift that piled up where he had lain.

"Must have been heat exhaustion," he said, looking up at the sun. When a cool breeze again ruffled his hair and chilled his dampened clothes, however, doubt emerged. After all, the morning had been the perfect temperature for a walk. He also noticed the sun was to his left when he looked out at the sea, which meant the sun was on the rise and it was still morning.

He tried to stand but wobbled and dropped to one knee, before he regained his balance and finally stood upright. As he looked around, he took more deep breaths. Apart from the birds, Dan was alone.

He took a few steps to gauge his coordination. His body seemed to be working again, somewhat; he stumbled only once. He also noticed that his khaki shorts were wet and when he looked down, he caught a faint odor on the wind and, for a few seconds, wondered if he had wet himself. It felt like that might be the case, but he could also feel that his shorts were wet all the way round. The sand he felt in his nether regions made him wonder if he had fallen into the surf. But if that did happen, how did he get back out?

As he pondered this, he stretched and perceived how something seemed to give way. A sensation of strength emerged in a wave of rejuvenation that couldn't be accounted for but which he welcomed. Again, he drank, swallowing over half of the contents of the bottle. If he had in fact passed out from the sun and heat, he knew it was important to rehydrate.

When he turned to look back at where he had been lying, Dan noticed the remote-control unit for his drone, and the drone sitting nearby on a small patch of dry grass. The sight opened more mental doors, and his mind started to come back online.

"Yes, I'm here, in Puerto Rico, and using my drone to capture video files of the damage to the shoreline and the erosion caused by the earthquakes, hurricanes, and the sea."

Starting to connect more puzzle pieces together, he continued to talk softly to the sand. "I am an independent freelancer on assignment with the department of Environment, Great Lakes, and Energy." He pressed the palms of his hands across his eyebrows and forced his eyes to open wide.

"I'm here with my cousin Alex and an engineer named Megan. Right? Right." He ran his hand back and forth over his hair; he could feel sand laced throughout.

He began reciting the words he had used to describe what he was doing any time someone had asked before his trip. "We are a part of a study program requested by the Puerto Rican government. I'm a member of a three-person team sent to gather data and images." Then he included what he only said to himself or to a team member. "My reports will hopefully inspire a group of self-worth–bloated meat puppets to report to their bosses, who will then approve the aid required to help Puerto Rico and prevent additional problems."

Dan grinned and repeated, "Meat puppets."

He recalled the morning's assignment and wanted to make sure he was on schedule. Out of habit, he tried again without success to activate his iWatch. He frowned and tapped the watch face. He didn't know how long he had been lying there, but it was still morning and he wasn't sunburned. He wondered if Alex would be waiting to give him crap about being late.

Again, the unexplained energy surged and forced him into action. He retrieved the remote and considered the drone that was sitting on the small patch of grass. It must have been placed there safely, as the auto-home feature wouldn't have set it down there. The lack of active lights also made Dan think it had been there long enough that the drones automated systems deactivated the light to conserve battery life, but not long enough to shut off completely due to inactivity.

He recovered the drone and gave it a visual once-over; everything seemed fine. Using muscle memory, he reached behind himself to retrieve a fresh battery from his large back pouch. When he grabbed nothing but the back of his shirt, he halted. The pouch was always there when he walked. It was where he kept his spare batteries and the supplies he might need on his walks. He looked around and spotted it nearby. It, too, was covered with a dusting of sand.

Dan picked up the pouch, shook off the loose sand, and unzipped the top. Everything seemed to be as it should be, so he pulled out a fresh battery to replenish the drone's power. He then pulled the belt pouch around his waist and clipped it in place before swapping out the drone's batteries. He realized he felt better and stronger, so he decided to continue his walk. After all, what choice did he have?

He also decided to continue the voice recording for Aleecia. Retrieving his iPhone from his shirt pocket, Dan tried to unlock it.

Nothing happened.

He tried swiping and touching multiple times, but there was no response at all. He tried to power down the device but still couldn't get a reaction. Puzzled, he stowed the phone back in the pocket and tested the controls to the drone. The drone lifted off without a problem, with Dan raising it into the air and taking three steps before something flashed in his mind and stopped him mid-step.

"The stone!"

The memory startled him, not because he'd had it but because of the way he'd felt as he had it. It came to him abruptly and seemed unnaturally wedged into his mind as if it were a movie scene he was forced to watch, and Dan's mouth dropped open. He remembered, unmistakably now and with clarity, what had happened to him.

He stood frozen to the spot, the memory frightening him into an instantaneous nervous perspiration.

"It's dangerous," he said sternly, as if warning a child of a hot stove. The idea of the stone having something to do with his passing out he considered ridiculous, but Dan *knew* something had happened.

Despite the red flags coming in droves from the guys down below, he began looking. He searched for almost a full minute without seeing anything, actually finding himself hopeful that it had somehow rolled away and he wouldn't be able to find it. But hope vanished when a glint of red caught his eye.

He just stared at the stone for a while, afraid to do anything. The thought of walking away came to his mind, but something wouldn't allow him to make an attempt. Instead, he turned back to the young mangrove tree and retrieved the box and lid of the vase; the vase itself was lying not far-off. He was relieved to see it wasn't damaged when he'd dropped it into the sand. Holding the vase in one hand—though being careful not to touch the stone—he used the lid to roll the stone back into the vase and then fastened the two pieces together. Afraid to investigate further, he slid the vase back into the box, quickly secured the latch, and slipped it into his back pouch.

No sooner had he pulled the zipper shut than the strange energy washed through him once again. He stepped back into the surf to rinse his shorts, then regained his bearings, relaunched the drone, and completed the last three miles of his walk in just under forty minutes.

4

Something Strange in Your Shorts?

It was ten-thirty by the time Dan reached the rendezvous point where Alex and Megan were waiting in their aging rental minivan. He waved hello as Alex popped the hatch to the cargo area. Dan stowed his drone and controls in the back and glanced at his coworkers in the front seats, wondering what he should tell his team members. Alex possessed the character traits Dan associated with an absentminded professor type and was a happy mix of Shrek and Donkey rolled into one person. He suspected Alex might overreact. He also expected Megan to find the humor in what had happened to him.

Megan had earned her engineering degree before she'd met her husband. Now a thirty-four-year-old wife and mother of two, on this trip she acted as back-seat caretaker and lead sarcastic wiseass. She had taken the extended assignment to get a break from the everyday tasks and routine she had honed over the last eight years. Neither thin nor fat, Megan had long been comfortable in her girl-next-door appeal. Dan found her to be cute and saucy and could imagine her being involved in one of the hot and steamy affairs found in the kinds of romance novels she read and referred to as women's porn.

"Beat you by half an hour, D. See anything of interest?" Megan asked as she raked her fingers through her long brown hair while examining the red tint the sun had painted in it over the last few weeks.

"I'm not sure," Dan said after a short pause.

She turned in the front passenger seat to face him. "Dude, you look like crap!"

The remark pulled Alex's attention away from the map he held, and he peered at Dan in the rearview mirror.

"Thanks, Megan," Dan retorted. "You always know how to make me feel good."

"You're welcome, big guy. But this time, I mean it more than most. Did something happen, dude?"

"Kind of sure something happened, but not sure what. I think I passed out."

Alex turned to look at Dan, peering over the top of his thick, black-rimmed glasses.

"Are you okay? What happened?"

Dan shrugged and told a trimmed-down version of what had happened or, more accurately, what he wanted them to know about what had happened. He told them about finding the cavern just before it collapsed and waking up in the sand to find his stuff lying safely nearby. He didn't tell his team members about finding the box, the stone, or almost being buried alive.

Megan grinned. "You woke up in the sand, can't remember what happened, and there was no alcohol involved? I'll bet few people can say that with a straight face."

Alex removed his wide-brimmed hat and rubbed his hand across his balding head and graying hair. When Alex pushed his glasses up his nose with his middle finger, Dan grinned. Alex had inadvertently given someone the finger every time he repositioned his glasses as long as Dan could remember; though he never mentioned it, the act always made him smile.

"Are you sure you're all right?"

"I feel good," Dan said. "Energized, with just a bit of a headache."

"You sure you didn't mash your melon when you went down?" Megan asked with too wide a smile.

"I don't think I mashed my melon," Dan repeated. "I mean, there's no bump," he said, while rubbing the stinging spot on the side of his head where he'd pulled out his own hair. "I think I just got too much sun and blacked out."

"Maybe we should have you looked over by the local doctor," Alex suggested. "Just to be sure."

"What's the point? I'd only waste the rest of the day waiting for somebody to tell me I got too much sun." Dan shook his head. "I think that I'd rather just relax for a little while, get some lunch, take a few aspirins, and forget about the whole thing."

But forgetting was something Dan was having some difficulty doing. In fact, his mind was starting to recall the kinds of strange images and vivid dreams that may come when one passes out, except he was awake. The most disturbing were the images of men in trenches, dead and dying. If Dan's memory—if in fact it *was* his memory, as Dan wasn't certain of anything at the moment—served him well, the men were soldiers from the First World War.

Alex considered Dan for a few seconds and, as if in concession, returned his hat to his head and turned his palms to the sky. Then he turned back in his seat, put the red minivan in gear, and headed toward the town of Guánica.

As they drove, Dan noticed how the strange energy kept him fidgety and made it difficult for him to sit still. He focused on gazing out the window, and unconsciously rested a hand over the bulge in his back pouch made by the box. When he realized he was holding the box, he jerked his hand away as if it had been burned and fidgeted some more. Alex noticed his uneasiness.

"Are you sure you're okay? You're acting like you've got something strange moving around in your shorts."

"I feel fine, Alex. Honestly, I feel good. I'm hungry and have a slight headache, but there's nothing wrong."

"Again, something most people can't say," Megan said. "Something strange in your shorts yet no alcohol involved."

Alex pushed his glasses up, unwittingly flipping Dan off, and contemplated his cousin in the mirror. "Well, it may be your head, but you're my responsibility. We'll get some lunch and if you still feel all right and can calm down, we'll forget about the doctor."

"That's fair enough," Dan said.

It took some effort for him to control his fidgeting. He also found his appetite increasing despite the breakfast he'd eaten that morning. When they arrived in Guánica, Alex pulled the minivan into the parking area for a restaurant called Brisas del Mar. Instead of following the routine of going to the restroom to clean up, Dan went straight to a table and ordered lobster, grilled mahi-mahi fillet stuffed with seafood, and the seafood turnover. Megan and Alex, who upon arrival had washed their hands, were still pondering the menu when the waiter brought Dan the first of his plates.

As lunch progressed and Megan watched Dan eat, she realized she couldn't ever recall anyone eating so much in one setting.

"Dude, if you eat any more, I'm going to throw up, and I'll make sure it ends up on you," she warned him.

"Yes, there's certainly nothing wrong with your appetite," Alex said, adjusting his spectacles and unknowingly flipped off the waiter as Dan finished off his second plate.

"Nope, I feel fine," Dan said. "What's on the itinerary for this afternoon?"

Alex considered Dan for a few more seconds, then shrugged and pulled a small map from his shirt pocket.

"We need to take a ride farther west, near Punta Brea. I think we should split the route again. "Just be careful," he said, looking at Dan. "I don't want one of us to become a statistic on a report. Dan, I want you to . . ." Alex stopped when he noticed Dan's sweating despite the restaurant's cool air-conditioned temperature. "Are you sure you're feeling okay?"

Dan nodded in the affirmative as he took a drink from his small glass of water. But when he moved to set the glass back on the table, he froze. He began twitching as if someone was pinching him, and he spilled a small amount of water. He twitched again. He started to twitch a third time, but in mid-twitch he seemed to seize. As if he were made of granite, his body stiffened.

"Danny?" Megan asked softly, as she reached over and touched his arm. "Danny? Oh crap, Alex, he's cold."

Alex leaned over to touch Dan's other arm when the twitching continued, the sudden movement causing both Alex and Megan to jump. Dan's head bobbed forward as if he had dozed off, and the water glass dropped from his hand and clanked on the table. The sound seemed to arouse Dan, who jerked awake and looked across the table to Alex, as if waiting for him to continue speaking.

"Go on, I'm listening. We'll be careful, split the route, and . . . What?" he asked, reading the concern on Alex's face.

Alex looked at Megan, who hadn't taken her eyes off Dan. "Woah, dude, that was some freaky shit," she said.

"What was?"

"It looked like you just winked out or something."

"What?"

"It looked as though you just had some sort of seizure," Alex tried to explain. "But it was the damnedest thing I've ever seen."

Dan waited for them to continue, but instead they just continued to stare at him.

"Whatever," he said. Though he felt lost, he did notice the spilled water in front of him, which he used a napkin to sop up.

"No, I think this warrants a lot more than just a 'whatever,'" Alex said. "I'm going to insist that you stay in this afternoon and see the doctor."

"I feel fine," Dan said.

"I'm sure you do, but I've never seen anyone do what you just did, Dan, and I want to make sure you aren't going to just pass out and fall into the sea."

"I feel fine," Dan tried to argue.

"No," Alex said, raising his hand. "It won't be me explaining why you ended up washed away with the tide. You're going to stay at the hotel this afternoon, and I'll ask for the doctor to see you. End of discussion."

5

The Call

It had been four hours since Everett Koltz started his day by inadvertently ordering a man's death. The early morning session with Jim Talbert didn't go as smoothly as it could have. Zack had assured him that Jim's resistance and weaker physical state had been important factors in his death, but Koltz also knew that Zack was often more forceful than he needed to be and was sure that was the case now. Zack had used the duplicator on Jim for such a long duration of time, he'd drained the power source. He'd done it not because he needed to, but because it hurt Jim Talbert. Even that was apparently not enough to curb the violent tendencies that had arisen in Zack; the toothpicks under Talbert's thumbnails serving as the evidence. Koltz knew Zack's cruel new tactics had to be tamed, but he didn't know how to go about doing it. He was afraid of Zack, but he also refused to let it show. He couldn't. Besides, pain was a part of Zack's job.

Koltz was thinking about this when he was startled by a scream loud enough that it came through the closed door. Everett Koltz recognized the scream for what it really was: a statement. His boss's way of reminding him, reminding all of them, just who was in charge. Koltz put his head in his hands and leaned forward over his desk, wondering if Zack and John were going to have to dispose of another body. It was something they were becoming quite good at doing.

He lit a cigarette and intentionally allowed some time to pass before getting up from his desk and heading for the door. He needed to give Doc a chance to get to the fallen before he started asking questions. Doc's demand that he be permitted time to at least evaluate a patient was a nonnegotiable stipulation that Koltz had told him he respected. In truth, it was Doc's ability to quietly remove someone and not raise suspicion that Koltz respected. Since Doc had lost his license by participating in a questionable assisted suicide, Koltz was unsure of what Doc could get up to if he was pissed off enough. He found it easier to be amenable than to wonder if there was something in his food.

After a reasonable amount of time, Koltz crossed his office and entered the adjoining room. Unlike the watch room, these rooms were more to Koltz's liking. He had personally furnished his office and had overseen the decor with care. His desk and other furniture were cherrywood and reminded him of the nicer things he'd left behind, before he became a prisoner of the truth.

Except for his bedroom, this was the only space he considered his own. The hardwood floors complemented the rich dark paneling that rose to a height of four feet, and a warm cream color was painted to a few inches below the ceiling. There, a thin molding separated the cream from the white with its touch of blue. In the past, Everett Koltz had loved the outdoors; these days, this scheme was the closest to nature he could get.

The adjoining room was larger and brightly lit. The same hardwood graced the floors, and the beige-colored walls and white ceiling were welcoming. Twenty-five computers sat on desks in a horseshoe-shaped array, the open end located near Koltz's office. This way, he could quickly walk to the center and "inspire" his people. This was the wit room, where the research and other intellectual work was done. This was where everyone tried to outwit everyone else. At present, two-dozen people sat at the stations, all too nervous to stop working, especially now.

When Koltz entered, Doc was still checking the vital signs of a man who had recently been picked up off the floor and laid on a gurney. Being tall, older, thin, white-haired, and wearing round thin glasses and the typical lab coat, at least Doc looked the part. Koltz decided another minute was in order, so he stopped at the first computer station where Mary Reyes sat.

"I'm assuming the call came in," Koltz said.

"Yep," Mary answered, nodding to the unconscious man. "Larry's watch."

"He was evidently searched, how much fault did they find with him?" Mary shrugged.

"Did Larry recite any instructions?"

"Nothing directly to the point," Mary said. "He said the Reti has started an investigation and to expect a second call as soon as the location is confirmed."

"Well, that's just fuckin' great, another call," Koltz said. "Doc will love that."

"So will the person on watch."

Koltz nodded. "Make sure you keep up the rotation. I don't think it will take them long to determine the origin."

Mary nodded and glanced briefly in the direction of Doc and Larry, before turning back to her work.

Koltz walked to the side of the gurney and looked at the face of the man stretched out on it. The look was one Koltz knew well: the pasty skin; mouth and eyes opened wide and frozen in a state of terror and shock; and the blank emptiness behind those eyes. He wondered if Larry's mental lights would ever come back on. Sometimes they did, but sometimes the person searched would remain that way—locked in a suspended state of *'wholly shit!'* for the rest of their life.

Without taking his eyes off Larry, Koltz asked Doc, "Was the boss in a forgiving mood?"

"He's not dead, if that's what you're asking," Doc replied. "Not yet, anyway, but he's gonna have one hell of a headache when, or if, he wakes up."

"Do what you can for him, Doc."

"I always do," Doc said as he began pushing his patient toward a door on the opposite side of the room. Koltz unexpectedly reached out and stopped him and Doc watched as Koltz gripped Larry's wrist and pried open his fingers. A transparent black stone with a reddish tint fell out of

Larry's motionless hand and landed on the floor with a soft knock. Koltz nodded and Doc resumed his pushing. Koltz bent down and retrieved the stone, then held it out to a woman sitting at the next desk.

"It's not my turn," she said, withdrawing her hands and plunging them into her lap.

"It is now," Koltz said as he reached out, took her by the wrist, and forced her to accept the stone.

There was a thump on the other side of the room as the gurney pushed through the double doors. When they opened, Zack and John were standing on the other side. Koltz whistled through his teeth and, in response, the pair came in.

"Boss is looking for the origin of the blip. I'm guessing it will take them only an hour or two to find. I want the two of you ready to board a plane as soon as we get the coordinates."

Zack exchanged toothpicks, old for new. "No trouble, mate."

Koltz looked at the toothpick and sighed. "I liked you better when you smoked."

"Unhealthy habit," Zack replied calmly, "Something you should consider."

"For what? Do you think either of us will live long enough to contract cancer, Zack?"Zack shrugged. "You never know, I could get lucky."

"Luck has nothing to do with it. Besides, our bosses created cancer, I'm sure they can cure it."

"Right you are," Zack said. "But the question is, will they?"

Koltz shrugged. "That depends on how well you do your job."

"We do it well enough," John answered.

"Shut up, John," Koltz barked. "You're lucky to be here, and the last thing I want from you is talk."

John simply stared at Koltz without reply.

"All we need," Zack said, diverting Koltz's attention back to himself and away from John, "is for these people to do their job and tell us where we're needed."

"Don't worry, they'll get it done," Koltz replied. "You just be ready."

Zack nodded in response and Koltz returned to his office to wait.

Koltz only had to wait for an hour before the second scream of that day achieved three things.

First, it announced the arrival of the second call. Second, it scrambled the brains of a man by the name of Joe Moss. Third, it started a battle that would come at a cost of many lives and alter the numbers included in all three groups.

Unlike the first time, when Koltz was somewhat insulated from the effects of the call made to the person on watch, this time his office door was open. He also just happened to be watching Joe. When the call came in, Joe's body suddenly stiffened and he spoke in a monotone voice.

"The point of origin of the unauthorized transmission by an unknown user occurred at the coordinates 17°58'17.87"N, by 66°54"28.62"W. This is on the shoreline of the Caribbean Sea in the country of Puerto Rico, between the areas listed as Guánica and Indios. Locate this stone and return it."

Those were the last words ever spoken by Joe Moss. In truth, these were the last words formed by Joe's mouth, as the words weren't his to begin with. He shuddered and opened his eyes wide in horror and pain as the color drained from his face and he let loose a scream that echoed off the walls while he collapsed to the floor.

Zack and John had also been there. As soon as Doc had Joe on the next gurney, Koltz motioned for the pair. They met at Mary's desk.

"Mary, call the airport and have our guy prepare the jet."

"Already done, he's just waiting for orders."

"Good, tell him Zack is on the way," Koltz said, seemingly ignoring John's existence. "And tell him to plot a speed route to Puerto Rico. I want him there as soon as humanly possible."

"Yes, sir," Mary said, finding comfort in the thought that she may have survived another encounter.

"Zack," Koltz said. "I'm going to call the post in Florida and tell them to get to Puerto Rico and start looking, but they aren't going to make contact. I want you in charge of the capture. Bring the stone and whoever has it back to me alive. Kill anyone else who gets in the way, but I want the person who used that stone alive. Do I make myself clear?"

Zack paused long enough to change toothpicks. "No trouble."

"Then, go. And Zack," Koltz added, causing Zack to pause after he and John had already turned to leave, "this is the most important mission we've had in the last sixty years. You foul this up, and we could all be dead."

"Koltz," Zack replied, "that's not much of a threat, mate. Considering what we do, death isn't a bad exchange."

Zack grinned, winked at Koltz, then left to catch his plane.

6

Dreams or Lessons

Dan paced his room at the Copamarina Beach Resort in Guánica. The warm colors in the wallpaper and the floral throw pillows did as little to calm him as the tropical view beyond the window. The local doctor couldn't see him until the morning, and Dan had thought several times about ignoring Alex's orders and finding a way to catch up with him and Megan. But the possibility of what Megan called his "Freakin' turning to stone" tugged at the back of his mind. He didn't feel sick, but something had happened at lunch. Alex's and Megan's testimony were all the proof he needed.

He'd taken the small treasure box out of his back-pouch hours ago and, without removing the vase from the box, had set it on a small side table. In truth, he was afraid to even open the lid. The idea that a stone could have anything to do with his blacking out seemed ludicrous, but as crazy as it sounded, he also had to consider whether it could be true. There were, after all, other things that needed to be considered when mulling over the possibility.

His iWatch, for example. It had stopped working, which alone wasn't strange, as watches stop working every day, but the fact that the watch was only a few months old bothered him. The fact that it had stopped working at the same time as he'd found the stone only added to the oddity.

But this he could have written off as a coincidence, had it not been for his iPhone. It had worked fine in the morning, but now was totally locked and wouldn't give him any response. Dan had removed and replaced the battery to no effect. He had even hooked it up to his laptop and tried to call up the files, but his computer had declared the device incompatible with his software. That anomaly was one Dan could not ignore.

"I have to stop thinking about this or I'm going to go nuts," Dan said to the walls. "I'll just tell Alex the truth."

He paused for a few seconds, and then responded to his own statement. "Are you batty? Alex will have you looked at by every doctor he can find, and you'll end up on the next flight home."

He paused. "Can't talk to Megan, she's already freaked."

Another pause. "Leecie," he said with a knowing nod.

He stopped pacing and walked to the small desk, pulled the phone close, picked up the receiver, and began dialing the number of Aleecia Donnelly.

"Leecie will listen. She always at least listens to my problems." Dan talked as if he was trying to convince someone else who was in the room with him. "Oh, she'll shake her head no, because that's what she does, but Aleecia will listen and know I'm not making it up. She'll listen and give me an honest opinion and . . . and . . . and she'll worry about me and tell me I should come home." Dan hung up before the call connected. He sighed and started to walk in a small circle, rubbing his face in frustration.

He picked up the phone receiver and pushed redial.

He hung up and pushed the phone back on the desk.

Then he sat on the bed, found the TV remote, and forced himself to sit and try to watch the television. Nothing could hold his attention. Historical narratives he might have considered interesting yesterday he now found dimwitted and even inaccurate. Why he felt this way, he couldn't comprehend, but he seemed to disagree with almost everything he heard.

He walked to the window and looked out at the ocean; then, he looked down at the treasure box. He decided to run the events through his mind again, but slower this time to see if he could put together any more of what had happened to him. He closed his eyes and pictured himself walking the shoreline, finding the cavern, spotting the box, stupidly going in and retrieving the box only to almost get buried alive, opening the box and the vase, seeing the stone, dumping it into his hand . . . but at that point, his memory failed him.

When he opened his eyes, he realized he was suddenly feeling extremely tired. The events of the day, it seemed, had finally caught up with him. Hoping to get back to feeling normal, he curled up on the bed to take a nap.

He fell asleep within moments of lying down, but the rest he had sought never came. Instead, Dan endured a series of restless naps and bad dreams. Instead of feeling better when he got up, he felt worse. Not just from not getting the rest he'd needed, but because he now had to ponder what the dreams meant. They were, after all, more like visions than dreams, and there was no way he could push these visions out of his head when they were so vivid and horrible.

In one of his dreams, he was standing beside French soldiers who were huddled together around a small fire as they attempted to fight the effects of a biting cold. Noses and ears were already black from frostbite and would need to come off. One soldier pulled his knife and braved the cold long enough to waddle to a horse that was more dead than alive. The animal, too numb and weak from starvation and the cold, couldn't fight back when the soldier cut a piece of meat from its hind quarter. Around the fire, some soldiers cursed the weather as others cursed Napoleon Bonaparte.

In another dream, Dan was standing beside a Nazi soldier as they reviewed the results from a gas chamber. Dozens, no hundreds, of bodies were piled in a mass grave and covered with a moving blanket of black flies, whose little wings stirred the horrific stench into the air.

But the one that pulled him from his sleep was a vision he wasn't just watching but somehow participating in. In it, he was looking through the lens of a rifle scope, the butt of the weapon snug against the front of his right shoulder. The scope's view was focused on the pavement of the street below, then on the back of the black limousine, and finally came to rest on the head of John Kennedy. He didn't willingly pull the trigger, but Dan felt the butt of the rifle kick hard against his shoulder; he saw the president slump forward toward the backside of the front seat. The scope remained focused on the president until a shot that didn't come from Dan's rifle slammed the president's head against the back seat of the limousine and caused pieces of skull and brain matter to explode and spray backward.

At that point, Dan let out the short scream that must have woken him. As he sat sweating and rocking back and forth, he attempted to push these images from his mind. But they were infecting Dan in a way he couldn't escape—like poisoned gas filling a locked room.

He decided to shower and shave, thinking freshening up might make himself feel better. He stood and allowed his body to soak in the steam as an attempt at relaxation, however, his mind was racing and it was clear that if he was going to get any rest, he would need something stronger than hot water to calm him.

Dan stepped out of the shower and strode, naked and dripping, over to the mini bar. He opened a bottle of Jack Daniels and considered ice and a Coke, but since there were approximately three swallows in the small bottle, he slammed it down in two gulps. The whiskey caused a mushroom of warmth to rise in his gullet, which he allowed to settle before heading back to the bathroom.

Dan used a clean towel to wipe away the haze from the fogged-over mirror, so he could shave. He plugged in his electric razor and put it to his face. Then he froze. What he saw in the mirror forced him back to the mini bar. This time, he would need several drinks.

His right shoulder, where the butt of the rifle had rested in the assassination dream, was bruised.

7

Killers

I n his seat on the Phenom 300E jet, Zack reached into the pocket of his sport coat and retrieved a fresh toothpick. He was chewing them to shreds in minutes, so this was something he was doing often. In the old plane, he would have just flicked the used picks toward a trash can to see if he could hit it and not bother to pick them up if he missed, but this was the new plane. The Phenom 300E was only three months old; it still smelled new. It was luxurious and comfortable and quite a contrast to most of the other Bound environments. It was a nice change, and he wanted to enjoy the novelty.

Change was something that happened often for Zack, but rarely in a good way. His missions provided him with his only real sense of freedom, and Zack loved being out on a mission, even if he had to kill people or, when the situation demanded it, run for his life. It was the only time he felt in charge of his own life, and if he did his job well enough, his life was his to keep. It usually felt good to be out where others weren't constantly looking over his shoulder, but now he looked out the window and sighed audibly.

"What's that noise all about?" John asked without shifting his eyes from the book he was reading.

"The time," Zack said while turning to face John. "I'm feeling there's something big happening, and I think we need to get there as fast as we can. It's taking too damned long."

"We're going as fast as we can."

"I know, but it was four hours between the blip and the first call. We waited an hour for the second call. It took us an hour to reach the plane at Midway, and another forty-five minutes for clearance to take off. The airport in Ponce won't accept us because of the earthquake damage, so we'll have to land in San Juan. The way I see it, it's going to take us four and a half hours until we land, two hours to get to the coordinates, and a few hours to figure out what happened. I'm guessing between sixteen and twenty hours from the time of the blip, before we have a chance to get the stone."

John let his book fall to his lap and stared across the cabin at Zack.

"Thought about this much?" he asked with a little sarcasm. "What the hell has got you freaking out about the time? Your watch says *now* across the face, you've never worried about time lags before. Aren't you the guy who always says we'll get there when we get there?"

Zack grinned. "Deadset, mate. But there's something different this time. I guess I just got a bad feeling about this one."

"A bad feeling about what, precisely?"

"This is all going to go to hell, I suppose."

"You serious? Because I thought it all went to hell a long time ago."

"Well, that's right, mate, bloody oath. But I just got an uneasy feeling there's something bigger on the horizon that we might not be able to stop."

"There has always been something bigger on the horizon we might not be able to stop. It's the same world we've lived in for the past few years. Why the unease now?"

"Not sure, maybe because things have been more tense at the den lately, or maybe because Koltz has been acting mongrel the last few months."

John folded his arms across his chest. "I get that. He's been an asshole with me."

"Yeah, what the hell is going on there? He seems to have taken a big dislike to you. Why's he so eager to piss in your pool?"

John chuckled. "I did something he won't forgive me for."

"And what's that?"

"I saved his life."

Zack looked across the cabin at his partner. "Fair dinkum?"

"Honestly."

"How?"

"Remember that big scrap with the Crew a few months ago?"

"I do but that turned out all right, as far as I remember."

"I thought so too, but during the fight Koltz got himself into a spot and one of the Crew members got a bead on him. Had him in the sights of a nine-millimeter, dead to rights. Koltz spotted it around the same time I did, but he didn't move."

"You mean, he froze."

"At first I thought so. I gave him a shout that made him jump, and I squeezed off a round with the Eradicator as I did. It was just enough to make the shooter miss, and Koltz shot back and killed the guy. I went over to him expecting a thank-you, but instead he punched me on the chin and said something about controlling his own fate before stomping off."

"You think he was just going to let himself get wasted?"

"Who knows? But I owe him something for the sucker punch."

Zack grinned "Planning to clock him, are you?"

"Not really. He can't punch for shit, so it didn't hurt, and I found it kind of funny. Besides, if I do thump him, I'd have to hold back or I might take his head off, and I don't want to do that. If I ever decide it's time to tag Koltz, it will be with everything I've got."

"It might do him some good. His thinking's been iffy lately. Telling us to use the duplicator on Talbert, that's just drongo. Now we can't use it because it won't charge up again for a few days, and I'm betting we're going to wish we had it. Maybe you should let him have a good one."

John chuckled. "He has been acting weird lately, I'll give you that, but I'm not planning anything just yet. Hitting him would just give them a reason to try and have me killed, and I really want to avoid the afterlife for as long as I can."

Zack raised his eyebrows. "You're afraid of death. A man who kills for a living, afraid of death, that's interesting."

"Kind of, but not why you think." John smiled a little and looked out the window. "I never knew religion, but as a kid I had an aunt who took me to church a few times. Not much of it stuck in my head, but the whole 'going to hell' did. Don't get me wrong, I've seen enough to know there's no real god thing going on, but is there a special nasty place for us later? A place just for those of us who do what we do. Lately I've been wondering what will happen to me when I'm offed. If I'm lucky, nothing, and I'll fade into oblivion. But if the church ladies' delusions are even close to some kind of truth, then what? I'll be punished forever. No thanks. Even if there is some way to be granted forgiveness, I have no right to ask for it considering the things I've done. No, if there is a life after this one, I'm pretty sure it'll be some sort of ugly place. I'll just put it off for as long as I can, even if I have to listen to Everett Koltz bitch and whine. Besides, I'll outlive him then grin and piss on his memory."

Zack stared blankly at his partner, trying to determine if John was playing with him. He soon decided he wasn't.

"Never heard you speak about religion before, Mate."

"Not religion, though, is it? More like a philosophy, I'd say. You, on the other hand," John said, turning back to face his partner. "You don't seem afraid of dying. I heard what you said to Koltz as we were leaving. You said, 'Death isn't a bad exchange.' You look forward to the afterlife, do you?"

"Not really, but I hate what I've become, Mate. All I do is what I'm told, and most of the time it involves hurting people who are trying to save our world. What good am I? That's the question I've been asking myself lately, and I always come back with the same answer. I'm a damned good killer. But recently I've been wondering why."

"Zack, if you want out, why not just bolt and see how long you can make it on the run? Most people, like me, would never make it far, but you, you're resourceful and damned clever. I think you'd be one of the few who could make it out. Why not give it a go?"

"Because, if my daughter is still alive, she won't be for long if I suddenly go bush. Can't take that chance. Besides, I've got other plans."

"Really, like what?"

Zack shook his head. "No. If I tell you about them, they become a part of the record. And if they ever search either of us, then it's all out in the open. If they're just thoughts, they're all mine, and maybe, just maybe . . ."

John nodded in his understanding that experiences may be vulnerable to being hacked, but thoughts are impenetrable. For several seconds he considered his own plans and how he might find his wife. He wondered if she was still alive, and if this mission might be the one that raises his status enough to allow him a visit. But, as John knew, these thoughts could drive a person mad. He stretched his thick neck and went back to reading Erich von Däniken's *Chariots of the Gods*.

8

The Second Touch

Much to Alex's disappointment, Dan had gotten drunk. With there being nowhere for him to go and no other way for him to escape his own mind, what else was there for him to do? He had drunk himself into a stupor that left Alex unimpressed when he checked on Dan later that evening. Dan, however, was past feeling guilty and didn't try to explain. How could he? 'Hey cousin, I just shot John Kennedy and have the bruise to prove it, what do you make of that?' But the drink had paid off and no sooner had Alex left him than Dan finally fell into a peaceful sleep.

For a couple of hours.

Then drops of sweat formed on his forehead before gathering enough weight to be pulled downward across his temples. More followed to soak his hair and finally the pillowcase.

Dreams came in a crisscross barrage of images that left him gasping for air. His survival instinct tried to pull him from his murky state, but the dreams held him in their authoritative grip. Whatever this was, it was stronger than him and he was bound to it—a prisoner of its supremacy.

When release came, he wasn't allowed to awaken and instead was thrown back to consciousness with crudeness resembling a bouncer removing an obnoxious drunk from a nightclub. His eyes shot open and then he sat, spun, and stood in a single motion. He was two steps away before the sheets could settle back to the sweat-soaked bed. After he walked to the balcony door, Dan flipped the latch and stepped out into the night air, gasping for breath as if he had just run a marathon and drawing the attention of a few guests who were just calling it a night. Dan ignored them as he stood sucking in air and trying to calm himself.

It took several moments for his mind to catch up to his situation; when it did, he discovered two things. First was that he felt totally sober, and the second was that he was totally naked. He looked back down at the people who were grinning up at him while waiting to see what he did next. Despite the cool temperature, Dan's cheeks flushed.

Filled again with an energy that seemed borne from the strange dreams, he went back inside, shut the door, and began pacing the floor. Out of habit, he checked his watch. Out of disgust, he tossed it on the nightstand and checked the bedside clock for the actual time. 11:40 p.m. He had the urge to get dressed and go for a run to burn off the strange energy he was feeling.

And why not? Sleep was something he couldn't do and something he wanted to avoid, so why not go out and enjoy the night air. After he dressed and as he tied his shoelaces, he caught a glimpse of the treasure box still sitting on the small table.

He stopped and stared at it and, for better or worse, forced himself to consider what it was all about. His logical brain told him he had to be suffering from some sort of mental breakdown. There was no way a stone could have had anything to do with his dreams or whatever had happened to him. Simple reason and common sense prevented it from being true.

He crossed the room and sat down in the chair at the table and stared some more at the box. It was stupid to think that this had anything to do with his passing out on the beach. He had simply gotten too much sun. Right? It was nothing more than the overwhelming heat.

At this point, the little voice of self doubt in his mind cleared its throat and spoke up. *If it was just the heat, then why the strange dreams?*

"That could be anything," Dan said aloud in response to his own thoughts. "It could have been something I ate. Like Ebenezer Scrooge said, 'It could have been an undigested bit of beef or a fragment of underdone potato.'"

Is that so, asked the self doubt. *And would those things also freeze your watch? I don't ever remember a story about somebody eating something that stopped their watch.*

"Defective battery," Dan retorted.

Right, sure. And the phone?

Dan knew these to be valid questions, but he pushed them away.

He reached out and picked up the box to look at it more carefully.

"It was obviously manufactured by someone who wanted it to be recognized as special. It's finely crafted, and the metalwork is elaborate."

He spoke as if he was a coroner documenting an autopsy. He cautiously released the latch and lifted the lid to look at the vase inside.

"The vase is also finely crafted, and it looks older than the box. Like the vase was made first and the box crafted sometime later for the specific purpose of holding the vase."

He pulled the vase from the box and set both down on the table so he could study them.

"I'm no expert, but the artwork on the vase reminds me of that done by the Aztecs or Mayans. There are images and characters on the side that could be some sort of writing." He hesitated. "Or warning," he said a little more softly. The thought of being the victim of some sort of curse entered his mind and caused him to ponder for a few seconds. Then he shook his head in disbelief and continued the vocal report.

"I'll take this to a museum for more information."

He pulled the lid off the vase and peered inside at the stone.

"The stone is there and was obviously manufactured by someone. It looks entirely round and so smooth, nature wouldn't be responsible. It's possible, but not likely."

He sniffed the air inside. "Nothing abnormal about the odor."

He held out his other hand to again dump the stone into his palm, but then he thought better of it. Instead, he looked around for something to drop the stone into. When he noticed one of the resort's monogrammed wooden drink coasters, he placed it in the center of the table and carefully tipped the vase until the stone rolled out and landed in the coaster. The lip of the circular-shaped coaster allowed the stone to roll around the circumference twice before settling at the low side that happened to be the part nearest Dan.

With the word "curse" stuck in his mind, Dan dropped to his knees and stared at it some more.

"This is stupid," he muttered, moving his hand over the stone. When his hand hovered an inch above it, he said, "Nothing" into the invisible microphone. "Or maybe just a tingle, but it's so small it might just be nerves."

He withdrew his hand and formed it into a tube, blowing through it as if his fingers were cold.

"A fast touch with just a finger," he said to no one. "I'll touch it like I want to see if it's hot. I'll just touch it and pull back, a quick on and off."

He checked the clock on the nightstand: 11:55 p.m. Then he extended his right index finger, took a deep breath, and very quickly touched the stone with just a fingertip. The contact between his finger and the stone was very brief, but it was long enough.

Dan hit the floor.

9

The Crew

It was getting late in the small office building in Maple Grove, Minnesota. The clock had been running since seven that morning, yet they were no closer to solving the mystery of the blip than they were when it had first happened. The stress was once again starting to press on Niles Jority. Thinking back, Niles realized he couldn't remember a time when stress wasn't pushing on him, and that certainly wasn't helping his health or his looks. He was forty yet looked sixty. His once-black hair was receding and gave him more forehead than he liked; it also seemed to have skipped the gray part and was now mostly white. But he knew, in the long run, it wouldn't matter one bit.

He would never need to be considered handsome again, and he wasn't interested in forming another relationship. With the murders of his wife and children, he learned that if word got around that you cared for someone, they only became bigger targets for the Bound.

Niles didn't consider his appearance overly worrisome, but he was concerned about his health. Although he was at an optimal body weight, the stress was taking its toll and for the first time in his life his blood pressure was now running high and there wasn't a night when his stomach didn't cause him worsening fits of indigestion. Yes, the stress was getting to him, all right, and why wouldn't it? The only thing that hung in the balance of his and the Crew's work was the entire human race. A huge jump from back when he was in the mortgage game.

Luckily, his health could be fixed the next time one of the Renegades came to see him. Of that, he was confident. After all, they had healed him when he had been shot. As they put it, experience was easier to preserve than to obtain. So, the next time one came around, he would ask for healing and was relatively sure they would give it to him. Provided he could live that long. Renegades didn't make regular visits and unless it was of major importance, visits simply didn't occur. After all, a visit from a Renegade would mean they were risking their life, and theirs was a voluntary risk. The Renegades were not the ones who would suffer and die in this fight, if they stayed out of it, yet they chose to help. Whether that help was borne of kindness or guilt, Niles wasn't sure, and in truth, it didn't matter much. But it was one of the reasons he considered it his responsibility to make things happen when he was asked to do something.

Among the Crew members, Niles was senior by almost eight years, which was a year more than the next-most-senior person, David Mills. According to the unwritten rules, this put Niles in charge. The fact that you gained seniority by staying alive only made you more of a mark and as Niles learned, as most did, the possibility of death was a huge motivator.

He paced behind eight people sitting in a row of office chairs at a line of white plastic folding tables looking over their shoulders at computer screens. Each monitor showed a different image of an ocean and shoreline, as the row of workers sat clicking, typing, and searching the web. They were a good team. Maybe the best Niles had had, which saddened him. He knew well enough that some of them weren't going to live long.

The thought caused him to glance at a younger couple sitting together. They represented the only husband-and-wife team Niles knew of in the Crew. It wasn't uncommon for couples to form unnamed relationships, because people felt the need to cling to someone, but what made Cavan and Tami Lillia special was that their marriage predated their becoming members of the Crew. This wasn't just an oddity but a downright miracle. They had been with the Crew for the last two years and came the way a lot of members did: because they were connected to someone who learned something they weren't supposed to, they were paid a visit by the Bound. In Cavan and Tami's case, a mutual friend. Fortunately, they had watched a lot of *CSI* and learned a little something about living off the grid. This made it harder for the Bound to find them. The couple found the Crew while they were doing their own research into the murder of their friend and, as they put it, teamed up.

When Niles had first met Cavan and Tami, he thought they would make good king and queen material for any prom. Cavan had just turned twenty-six and was three years older than Tami; at 5'9", he was taller by five inches. Both partners looked like they were cut from the same cloth. Their hair color was the same dusty brown, though Cavan's was a shade darker. Both had blue eyes and well-proportioned features and would be considered attractive by many members of the opposite sex. Neither felt it necessary to mask the attraction they felt for each other, and they were often observed in public displays of affection. Hugging, kissing, and holding hands were the norm for the Lillias.

Only one other time in the Crew's history had a husband-and-wife team survived together. As a result, Niles had a hard time giving Cavan and Tami separate assignments. In truth, it was working out well. Cavan would fight harder than anybody to save Tami, and vice versa.

Also present was Jammie Holmes, a construction worker and muscular man; Glen Stover, a waiter who'd proven tougher than he looked when the Bound had left him for dead in a ditch; Craig Audamchik, a computer programmer with a talent for electronics; Bethany Pickering, a gal who, along with her husband, had returned home to find the Bound in the process of killing her children and whose husband had sacrificed his life to save hers; Derick Gates, a former college football player; and Debbra Sorensen, a dentist who looked more like a scientist. They all came from different parts of the country and had their own reasons and stories—stories they all knew well—for becoming Crew members. There were others, of course, scattered across the globe yet united in the same cause to ensure billions of people would survive.

The ninth Crew member in the room, Breanne Coombs, sat quietly with her eyes closed and her hands folded gently around a small transparent black stone. Niles touched the locks of her long red hair as he passed, drawing a small smile from Breanne that highlighted the light freckles which speckled her full cheeks, like tiny pebbles on a white sand beach.

Niles continued to the desk where Cavan punched at a keyboard.

"What do we have?" he asked.

"Still not much, it's like the proverbial needle in a haystack."

"I know, I know," Niles said. "We need to do better, people." His voice rose to a volume detected by everyone in the room. "You know who's working against us."

"Yes, we do," Cavan replied, "and we're doing the best we can, but you saw what we've got. A few seconds of a sandy beach or shoreline and a hand, not much to go on."

"I know, but we got a glimpse of something and we need to find out what it was, where it took place, and who used a stone."

"If you ask me," Debbra said from where she was sitting at the next table. "It would almost seem that a Bound has a Perception Stone."

"If that's the case," Cavan said, "then this has got to be some kind of a trap."

"No, if this was a trap, they would have given us more detail," Niles said. "They wouldn't let us come to the wrong conclusion."

"What if it was an accident?" Debbra asked.

"I don't buy that, either. The Reti would never allow a Perception Stone to have an accident."

"Never." Repeated a man from the doorway.

Niles turned to greet David Mills. David was 6'3" and slim, almost too thin, as far as some were concerned. There was a sharpness to his facial features, with above-average points on his chin and nose. High cheekbones sat below blue eyes, and even though he was not quite thirty, David had a touch of gray that merged with his short brown hair. He looked pale and near sickly. In truth David was surprisingly strong in body and mind and could fight like a wild man when necessary. He always dressed in slacks and a dress shirt—business casual, as he called it—a remnant from back when he still had hopes of running his own real estate office.

Niles walked over to shake his hand. "David, it's good to have you back, we could use your help."

"I heard we got a blip, any idea what's happening?"

"None yet, and I'm afraid we're running out of time. Are we all set up in Canada?"

"Yeah, we're in Saskatchewan, near Stalwart, north of Moose Jaw."

"Good, we'll need to make the move as soon as we figure this out."

"You sure you want to move now?"

"We have to. We've been here too long as it is. It'll be a bigger risk, staying any longer."

David shrugged his slim shoulders. "You're the boss. Which stone was it?"

"I'm not sure. When we try to look back, we can't get anything."

"What do you mean?"

Upon hearing the question, Cavan turned and held up a small clear tube with a hinged lid. Inside it was a second stone, twin to the one Breanne was holding. Cavan flipped the lid open with his thumb, and David held out his open hand. Cavan tipped the tube and the stone rolled into David's palm. He closed his eyes, drew a deep breath, and stood perfectly still for twenty seconds before opening his eyes and returning the stone back in the tube. Cavan fastened the lid and set the tube down on a table.

"Just black air before the hand," David said.

Niles nodded. "That keeps bringing a suspicious thought to my mind."

"What suspicious thought would that be?" Debbra asked. "Have the Bound developed some new trick?"

"Maybe," David said. "Or maybe, just maybe, this Perception Stone is catching up. Maybe this stone has been out of the system for a long time."

Every head turned to David and a silence fell over the room.

"One of the lost stones?" Tami asked reverently.

David shrugged. "It would explain the blank spot."

"Exactly what I've been thinking," Niles said bluntly. "If we do have a lost Perception Stone out there, we need to get it. If the Bound think the same thing, they'll stop at nothing to find it, and we know the Reti are paying close attention. David, I alerted the other post, but contact each one again and make sure they're ready. I don't want any lag—"

"Blip!" Breanne's shout cut off Niles midsentence. Her hands closed tightly around the stone in her hand and she sat still with her eyes closed. No one moved, as every eye was now on her.

"We've got a name!" she said, the excitement rising in her voice. "Copamarina Beach Resort!"

Niles turned back to Cavan, who was already typing the name into the search engine. Every other person at a desk did the same. David picked up the clear tube and dumped the second stone back into his hand and closed his eyes.

"Where?" Niles asked.

"Looking," Cavan answered. Except for the clicking of the mouse buttons, the room was silent for a few seconds as everyone sat glued to a monitor.

David open his eyes just as Tami shouted.

"Got one! Puerto Rico."

Niles and David moved to her and each leaned over a shoulder to look at the images she'd pulled up. Pictures of the hotel and beach dominated the resort's website, and the circular logo stood out in the upper corner.

"That's it!" David said. "It's the same font and logo design."

"Okay, let's go with that!" Niles said. "Debbra, where's our nearest post?"

Her fingers punched the keyboard. "Looks like we still have quite a few people in Teotihuacán, Mexico," she answered, "but three of them are in Jamaica looking into the Folly Ruins project."

"Give them a call and get them to Puerto Rico," Niles said. "If this is a lost stone, it's the first one since the Kaiser found his, and we all know how it passed to Adolph Hitler and what he did with it. We need to get it first."

10

The Run Begins

It was the floor. The carpet, to be exact, but Dan knew it for what it was as soon as his eyes opened. Unlike before, when he had needed some time for his senses to come online and recognize where he was, this time the instant he came awake he knew he was face down on the carpet of his room at the Copamarina Beach Resort in Guánica.

He was also quite chilled. Not because the temperature had dropped, but because he was drenched in his own sweat. But this time was different. There was something new. A feeling of awareness he'd never had before, one of knowing. He knew exactly where he was, what was happening and, more importantly, what he needed to do. And what he needed to do was run, and run fast. They were coming for him. He didn't know precisely who they were just yet, but they were coming; there was no mistake about that.

Take only what you need! screamed the little voice in his head, as the survival guys in the back of his mind threw up red flags as fast as they could. Instead of arguing with the little voice the way he'd done before, this time he agreed wholeheartedly. *Take only what you need and get out. Now!*

Dan grabbed his duffle bag and shoved in his laptop along with whatever else he had left in there. He ran to the table and, being extremely careful not to touch it, rolled the stone into the vase, sealed it with the lid, placed it into the box, put the whole thing in his bag, grabbed his hip pouch, and ran from the room. He ignored the elevator and sprinted to the door leading to the stairway. After bashing it open with his shoulder, he took the stairs three at a time and bolted through the door into the lobby. Crossing the lobby in an all-out run, he hit the glass entry door hard enough to make the hinges groan from the stress.

On the other side of the door was a man dressed in shorts and a floral shirt, who was shocked to see a half-crazed Dan burst from the hotel. That same man was livid when a frenzied Dan collided with him and bowled him over. Their legs tangled briefly, but Dan righted himself and bolted off into the night.

II

The Morning After

The sun was coming up and shone on the police who stood in the main doorways of the Copamarina Beach Resort to keep the media and gawkers at bay. Everyone had questions, but few were getting answers. In the corner of the lobby, three men who were dressed to look like tourists were talking quietly. One of them reached into his pocket, pulled out his phone, pressed the call icon, and waited for the connection. The call was answered on the first ring.

"Talk to me, Rashan."

Rashan Palmer glanced around at the disorderliness of the lobby, then turned toward the corner to gain what privacy he could as the other two men safeguarded his back.

"We're too late here, Niles," he said, his English heavy with a Jamaican accent. "It seems the Bound got here first."

On the other end of the line, Niles's heart sank. He had been pacing but now needed to find a seat. "Damn it!" He had to take a few seconds to calm himself, so he could think clearly. "Tell me what you've found."

"Craziness by the time we got here, some people dead and a few rooms torn apart, but . . ."

"But what?"

"Niles, if this was a Bound thing, then they have a problem, because things are not adding up."

"Tell me, Rashan."

"Things are too messy for it to have gone right for the Bound. First, there is not just one person, but several who woke up dead this morning, and not thanks to typical Bound execution."

"Go on."

"According to the rumor mill, the night clerk jotted down a note that she received a noise complaint from one of the upper rooms. She was going up to investigate, but she evidently never came back down. They found her dead in a room this morning, apparently with her neck broken."

"Neck broken? That's not Bound protocol."

"I know, and we hear there's worse."

"How are the authorities there handling it?"

"Rumor is one of you American boys, some guy named Daniel Knocks, went berserk."

"Who's Daniel Knocks?"

"We don't know the details yet, but he signed in as a guest with a team of engineers, and it was in his room that they found the clerk."

"Is he Bound?"

"We don't know, but he is involved up to his armpits."

"Is this Knocks guy responsible for the killings?"

There was a slight pause before Rashan answered. "From what we can gather, the police are leaning that way right now, but . . ."

"But you think they're wrong?"

"We think they're wrong."

"Tell me why."

"We talked to a hotel guest who was busy nursing a hangover and a bruised backside. He told me he had been out celebrating and returned late. He was bragging about how lucky he is that he wasn't killed, too. Said he thinks this Knocks guy was the man who ran him down as he left the hotel and he didn't even break stride, just ran him over and kept on going. He's convinced it was Knocks and he was running because he had just killed those people, but, Niles, the timing doesn't work."

"So, you think if this was Knocks, he left the hotel before the murders?"

"I think so. If it was Knocks, then the collision definitely happened before the girl went up to investigate the noise."

"If he isn't involved in the murders then why would Knocks be running?"

"We don't know for sure, but our guess is maybe he got a tip or somehow knew about the Bound and this shit coming his way, and he wanted out before they got here."

"I'm listening." Niles said as he got up and started pacing again.

"Maybe this Knocks guy is the one who has the stone, and he took it on the run. Maybe he's a Bound and he decided to go rogue."

"Explain why you think that."

"I went upstairs for a better look, but I couldn't get close enough to do much investigating without the local police throwing me out, though I did get a glimpse at a few things and overheard some talk. We all know how Bound usually kill, natural causes, but this isn't the case here. It looks like something must have gone wrong in a big way."

"How so?"

"It sounds like these people were interrogated and tortured. I heard some poor guy had a shirt shoved in his mouth and toothpicks jammed through his eyelids into his eyeballs, for Christ's sake, but Niles, the Bound don't torture for sport. Whoever did this was looking for information, but I don't think they got what they wanted. I was able to walk by an open door, and the debris I saw suggest the rooms were tossed hard. If they did that, they didn't get what they were after and had to resort to a physical search. Probably what caused the noise complaint. Judging by the damage I saw, I don't think they got what they were after."

"You think they were looking for the stone," Niles concluded.

"I think that's it, and anybody who may have asked questions, or got in their way, is dead."

"And the police over there think this Knocks guy is responsible?"

"I don't know if that's the official stance, but that's what's going around. But it's hard to believe one engineer did all this."

There was a pause while Niles thought.

"Rashan, even if the stone is there, you won't get a chance to look for it. See what information you guys can gather on Knocks, ask around and see if you can find anything about what he was doing, who he's with, where he spent his free time, and who he talked to. If this guy has the stone and took it on the run with him, he might still have it and he might still be in Puerto Rico. We'll start looking for him on our end.

"I am already looking, but Niles . . . what if Bound did find the stone?"

There was silence on the other end as Niles considered the question.

"My best guess is a pandemic that will kill more people than the past three combined."

12

Aleecia Donnelly

"**L**et's go crazy!"

The music of Prince & The Revolution filled Aleecia Donnelly's living room in her Troy, Michigan, home. Sweat ran from her forehead through her eyebrow, and onto her eyelashes. She stopped to grab a towel and wipe her face before pushing the stop icon on her phone, which was Bluetooth-connected to an external speaker. Aleecia had exercised to *Purple Rain* since she'd started her on-and-off workouts several years ago. It was a tribute to her mother as much as anything else, the album being her mom's favorite; Aleecia had come to appreciate the music.

As she walked around her room to decrease her pulse, Aleecia looked at the app displaying her time. She had gone almost two full minutes longer than last week, better than she had done in years. She had decided six months ago to lose the fat that had started to gather on her butt and thighs, and now she was a lean 5'4" and 115 pounds. When she glanced in the mirror, she grinned.

Her hair, kept long enough to cover her shoulders, fell in loose black ringlets and framed her round face. Her full lips looked perpetually on the verge of a smile, and long rich eyelashes accentuated her deep dark-chocolate brown eyes that caught the light and echoed it back with a soft sparkle. Aleecia was happy with what she saw.

She went through a series of stretches and shook out her legs, the muscles waggling under her brown skin.

When her phone chirped, she answered it slightly out of breath.

"Hello?"

"Hey, Leecie."

"Danny?" she asked excitedly, though she already knew who it was.

"How come your number didn't come up and I didn't get your ringtone?"

"Sorry, I'm using a different phone. I broke mine."

"Well, that stinks. But, hey, sweetie, it's good to hear from you, how's Puerto Rico?" Aleecia moved to the window and looked out across the street at Dan's house. The shades were drawn just as she left them the last time she had gone over to feed the fish and water the plants.

Dan's pause was longer than normal, so she turned her attention back to the phone.

"Danny?"

"I'm here. It's been tougher down here than I thought it would be," he said, though he quickly realized he sounded depressed and changed his tone so as not to arouse Aleecia's suspicion. He needed her and didn't want to make this any harder than it was already going to be. "But that's just because you're not around to cheer me up," he forced himself to say cheerfully. "How you doin' back in the States? Anything thrilling happening?"

"I'm doing great. And no, nothing thrilling at all, thank you very much."

"That's you all over, always looking for a way to avoid anything new. Gets kind of boring, doesn't it?"

"You know me, the more 'nothing out of the ordinary' the better. I go to work in the morning, come home in the evening, and go shopping every Wednesday. Besides, I like boring, there's no anxiety involved."

"I suppose," Dan answered, well aware that what he was about to ask would be a huge deal to Aleecia.

"How about you?" she asked. "Anything stirring with you?"

If you only knew, Dan thought. "Sort of. I've decided to try something new."

"Nothing dangerous, I hope."

"Too late," he mumbled softly.

"What?"

"Nothing, just thinking out loud."

"When do you think you'll be coming home?" she asked. "Not sure," he said, "but listen, Leecie, I called to ask you to do me a huge favor, and I mean huge."

"Oh great, last time you asked me to do you a favor I had to buy a dress and go to your cousin's wedding with you."

"Yeah, I remember. You gave me a lot of trouble about going, and we ended up having a wonderful time."

"Yeah, I remember." An awkward silence passed between them, as the wedding was the first and only time in their ten-year history when they had crossed the line from friends to lovers. Although neither had any regrets, other than that it had never happened again, they didn't talk about it much.

"What do you need?"

"Please don't freak, and try to keep an open mind. I understand this will be way out of your comfort zone, but I have nobody else who can be there."

"Oh boy, I can already tell I'm going to hate this."

"Probably, but it won't be as bad as you're imagining it to be."

Aleecia drew a deep breath. "What is it?"

"I need you to drive up north to Charlevoix and represent me when I sell my boat." Dan listened to the long pause and imagined Aleecia shaking her head no.

"Leecie, please stop shaking your head and listen to me. I know this is something you're not comfortable doing, but I need someone I can trust."

"Danny, you know I hate stuff like this. I don't want to do this."

"I know, Leecie, and if it weren't really, really important, I wouldn't ask," Dan pleaded.

"Why is it so important? Why can't it wait until you come back?"

"It can't, something has come up and I need the cash now."

Another uncomfortable pause filled the phone.

"Come on, Leecie, I really need you to do this for me."

"No, Danny, no, you told me your uncle gave you that boat, and you said you'd never get rid of it."

"I know, but something's happened and I don't have much of a choice. I need to do it."

Aleecia picked up on another longer-than-normal pause. "Are you in some kind of trouble?"

"No, nothing like that." The pause wasn't caused by any desire on Dan's part to lie to Aleecia, but at this point he thought it necessary.

Aleecia was shaking her head, trying to find a way to say no without sounding illogical.

"Look, Danny, if you need some money, I'll give you what you need."

"I know you would, Leecie, you're sweet like that, but I need a lot—all I can get—and that boat is worth a lot."

"And who would you sell it to? It could take a long time to find the right buyer."

"You remember when we took her out on the Fourth of July last summer?"

"Yeah," Aleecia said, and she did remember the trip, quite well. "Remember that guy, Tom Howard? He asked if I'd be willing to sell her. Came on board, looked around, and made me an offer?"

"Yeah, I remember, the guy with the bad toupee. Hairpiece worse than Trump's. You told him no."

"That's the one. I found his number in an old file I've never deleted. I called him, and he said he's still interested. He wants to look at her, and if she's still in good shape he'll buy her. He's willing to meet you up in Charlevoix to do the deal."

"Oh, Danny," she said, the anxiety rising in her voice.

"I know, Leecie, but you can do this, and I really need your help."

She sighed heavily, and Dan knew this reaction as well as her shaking of her head. She was going to give in, despite her head telling her not to.

"Thank you, Leecie. I can't tell you how much this means to me. Today, you're my hero."

"Yeah, right," she said. "And when and where am I supposed to meet this guy?"

"He's going to meet you Monday morning at the boat, it's in the same slip as last year."

"Monday? That means I'll have to miss work."

"I know, but I also know you have a ton of banked vacation time, and I'm sure you can swing it. And stop shaking your head."

"This deal just keeps getting better and better. What time, Monday?"

"Nine."

"Nine in the morning, which means I'll have to leave here around four-thirty just to make it on time."

Dan heard the frustration and knew he was pushing the limits, but he needed the cash. And the risk, well, that was minimal. At least for now.

"You won't have to leave early at all, Leecie. I called the dockmaster and he put me in touch with a guy in Charlevoix who's getting things ready for you, so the boat will be all set when you get there. You can go up there tomorrow and sleep on board. I know how much you like staying on the boat, and you liked it when we walked all the shops in town. Go up to Charlevoix tomorrow, enjoy the day, walk the town, and meet Howard Monday morning."

"Daniel Knocks, I can't do this."

"Yes, you can, Leecie. It will be relaxing, and you can de-stress. It'll be good for you."

"No, not going would be good for me."

"Come on, Leecie, you're the only one I trust to do this for me. I need your help, Aleecia, please?"

Aleecia sighed again. "Okay, mister," she said after a long pause. "But do you owe me, big time."

"Anything you want, Leecie, anything you want."

"Yeah, well, you just remember this because . . ."

"I will, sweetie, I promise," Dan said, cutting her off. "I have to go, but I'll call Howard and let him know you'll be there. Thank you so much, Leecie. Love you, bye."

He hung up before she had a chance to change her mind. She closed her phone app and shook her head. He knew how much this sort of thing stressed her, and yet he had asked her anyway; that was an indication to her of how important this was to Dan, and why she finally agreed. But a nagging thought kept raising its hand: How could he trust her to sell his boat but not trust her enough to tell her why he needed it sold? That was something she would undoubtedly ask him later, when she got hold of him, and when she did . . .

She could already feel her stress level increasing, and she knew she shouldn't get so nerved up. She couldn't help it; that was simply who she was. New things bothered her. She often considered why this was so. Of all the times she had tried something new, there were very few that had turned out as what she would deem badly, but she had always feared change. Every time she held this inner discussion as to why, she always came to the same conclusion: it was just the way she had been raised. Her parents were on again, off again for most of her life and Aleecia, her sister, and her two brothers had spent a lot of time with their grandparents while growing up.

Her grandfather, like many African American men of his age, was drafted and had fought in Vietnam. From what Aleecia could gather, the reason he hadn't talked a lot about that time in his life was because he had seen a lot of killing.

One of the lessons he had repeated over and over to her was that she should keep her head down and not volunteer for anything.

"The less you make yourself a target, the happier you'll be," he'd told her.

This lesson was both ignored and confirmed by Aleecia's brother, Tyrese, who had enlisted in the military and fought in Afghanistan. His fight, however, didn't turn out as well as their granddad's, and Tyrese made the trip home in a box wrapped in a flag.

That drove the lesson home for Aleecia, and she found it easier and more pleasing to establish routines and stick to them. There is much less stress in a world that doesn't change.

But this was change, even if for a day or two, and it was enough of a change to cause her to think better of agreeing to help. She wanted to call Dan's cell and tell him that she couldn't do it. Now that she had agreed, however, she didn't want to go back on her word. As it was, she already felt too obligated to not show up.

13

The Lazin-About

Aleecia left her home around 8:00 a.m. Sunday morning. The drive to the northwestern coast of Michigan's Lower Peninsula, and Charlevoix, would take more than four hours, and give her a lot of time to stew about Dan.

She stopped for lunch around noon and reached Charlevoix around 1:30 p.m., parking in the grocer's lot across the street from the docks. She grabbed her overnight bag from the trunk and slung it over her shoulder. The gold stitching that bordered the wings of dozens of red dragonflies transformed the sun's rays into twinkling sparkles.

Aleecia found the Lazin-About in a slip near the end of one of the docks in Round Lake, the small lake connecting Lake Charlevoix to Lake Michigan. Because of her 7.5-foot draft, and need for deeper water, the Lazin-About was farther from the main docks than most yachts. Aleecia stopped and stood to admire the vessel for a few seconds.

Designed by William Hand and R. O. Davis, the 55-foot motor sailer was built in the Wheeler Shipyard of Brooklyn, New York, in 1934. She was a beautiful example of older craftsmanship; her white hull and brass fittings glittered in the sunlight and her boxy pilothouse made her look warm and inviting, like grandma's house.

True to his word, Dan had ensured someone had prepared the yacht for Aleecia's visit. She smiled as she climbed aboard and took a few minutes to walk the teak decking and touch the wood and brass helm before heading below.

The air below was a little stale, so she left the hatch open. There were several places she could choose to sleep, but the main stateroom at the bow was where she would spend the night. At a minimum she deserved that. Aleecia opened the portlights on either side to allow the fresh air to circulate, as she stripped off the sheets and made the berth with ones she had brought from home. The ones on the Lazin-About were clean, but the last time she and Dan had taken the Lazin-About out, the sheets had smelled musty and made her feel like she was sleeping in a tent.

She folded the sheets and opened a storage compartment to store them when something caught her eye. It was a greeting card Dan had given her when they took the Lazin-About out for their trip over the Fourth weekend. They'd sailed her to the straits of Mackinaw and had visited Mackinaw Island. Although the hustle and bustle of the crowd didn't appeal to Aleecia, the romance of an island that had outlawed motorized vehicles a long time ago did. Horse-drawn carriages, on foot, and bicycles were the only modes of transportation, which slowed the pace and was something she'd enjoyed immensely.

Dan had given her the card and signed it *Danny*; he had drawn a small *A-N-D* in the lower right corner, the way young lovers might carve their initials into the trunk of a tree. They had spent the night on the yacht, with a view of the five-mile-long Mackinaw Bridge just out of her stateroom. The thought of a second romantic interlude had danced in Aleecia's mind and although they had come close, it didn't happen and in the end, they fell asleep in each other's arms. *Maybe next time* was what she had thought at the time, and it probably would have come to pass, but now Dan was trying something new and she understood there wouldn't be a next time, at least not on the Lazin-About.

The weather was beautiful, so she left the portlights open and went above deck to look at the town. When Dan brought her here, he had taken her to dinner and afterward they had strolled the streets, and she remembered she enjoyed the little shops of souvenirs, sweets, and even art.

"So what do you say girl, should you be bold and walk the town?" she asked herself. Most people who visited for the weekend left Sunday afternoon so there would be no crowds; she grinned and nodded her head. "Why not, I'm on vacation."

She was hesitant at first, but she retraced the same route she and Dan had taken and visited the same shops. The things inside were fun to look at but held little necessity, so Aleecia bought nothing until her resistance fled when she walked into one of the fudge shops and the chocolate peanut butter called her name. She bought a quarter pound and, to ease the guilt, nibbled at it while she walked the pier to Lake Michigan and strolled along the beach where she and Dan had taken a moonlight dip.

She treated herself to dinner at the same restaurant, called the Villager, and caught a movie at the cinema next door, before returning to Olson's Market where she bought bread, bacon, and eggs for breakfast. She got back to the Lazin-About around sunset.

That night, she lay quietly in her berth listening to the sound of the water softly lapping at the hull. Dan was right about one thing—this *was* relaxing. She folded her hands behind her head and watched the waltzing shadows the moon and water scribbled on the stateroom ceiling and, for the last time in the years to come, Aleecia fell into a deep, peaceful sleep.

In the morning, her sleep was broken by the sound of warning bells as the drawbridge rose to allow the boats on Lake Charlevoix access to the channel leading to Lake Michigan.

She got up, showered, dressed, and packed, before going to the galley to make breakfast. When her food was ready, she took it up on deck to eat in the morning air. Over breakfast, she cleared her vacation day; when the HR department had noticed how much time she had banked up, they insisted she use five days. Aleecia was on forced vacation and was thinking of what she wanted to do when Tom Howard approached from the dock.

"Ahoy, Lazin-About," he shouted in a robust voice that startled Aleecia, given he was twenty minutes early.

"What? Oh . . . yeah . . . ahoy," Aleecia said around a bite of toast.

Howard stood on the dock smiling, and Aleecia recognized the same bad toupee; but that was all that matched her expectation, because

Howard was now approximately thirty pounds heavier and his dark-blue slacks were just a tad short and showed off his white deck shoes and argyle socks. He was also carrying a small briefcase, which made him look more like a salesman than a potential buyer.

"Permission to come aboard," he said, but he didn't wait for a reply before climbing the brow to the deck. "You must be Aleecia," he said, moving the briefcase from his right hand to his left before shoving the beefy right in her direction. "I'm Tom Howard. I assume you were expecting me."

"I knew you were coming," Aleecia said, wiping her mouth with her napkin before shaking his hand.

"Great," Howard said. "I was surprised when Mr. Knocks called me, just a few minutes ago as a matter of fact, to say he couldn't make it personally. He said you would be representing him, is that correct?"

"I believe that's what he had in mind."

Howard nodded his approval. "I was excited to hear that Mr. Knocks had reconsidered. I was also somewhat taken aback by his insistence that the deal happen so quickly."

"I know this was sudden, and I'm as surprised as you are. I never thought he'd sell his boat."

"Yacht, my lady," Howard corrected. "This fine vessel is a sailing yacht, and I'd like to give her a once-over to make sure nothing's changed from the last time I saw her."

"By all means," Aleecia said, feeling suddenly out of place. After all, this was not her boat, or yacht.

Taking his briefcase with him, Howard went below deck and spent almost thirty minutes performing an inspection marked by quiet mutterings accented by the occasional bang or thump of a door or hatch, but when he finally climbed back on deck he was smiling.

"Everything seems to be in order. She's just as beautiful as I remembered, and she has been well cared for. I think the deal can proceed."

Howard looked around apprehensively, before sitting down at the small table with Aleecia and setting the small briefcase between them. "I must admit it was a challenge to meet Mr. Knock's . . . shall we call it his strange request. It has made me somewhat nervous. My attorney advised me not to do this, she told me there would be no safeguard once the deal went through." Howard looked sternly at Aleecia, but his expression gave way almost immediately to a smile. "But I knew I just had to have her."

Aleecia smiled. "She is very beautiful."

"Yes," Howard said through the smile, though it faded slowly.

"Can I ask you a question? You don't have to answer if it makes you uneasy."

Aleecia stared at him blankly and when she didn't answer Howard pressed on.

"Are you alone?"

Aleecia hesitated as her pulse quickened. "Why do you ask?"

"Well, it's just an awful lot of money to carry around."

"I'm sorry, money?"

"Yes, or did Mr. Knocks not tell you?"

"Tell me what?"

"He asked me to pay in cash. That's what has made me so nervous. I'm no stranger to money, but I don't often carry it around in large sums." Howard pressed the latches on the case, which sprung the locks, and turned the briefcase to face Aleecia. He took one last look around himself then proceeded to open the case. It was indeed full of cold, hard cash. "Two hundred and seventy-five thousand dollars, just as he asked for."

Aleecia's mouth opened gradually, but her stress level increased five times as fast.

"He didn't tell you, did he?"

"No, he didn't."

"You may count it if you wish, but I suggest you do it below deck," Howard said, closing the case and securing the latches. "I was hoping you'd be able to tell me why it had to be done like this. I suggested we just wire the money to him or transfer the funds to his account, but he wouldn't hear of it. He told me it had to be cash, or he would find another buyer. For the life of me, I can't figure out why . . . and I think, maybe now, it would be better if I stopped asking. The title's clear and we faxed the paperwork and signatures back and forth over the weekend.

My broker tells me this is the weirdest sale she's ever been part of, but it all comes back legit. As far as I'm concerned, the deal's a good one."

Aleecia was still stunned. Dan had set her up with 275K. He would have to do a lot of explaining when he came to collect.

"Mr. Howard, I am at a loss as to what all this is about," she said, trying to regain her composure, "but you were nice enough to trust Dan with a cash deal, and I believe you're an honest man, so I don't think I need to count it."

"That's fine, I can assure you that it's all there, but I would like you to sign that you did receive this."

Aleecia nodded and Howard retrieved a form from his inside breast pocket and showed Aleecia where to sign. After she did, he quickly put it back into the same pocket.

Satisfied, Howard smiled. "Mr. Knocks said I could have immediate possession, is that still the case?"

"I guess it is," Aleecia said, realizing that her trip was now over. "I have a few things below. I'll gather them and then she's all yours. If there's any problems, I'm sure you and Dan can work them out."

"I think that's best," Howard said with a smile. "You can stay as long as you need to, but I will have someone here in about an hour, so we can take her out and get to know her better. You're welcome to join us."

"That's kind, thank you, but I won't be staying. I just need to get my things."

Howard took the briefcase from the table and sat it on the deck near Aleecia's feet.

"Only you and I know what's in there, but for chivalry's sake, would you like me to walk you to your car?"

"That would be nice."

Howard nodded. "Let me know when you're ready."

"Thank you," Aleecia said as Howard got up from the table and again went below, this time as owner of the Lazin-About. Aleecia looked at the case. She had no desire to touch it; worse, she had no idea what to do. She was sitting on a yacht that now belonged to a stranger, who had just given her a boatload of cash, and although she had suggested Howard was an honest man, in truth she didn't know him from Adam. She decided that the best thing to do was to head out as soon as possible and get back to more familiar turf.

She left the case sitting where it was and took her dishes to the galley where Howard was taking stock of what was there.

When she dropped the dishes into the sink, Howard said, "Don't worry about those, I'm not sure I'm going to keep them."

Aleecia hesitated for a few seconds. "I'll get my things."

"That's fine," Howard said, clearly ready to see her leave.

Aleecia collected her sheets and Dan's card and put them in her overnight bag with the rest of her things. By the time she returned to the deck, Howard was waiting.

"Are you ready?"

"I am," Aleecia replied while glancing at the case.

Howard motioned to the dock. "Shall we?"

Aleecia nodded at the case. "Could you?"

"Of course," Howard said, picking up the briefcase.

As they walked, Aleecia became increasingly nervous about Howard and how much she didn't know about the man who, at this point, was her sole protection. The anxiety reached such an intensity that by the time they reached her car and Howard spoke, Aleecia nearly jumped.

"Where would you like me to put this?"

"I think it would be best to put it in the trunk," she replied as casually as she could manage. Having that much money close to her in the car, where it could be easily reached, made Aleecia uncomfortable. She pushed the button on her key chain and popped the trunk. Howard stepped to the back of the car and deposited the case. Aleecia stepped up beside him and dropped in her overnight bag, before closing the lid.

"Please tell Mr. Knocks that I said thank you and I'll take good care of the Lazin-About."

"I will."

They shook hands once more, and Aleecia got into her car and left the parking lot. As Howard watched her leave, suspicion again rose in her mind. She decided that she would not give him a clear idea of which direction she was headed, so when she left the parking lot, she turned toward the residential streets instead of taking the main road. She then circled the block and instead of heading south, turned north. Aleecia began driving US 31 toward the city of Petoskey, but after only traveling a mile she began to feel a little silly.

"Come on, girl," she mumbled to herself. "You're driving in the wrong direction and just getting farther away from home. Besides, if that guy was going to pull something funny, he would have done it when he had the chance." She looked down at her fuel gauge and decided she would fill up now, so she wouldn't have to worry about it on the way home. Nobody knew what was in her trunk, but, all the same, she didn't want to stop once she got going. She pulled into a Krist gas station at the northern end of town and filled up before heading back the way she'd come.

When she reentered downtown Charlevoix, she was stopped by the open drawbridge. When the bridge lowered and the traffic began to move again, Aleecia crossed the bridge and looked toward the Lazin-About. She could see Howard standing on the deck talking on his cell. Movement from the corner of her eye caught her attention, and she looked to the road just in time to stomp on the brake and avoid hitting two men hurrying across the street. Aleecia came so close to hitting them that the first man had to put his hand on her car's hood to push himself away and avoid being hit. She expected the men to stop and say something, anything, but they barely looked at her as they passed. When they began sprinting, their open sport coats flapped behind them as they ran. The only acknowledgment they gave to almost being run over was when the second man flipped a half-chewed toothpick onto her windshield as he passed.

14

The Detective

Aleecia's drive home was a little nerve-racking but otherwise uneventful. Traffic had been light, and there was only one time when her imagination got the better of her and she swore she was being followed. But the fear vanished when the suspicious car exited the freeway five minutes later. Afterward, there were no moments of alarm . . . that is until she turned onto her own street and spotted the police cars.

A wave of panic struck her as she thought they were at her house. But as she got closer she realized they were across the street at Dan's. She watched as a uniformed officer walked in the open front door. As she drove past, she could see debris on the floor just inside.

"Oh, Danny, honey, it looks like somebody wiped you out," she muttered as she pulled into her driveway and shut off the engine. She watched through her mirrors for a while as she thought things over. She felt bad for not being there to watch the house and she was torn as to what to do now. She wanted to find out what was going on, but the last thing she wanted was to have to answer a lot of questions; especially since she had just sold Dan's boat. She knew facts like that had a way of breeding more questions, and since history had taught her lineage to be leery of cops, she decided she would check things out and keep the boat sale to herself.

She got out of her car and walked over to Dan's front lawn. When she glanced over her shoulder at the trunk of her car, the thought of the cash made her decide this could wait. Before she could reverse directions, however, a man in a casual suit stepped through the door and began to examine something under the sunlight. When he glanced up, he spotted Aleecia.

"Hi," he said, as though he was greeting an old acquaintance.

"Hello," Aleecia responded. She couldn't help but notice a warm smile she would never before have associate as coming from a cop. The cops she met were always stone-faced; any smiles had appeared forced. She also noticed the man's smile was supported by a handsome face and tall lean frame that suggested his workout program was responsible for his athletic body.

"You live around here?" he asked.

"Across the street," she said, pointing apprehensively.

"You know the homeowner?"

"Somewhat."

He eyed her carefully. She eyed him back.

"What's your name?"

"Aleecia, and yours?"

He kept the smile as he walked across the lawn to her. "My name is Merle Rogiletti," he said offering her his hand. She took it half expecting a manly handshake, but she was pleasantly surprised when the grip he returned was gentle. "It's nice to meet you, Aleecia."

"It's nice to meet you, too," she said, smiling at Merle, who smiled back warmly.

His Italian heritage was obvious, and Aleecia noticed he had a firm, square, hero's chin, a lot like Danny's, complete with a dimple. His hair was dark brown, not quite black, with matching sideburns of a length that ended mid ear. Although his hair was cut and well-kept, it was long enough to show off a natural wave. Merle Rogiletti also had big brown eyes. Eyes that were soft, clear, and seductive. Eyes that Aleecia referred to as bedroom eyes. Her pulse quickened, just a little.

An awkward silence followed as Merle held her hand for just a little too long. He caught himself, released her hand, and cleared his throat.

"Sorry, but I . . . I'd like to talk to you about this guy, if I could. Do you think I could stop by your place in a few minutes?"

She raised an eyebrow at the question. "That's a little different for a cop Mr. Rogiletti, asking instead of telling."

"Well, in my line of work, I do enough telling. Asking is something I like to try first."

She smiled, feeling like she had to be careful. This guy appealed to her on some level. Aleecia thought it better to keep herself at an emotional distance. "What happened here?"

"That's what I'm trying to find out. Is it okay if I stop by?"

"I suppose it would be okay," she said, and for reasons she didn't want to think about, she felt warmth in her cheeks.

"Great, I'll finish here and be over to see you." He gave her a quick wink before turning back to Dan's house.

Aleecia's smile didn't fade until she was halfway across the street and what had just happened dawned on her. She'd agreed to talk to him, and now she would have to answer all of his cop questions. She cursed herself under her breath as she walked.

"What an idiot. You're acting like an adolescent schoolgirl. You invited this cop to your home just because he has a nice smile, a handsome face, and a sweet body. Stop it," she told herself. "You don't know him any better than you knew Howard. He could be a flaming lunatic." She decided she would be tougher on the cop when he came to ask his questions. She would tell him as little as she could. She didn't want to get involved, and there was no way she would tell him about the money.

She stopped at her car long enough to grab her overnight bag and the case from the trunk. She glanced over her shoulder to see if Merle was watching her. He wasn't, and she felt strangely relieved and disappointed. She went inside her house, closed and locked the door behind her, and dropped her overnight bag to the living room floor. Trying to decide what to do with the case, she looked around. She sat it down on the glass coffee table in front of her sofa, popped the latches, and lifted the lid. Through the eyes of dead presidents, $275,000 looked back at her.

"Dump it on the floor and roll in it," she said quietly and grinned. Instead, she closed the lid and took it into the bedroom where she slid it under her bed. It wasn't the best spot, but it would have to do for now.

She used the bathroom and was headed back to the living room when the doorbell rang its contemporary two-tone bell. She looked through the peephole and got the fish-eye view of Merle Rogiletti. Aleecia wondered what it would be like to date a man like Rogiletti. Would the first date involve a fancy restaurant and dancing? Or would he pack a picnic basket and find a nice grassy hill overlooking the prison yard, so they could watch the inmates play basketball while they sampled fine wine and cheeses? She took a breath, put on her poker face, and opened the door wide. She leaned against the doorframe and folded her arms across her chest.

"Hi," he said again with the same warm smile. "Got a few minutes to talk?"

"I suppose. But when I think about it, I only took your word that you're a cop," Aleecia said, not inviting him in.

Rogiletti grinned and looked past her into the house's interior. "Cop, no," he said as the smile became a smirk. "I'm just an average guy who likes to follow hooligans around and question the neighbors for a hobby. Cool luggage."

Aleecia glanced over her shoulder at the overnight bag. *Wow*, she thought, *sarcasm with a side of compliment. I like it.* She turned back to the man at the door.

"That's a really strange hobby you have. And thank you, I like the luggage a lot. Can I see a badge?"

Merle pulled his ID from his inside breast pocket and nonchalantly handed it to Aleecia. As he continued to glance around the room, she proceeded to look closely at the ID before handing it back.

"Detective Merle Rogiletti," Aleecia said. "Would you care to come in?"

"Thank you," Merle said, stepping inside and closing the door. "And your last name?"

"Donnelly, Aleecia Donnelly."

"That's a pretty name." He smiled. "Just one piece, Ms. Donnelly?"

"I beg your pardon?"

"The luggage, one piece or a set?"

"Oh." Aleecia smiled and the warmth returned to her cheeks. "It's from a set of four."

"My sister would love it," Merle said, placing the badge back in his pocket. "Remember where you got it?"

"Bought it online a few years ago."

Merle looked closer. "Really, it's a neat print."

"Thanks for the review, anything else I can help you with?"

Merle's smile faded. "I think you probably can. The question is, will you?"

Okay, here comes the cop, Aleecia thought and the psychological shields went up. "Let's find out."

"All right. I need to ask you some questions about the guy across the street. You know him." This was a statement, not a question.

"Somewhat," Aleecia said, suddenly feeling very uncomfortable as Merle Rogiletti, within seconds, completed his transformation into Detective Rogiletti.

"Quite well, I should think."

"Why would you think that, detective?"

Rogiletti reached inside his jacket's breast pocket and retrieved a picture of Dan and Aleecia slow dancing at a formal event. He handed it to her. "I found this in the debris that used to be his home."

She took it with a slight smile. "His cousin's wedding," she said, noticing how in the corner of the photo Dan had written the same *A-N-D* he'd jotted down on the card he had given her on the Lazin-About.

"Are you two dating?" Rogiletti asked with a shy smile.

"No, detective, we're just really good friends."

He nodded. "Any idea of who might have paid him a visit like this?"

"No, but I'm sure he'll be glad to hear he's been robbed," she added sarcastically.

"Will you break it to him gently?"

"Me? I suppose I could tell him, but isn't it your job?"

"It is, but there is more to this story than meets the eye. I have a feeling you might get the chance to talk to him before I do, and there are a few things you and I should talk about first."

Aleecia took two steps away from Detective Rogiletti. "What sort of things?"

"Well, let's start with where he is and what racket he's involved in."

Aleecia's arms folded across her chest again. "I'm sorry, racket?"

"Yeah, you know, drugs, stolen property, the mob? What's his trick?"

"Look, Detective Rogiletti, I'm sure you're a fine investigator, but you missed the mark on this guy. I've known him for years. He's not like that."

"Really, tell me about him?"

"Why don't you tell me why you think this is something more than a robbery?"

Rogiletti studied her face and smiled, but this one seemed forced and phony—a cop's smile. "Most of the time, I refrain from telling people too much about an investigation. Mostly, a need-to-know basis is best. But sometimes it pays to be open about what's going on, so I'm going to be straight with you, Ms. Donnelly. I only ask that you do the same for me." When Aleecia didn't respond, he continued, "Some curious things have happened over the past few days, and we need to discuss them with Daniel Knocks."

"And not just because someone has stolen his stuff, right?"

"And there, Ms. Donnelly, is the problem. The fact is nobody has stolen his stuff. At least, nothing that we know of."

"What do you mean?"

"I mean all of his valuables still seem to be there and were only tossed about and broken. I even found a twenty-dollar bill lying on the floor, so robbery wasn't the motive, was it?"

"Nothing was taken?" Aleecia muttered as questions began to race through her mind. Did Howard have it planned, so someone would show up and get his money back, except they accidentally showed up a day early?

"Well, let's not jump to conclusions," Rogiletti continued. "I didn't say nothing was taken. But whoever did this was looking for something specific. Whether they found it or not is the real question. Any idea of what they might have been looking for?"

How about the money under my bed? she thought, but Aleecia shook her head.

"Any idea of where he is?"

Aleecia wanted to stop talking. It was obvious something bad was happening. She wanted time to think things over. She wanted the cop out of her house.

"Right now, he's in Guánica, Puerto Rico. Know where that is, detective?"

"I certainly do. In fact, I know more about it today than I did yesterday."

"And why is that?"

"I received a call from the authorities in Guánica. That's what brought me to your friend's house this morning. Apparently, Dan's gone missing and they need to ask him some questions."

Worry altered her expressions. "Missing, what do you mean he's missing?"

Rogiletti studied her face in pursuit of signs that she might know where this was going. Seeing no deception, he continued. "According to the people I spoke to, a coworker by the name of Megan Tomsly and his boss, Alex Mayer, were found dead in their hotel rooms."

Aleecia drew a quick breath and felt her knees go weak. She made her way to the sofa, where she sat down heavily. Rogiletti moved to the side of the sofa and waited.

"A . . . Alex and Megan are dead?" she asked with stunned induced stutter. "Oh my God, how?"

"That's where things get weird. The autopsy report says heart attack and stroke, but there's much more to it."

"Like what?"

"Well, the information I have is that Megan was relatively young, in good health . . . and was tied to a chair before she suffered her stroke. Alex suffered a heart attack, which is possible because he was a bit older. But he was also tied to his bed, had a shirt in his mouth and toothpicks shoved into both of his eyes through the lids. Most heart-attack victims are able to avoid those particular symptoms."

"They were murdered?"

"It would seem so, but the coroner is positive the deaths were caused by a heart attack and stroke. Alex's heart attack, brought on by the violence, is possible. But Megan and a stroke?" Rogiletti shook his head. "In any event, it's clear that whoever killed the pair was looking for . . . answers. In my humble opinion, I'd say the information is tied to our missing Daniel Knocks." Rogiletti watched Aleecia for her reaction. It was one of shock and disbelief; tears welling in her eyes. Rogiletti retrieved a tissue from a box on the end table, offered it to her, and pressed on.

"When was the last time you spoke to Mr. Knocks?"

There was a lengthy pause as Aleecia struggled to find her inner strength. She looked at Rogiletti and wondered if he was friend or foe. In truth, it didn't matter. She was vulnerable and would have to be very careful with the information she gave him.

"He called the other day."

"And he called for?"

"He asked if there was anything new, what was happening."

"You mean like, hello, anything happening, did anyone ransack my house?"

"He never asked about his house."

"What did he ask about?"

"Me, how I was, things like that."

"Anything out of the ordinary?"

Aleecia didn't want to lie, but she was confused and frightened. She thought she owed Danny a chance to explain things, so she decided the sale of the boat could wait until later. And it would be later. If Rogiletti was worth his salt as a detective, he would find out Dan's boat was sold, to whom, and who had represented Dan in the sale. These thoughts kept Aleecia from speaking. Again, she shook her head no. Rogiletti, seeming to take this all in, drew a deep breath. Then as quickly as the cop replaced the friendly man at her door, there was another switch. To her surprise, Merle now sat next to her on the couch.

"I'm sorry to be the one to share this with you. At times, my job puts me in bad situations, and this is one of them. I hate bringing bad news."

Aleecia looked up into his face and noticed how he was gazing at her with an expression of genuine concern.

"I don't know your friend, so I'll ask a simple question. Do you trust him?"

"Yes," she answered as she wiped a tear from her cheek.

"That's what I was afraid of. Listen, Aleecia—" She was surprised to hear him use her first name. "It's obvious you live alone and this friend of yours is into something you either don't know about or are unable to accept. Either way, it could be dangerous for you. I'll be talking to you again soon, but until then I'm going to give you my card." As if by magic, one appeared in his hand. "If you can remember anything that could shed some light on what's happening, I want you to call. This is my extension at the station," he said, pointing out the number. "And this is my personal cell. Call me if anything happens, okay?"

Aleecia took the card and nodded.

Merle stood and moved to the door, then stopped. "Aleecia, I think you're a charming lady. I wish we could have met under better circumstances."

She simply nodded again as Rogiletti left, closing the door behind him.

15

The Exchange

For the rest of the day, Aleecia's emotions drained her, so by early evening she was running on empty. The thought of the case sitting under her bed caused her to get up and, more than once, check the door locks. She didn't live in a high-crime area; in fact, it was exactly the opposite. There hadn't been a serious crime in her neighborhood in over five years, so Dan's break-in was a major event. The money under her bed represented a few years of salary for most of her neighbors, and a bit more for her. That much money could cause honest people to think twice. She made sure her doors were locked. And, just to be safe, she closed the drapes and pulled the shades.

To take her mind off the events of the day, she selected a movie from her video library—*Fellowship of the Ring*—and sat down on the sofa. She was hoping to lose herself in the story, but the questions plaguing her kept coming back. If Rogiletti was right, Dan needed to answer some serious questions. For the first time in their ten-year friendship, Aleecia had a moment when she questioned Dan's character.

She recalled the conversations with Dan and Rogiletti and couldn't make sense of the situation. Finally, she could take it no more and forced it away. The events of the past few days had sapped most of her energy, and she found herself slipping in and out of the story. By the time the fellowship had reached the mines of Moria, she had dozed off.

When the doorbell sounded, Aleecia jumped. Startled from her sleep, she gripped the arm of the sofa with her nails. She sat dazed, her mind racing to catch up. Waking enough to recognize the sound, she got up and headed to the front door. Feet from the door, she stopped. The doorbell had only chimed once. The back button had been pressed. She was now fully awake, frozen by suspicion and surprise. *Who would use the back door? And why?*

Leaving the lights off, she moved to the back of the house and carefully peeked out the small window of her laundry room that overlooked the back porch. Dan was standing there, watching the door. At first Aleecia just looked at him through the glass, while she debated what to do. But when he rang again, she went to the door. Leaving the chain on, she opened it to find Dan smiling and waving—but a stone-faced Aleecia stood still.

"You gonna let me in?" he asked.

"I don't know if I should," she said, despite knowing she would. "You've got a lot of explaining to do."

"I know I do, Leecie. Let me in and we'll talk about it."

Aleecia didn't move.

"Come on, Leecie." Dan's smile faded. "I need your help."

"I'd say you need more help than I can give you. You know the cops are looking for you?"

"I know," he said, bowing his head.

"A detective was here asking about you. He said I should call him if I see you."

"If I didn't know you better, Leecie, I'd say that was a veiled threat."

"Maybe it is. Are Alex and Megan really dead?" She watched Dan's posture deflate like a beach ball when its plug is pulled.

"They might be," he said quietly. "I don't know for sure, but I wouldn't doubt it."

"Why would somebody want to kill them? What have you gotten yourself into?"

"I'm not sure yet, but I didn't do anything to deserve what's happening." Even in the dim light, he could see the doubt cross her face. "Listen, Leecie, Alex and Megan are not only coworkers, they're my friends. Alex is my cousin, for God's sake, you know that. I had no idea these people would go after Alex or Megan. I didn't even know they'd come after me until it was too late."Dan's voice cracked, and Aleecia knew he was on the verge of breaking down. Tears shone in his eyes. "Please, Leecie, you're the only one I can trust. I can't even go home."

Aleecia's defenses cracked and she unchained the door.

Dan walked in cautiously, looking around as if he were expecting someone else to be there. In the light, Aleecia got her first good look at him.

"You look terrible," she said, wrinkling her nose as he passed.

"I know. I haven't slept much lately."

"Slept?"Aleecia asked, looking him over. His clothes weren't only disheveled; they were downright dirty.

"Yeah, I also haven't had a chance to shower in the last few days."

"I can smell that," she said. They shared a small smile. "So, tell me what's happening, Danny."

He wiped his eyes with the backs of his hands. "Where do I start?"

"Start with what happened to Alex and Megan."

"I'm not sure. I wasn't there. I left in the middle of the night, and ..."

"And?"

Dan hung his head shaking it slowly. "I wasn't sure they were dead until you told me. I suspected, actually kind of thought they might be, but I wasn't sure until now."

"Who's after you? Who killed Alex and Megan?"

"I don't know," he said with an exaggerated shrug of his shoulders.

She folded her arms across her chest. "Look, you need to start explaining things to me, or I'm going to ask you to leave."

"I don't know who they are, Leecie. All I know is the less you know about it, the safer you'll be." She didn't move so Dan pressed on "Where's the money?"

"Oh no, you owe me an explanation for that too. You should have told me you'd asked the guy to pay in cash. Do you know how shocked I was when he opened that case? Do you have any idea how nervous I am just having that much money around my house?"

"I'm sorry, Leecie, but be honest. If I had told you Howard was going to give you cash, would you have still gone to get it?"

"No."

"I knew you wouldn't. That's why I couldn't tell you."

"Well crap, Danny, what can you tell me?"

Dan cupped his hands over his face and leaned against the wall. "I found something that belongs to someone else, and they'll kill, and die, to get it back."

"What did you find, and why not just give it to them?"

"Even if I did, they'd kill me for having had it at all."

"What do you have? What's so damned important? Tell me what's happening." Anger was rising in her voice.

Dan paused, turned away, and walked to the front window. After a minute of peeking through the blinds across the street at the yellow tape blocking his front door, he turned and looked into Aleecia's eyes. "Who do you trust with your life, Leecie?"

"What?"

"Your life, who do you trust with it? If you had to choose one person to count on to do something that could save your life, who would it be? If your life hung in the balance and was determined by what that person did, who would you pick to make decisions for you?"

"What kind of question is that?"

"Who?"

"I don't know, my mother, I guess."

Dan shook his head. "See, when it comes to a matter of life and death, the list of people you trust runs short. There are only a few people who are truly on your side." They stood quietly for nearly a minute. "I'm running for my life, Leecie. These people won't stop until I'm dead. The only chance I have is tied to the money."

Of all the things Aleecia didn't understand, one thing was clear: something bad had happened to Danny. He had been transformed into someone she no longer knew.

She went back to her bedroom to get the case. She'd expected him to follow; when he didn't, she was glad. She pulled the case out from under the bed and brought it to him.

"You should probably count it. I didn't bother when Howard gave it tome. I guess I was just a little nervous about handling it."

"I'm not worried about it." Not wanting to look at her. "Look, Leecie, I'm sorry I had to get you involved in all of this. I wish I could say it will pass, but I'm not certain it will. I'm kind of stuck on the run, and I don't know what's going to happen."

"Why don't you just go to the police? If you didn't do anything wrong, then you don't have anything to worry about."

"Do you really believe that?"

She lowered her eyes. They both knew she didn't.

"Besides," he continued, "I barely got out of Puerto Rico. You confirmed Alex and Megan are dead, and we both know that's why they're looking for me. Maybe there will be a time when I can go to the police, but now's not the time."

"What are you going to do?"

"Do you really want to know? I'd love to tell you and have somebody to talk to about all this, but I'm serious about you being better off not knowing. If you ask once more, I'll tell you everything I know. But if I do, you're in, you won't be able to get out, and you'll have to come with me."

Aleecia's first thought was to tell him to spill his guts, but she stopped to consider the consequences. "I don't think I want to hear anymore," she said quietly.

"That's probably best," Dan said. "I'll call you when I can."

Aleecia nodded and felt suddenly sad. She was saying goodbye to Danny and didn't know when, or if, she would see him again; the friendship they had developed deserved more than just a casual goodbye.

"Is there anything I can do to help?"

Dan smiled. "I'd like to shower, if I could. If you have any clothes that might fit, I could use a change."

"I guess," she said, pointing down the hall. "I haven't taken the bag of donation clothes to the Goodwill yet. I think I have some of your old stuff in there. I'll see what I can find."

"Thanks, Leecie."

Aleecia went to her spare bedroom and retrieved a plastic garbage bag from the closet. Sorting through it, she found some of Dan's old clothes. When she took them to the bathroom, she heard the shower running. She opened the door just enough to slip the clothes through before pulling it shut.

Dan showered and shaved with the razor Aleecia used for her legs. As he stepped from the shower, his wet foot slipped forward on the tiled floor. He would have fallen if he hadn't kicked the baseboard next to the toilet, clenching his teeth to stifle a cuss. He sat down on the toilet and rubbed his toe, looking down at the wall near the floor and noticing he had hit the baseboard so hard it had popped loose. Dan shook his head as he recalled the weekend when he'd helped Aleecia retile her bathroom floor. That baseboard had fit snugly when he'd positioned it just as they had broken for lunch,only for him to forget to nail it later.

"One more meaningless thing," he said quietly then started to dress. When he flipped his pouch to fasten the straps around his hips, he felt the weight of the box swing against his leg and he considered the stone inside.

He wanted more than anything to be honest with Aleecia, but he couldn't tell her everything. Hell, he didn't know everything. He couldn't tell her he'd almost been caught once and had killed to get away. That would shatter the remaining string of trust she had for him. He couldn't tell her he'd have to meet with them again, and if he did live some of them would not. First, he would have to find a place to hide the stone. He knew he would probably die within the next few weeks, maybe even within days,but he could make it more difficult for them by not having the stone on him when he was caught. How he would hide it was something he did not know yet.

He finished dressing as he contemplated his situation, and he fought the urge to throw up as he had done so many times before. His anger started to grow, so he clenched his fist and went back to the survival state of mind. Looking around the bathroom for something else he might need and could ask Aleecia for, Dan's attention went to a most unlikely item: the toilet paper.

Slowly, like a sprinkle of rain before a storm, an idea formed. He started to look back down at the floor but jerked his head away. Instead, he looked up at the ceiling. He drew a deep steady breath, clenched his fist even tighter, closed his eyes, and opened his mind to the past. He had learned a few things over the last few days, things that didn't make much sense to him but that he knew to be true. It was one of those things he would use now, so he concentrated on the events of the past few days and, when the images were locked in his mind, he began. It took him two minutes to do what he'd set out to do.

When he finished, he opened the door and walked to the living room where Aleecia was waiting.

"Thanks, I can't tell you how good that feels."

Aleecia nodded. "You look a lot better."

Dan put his nose under his arm. "I smell better, too." Aleecia smiled. He looked at the small pile of his old clothes that Aleecia had gathered.

"Do you have a suitcase I can use?"

"Will I get it back?"

Dan shrugged. "I don't know."

Aleecia looked at him, realizing it probably meant no. "I suppose," she said, and shook her head. "Giving you a suitcase is a small thing considering the problems you have."

She went to the spare bedroom closet and found the small case. It was bigger than the overnight bag she took upstate and would be easier to drag around than the bigger one. She brought it to Dan, who was standing at the front window peeking through the split in the shades.

"Will this one work?"

"Sure," Dan said as he turned away and let the shade close. He opened the suitcase and packed his old clothes, along with his dirty ones, in silence. She realized this was it: Danny was leaving, maybe forever. Tears formed in her eyes, and she walked over and threw her arms around him. He hugged her back.

"You're so much stronger than you know," he said, pulling her closer. "If you want answers to what's happening, study the past. All the answers are there." He kissed her on the cheek when they parted. Picking up the suitcase with one hand and the case full of cash with the other, he left through the back door after pausing only long enough to glance back.

"Lock the door, home might not be safe." He gave her a sad smile and then turned and disappeared into the darkness.

Tears slipped down Aleecia's cheeks. Danny was gone.

16

Soaked and Smoked

J ust after seven, the morning sun rose over the peak of Dan's house and pushed bright rays of light through the slits in Aleecia's bedroom blinds. Streams of sunlight shone on her eyelids and dragged her from her sleep. It was Wednesday morning, and just thirty hours since Dan had come and gone. The question of where he was or whether he'd be back was framed by what would happen when Detective Rogiletti returned. And Rogiletti would be back. Asking questions about the boat and why Aleecia didn't tell him during their first meeting. Maybe she should tell him what she knew; she could explain she was confused and frightened, and maybe he would understand. She wanted that very much, as another part of her wanted to see him again. He was an attractive man, both physically and in personality. If they had met any other way, she would be interested in knowing him better. The thought made her smile, and she felt the warmth in her cheeks again. Aleecia decided that she would tell him the truth about the boat, ask for clemency, and see if they could start again.

She rolled over, wanting to go back to sleep, since she didn't need to go to work today, but now that she was awake her bladder insisted it was time to get up. After reluctantly rolling to her feet, she made her way to the bathroom. Now that she was up, there was no going back to bed. She put her robe over her shoulders, but didn't bother to close or tie the front. Half asleep and half naked, she made her way to the kitchen where she got the coffee pot going. Next, she shuffled into the living room and turned on the TV to catch the morning news, paying little attention to the update on a warehouse fire that was now yesterday's news, and decided she might need more help waking up and a shower was in order while the coffee brewed.

She took her time in the shower, letting the warm water soak her pores before toweling off and slipping again into her open robe as she followed the smell of the coffee back toward the kitchen. She had only taken a few steps when the front doorbell sounded. She considered not answering it but decided to see who it was first. When she crossed to the door to look through the peephole, she got the fish-eye view of Detective Merle Rogiletti. Aleecia smiled to herself, unconsciously catching her breath.

Why this guy appealed to her so much escaped her, but she did have a brief but strong flirtation with the idea of opening the door before closing her robe. She hesitated for a few seconds as she imagined the look on his face, but quickly decided against it and closed and tied her robe—but not too tightly. After all, she was going to ask for his forgiveness and would need all the persuasion she could get. She opened the door slowly.

"Good morning," Merle said, smiling warmly.

"Good morning, detective, what a lovely surprise," she said, grinning at the fact that the sarcasm in her voice leaked out in just the right amount. "What can I do for you?" she asked, letting the door swing open and turning her back as she headed toward the coffee.

Merle took the open door as an invitation and stepped inside, closing the door behind him.

"Do you always let men you've only known a few days into your home like this?"

"No, but since most dangerous men don't use the bell, and you're one of the guys I'm supposed to call for protection, I think I'm safe."

Merle thought for a few seconds then shrugged his shoulders in surrender. "Fair enough," he said quietly. Then he cleared his throat and stood a little taller. Aleecia noticed a change of tone in his voice from over her shoulder as she entered the kitchen. "Have you seen the news lately?"

Aleecia returned to the living room but stopped at the kitchen doorway and pointed at the TV.

"Are you aware of the big warehouse fire?"

"Sure. Do you want some coffee?" Aleecia asked while already walking back into the kitchen.

"No, thank you," Rogiletti answered from behind her. "What can you tell me about it?"

"The coffee?"

"The fire."

She finished pouring a cup and sipped at it before walking back into the living room. "Is this a test?"

Rogiletti gave a half smile. "Perhaps one of character."

Aleecia rolled her eyes. "Is this your way of making small talk?"

"No, no, it is not. I wish it were, but unfortunately I'm here on business."

"I'm sorry to hear that."

Merle nodded and Aleecia read *me too* in his eyes, but when he spoke it was with authority. "The fire department fought the blaze for nearly twelve hours, trying to keep it from spreading. The investigators rummaged through what was left last night. Not much survived." Rogiletti paused, looking for a reaction.

"That is terrible, detective, but what does it have to do with me?"

"I want your opinion."

"My opinion of what?"

"Do you think the fire was an accident or arson?"

She almost laughed. "Why are you asking me?"

"We found the remains of six badly charred bodies in the building, and it's important that we learn all we can about what caused the fire."

No urge to laugh now. "And you came to me?"

"Shall I get to the point?"

"Please."

"Where's your luggage, Ms. Donnelly?"

Aleecia's heart skipped a beat. "I'm sorry, my luggage?"

"Yes, your luggage. You remember the last time I was here, we talked about the cute piece of dragonfly luggage you had. I told you my sister would love it."

"I remember."

"Good, where is it?"

"It's in the other room."

"May I see it?"

"Why?"

Instead of answering, Rogiletti reached into his breast pocket and retrieved his phone and touched the face a few times. Then he paused. "I really am sorry about this," he said as he held the phone, face down, out toward Aleecia. Doubting that he was sorry at all, she took it and turned it over. What she saw caused her to sit down on the sofa and almost spill her coffee when she sat it on her coffee table.

"I know it's graphic," Rogiletti said without looking at her, "but I wanted you to see it the way it was found."

The picture was a HD photo of what were unquestionably the remains of a human body. Black and charred and, if possible, melted. That was bad enough, but what caused Aleecia to sit down was the unmistakable piece of cloth that had survived the fire by being trapped under the body and spared by the fluids which had soaked it. Even as badly as it had been soaked and smoked, however, the red and gold dragonflies were clearly identifiable.

"Anything in the photo look familiar?"

Aleecia didn't say anything; she was just too stunned. There was little doubt in her mind about where her luggage was now. One piece, the one she had loaned to Dan, had been burned up in the warehouse fire along with six people, one of whom could be Danny.

"All we know about the person in the photo is she was a woman. Besides that, we've got nothing. But the luggage, it's not a common print. So, I ask again, where's your luggage, Ms. Donnelly?"

Aleecia's head was swimming. She needed time to think. The thought of being honest with Rogiletti was gone. She wanted to talk to a lawyer, but there was no time for that. The picture of her burned-up luggage was at hand. The other three pieces were in the spare bedroom down the hall, but the fourth was . . . well, there was no getting out of this now . . . or maybe, just maybe, there was. Perhaps not a way out, but at least a way through. A way to slow things down and allow her some time to think and talk to a lawyer.

"Your luggage, Ms. Donnelly?" Rogiletti repeated.

"It's down the hall," she said quietly while handing back his phone.

"I need to see it."

Aleecia nodded, stood slowly, and started down the hall. He followed her without a word. She took him to the spare room and pointed. "It's in the closet."

He crossed the room, taking in the contents, and opened the closet door. The luggage was sitting on the floor. He pulled out the top piece to look at the rest.

"Last time we spoke you told me this was a set of four, I count only three."

"There's a matching makeup case in the big one."

This was both the truth and a lie. The makeup case was there, but it was a part of the big case and not a separate piece. Aleecia refused to look at Rogiletti. She could tell he was watching her face to catch any change in her expression; although she steeled herself to keep her poker face, she knew it would be a wasted effort.

"Would you mind showing me?" Rogiletti asked.

Aleecia crossed to the closet and knelt to open the biggest case. She was aware most of her left breast was exposed by the loosely closed robe, but she didn't bother to adjust. If this would distract his train of thought, even if only for a few seconds, maybe he'd miss the deception. Besides, a few minutes before didn't she consider opening the door to him while exposed? She unzipped the suitcase and pulled out the makeup bag.

"That's the fourth piece?"

Aleecia nodded.

"Not much of a case."

"That's what I thought when I first saw it."

"Where'd you say you bought it?"

"I ordered it online a few years back."

"Remember the name of the seller you bought it from?"

"Sorry, no."

Rogiletti picked up the makeup bag and looked at the small tag sewn to the bottom. "Mind if I take this tag?"

"I'd like to keep it intact, but I have the feeling it doesn't matter . . . you're going to take it anyway."

"Not if you object. I don't need to."

He pulled out his phone and took a pic of the tag and checked it to make sure he could read the details. "Maybe with this I can track down the manufacturer and see if they have a record of who else bought a set of this luggage." As he stood up, he showed Aleecia the image.

"With any luck, this will do two things. It will clear you of any involvement with the fire, and it will help lead me to the person responsible."

"That would be nice," Aleecia said, but knew when Rogiletti came back she would have a lot of explaining to do, provided he even gave her a chance to explain. He might just throw the cuffs on her and take her for a ride. Their first date might be in an interrogation room.

Her anger grew inside her. Being in this type of situation was so out of character for her. She had gotten involved in a terrible mess. Her whole predictable and stress-free life was now turned upside down by one of the few people she trusted.

"Aleecia?"

The sound of her name brought her back. "Sorry, I was just . . . I mean, that would be a good thing. I hope you find out what started the fire."

Rogiletti nodded. "Has Daniel Knocks called you again?"

"No," she said. He hadn't called; he'd just shown up.

"That's probably a good thing. Trouble seems to follow this friend of yours. Not to mention bodies."

"What does that mean?"

"I got a call from the police up in Charlevoix. Do you know where Charlevoix is, Ms. Donnelly?"

Aleecia's heart skipped and she felt as if she might throw up. "Up north," she said.

"That's right, only about fifty miles this side of the upper peninsula. Do you know what they told me?"

"What?" she asked, her heart pounding in her chest.

"Daniel Knocks has, or should I say had, a boat up there. Evidently, he sold it to a man named Tom Howard, who paid a couple hundred thousand for it. According to Howard's broker, it was a good deal. Personally, I think he got screwed."

"Why?" Aleecia heard herself ask.

"As far as we can tell, Howard died shortly after buying it. A stroke, according to the coroner. But the strange thing is he was found floating in the lake. Now, my first thought was that he fell overboard when the stroke hit, but according to the medical examiner there was no water in his lungs. That tells us he was done breathing before he went for his swim." He paused, waiting for Aleecia to get up to speed. "That means Howard went overboard after he was dead," Rogiletti said quietly.

Aleecia stood frozen in shock. As it happened, this may have played out better for her. Her numb reaction hid the fact she was scared beyond any time she could remember.

"There is one more thing about Howard I found interesting," Rogiletti continued. "He had a toothpick jammed through his left cheek. Any of this sound familiar?"

Even if she wanted to, Aleecia couldn't answer. The toothpick was a definite link between Alex and Howard, and that meant the person involved had to have been in Puerto Rico and Charlevoix and knew to look for Alex and Howard. The only person who had access to both was Dan. There were so many questions. If Rogiletti was right about Dan, she would consider herself lucky to be alive. But he couldn't be right; this was Danny. The guy Aleecia considered her best friend and then some. This could not be happening the way Rogiletti thought it was.

Aleecia stood lost in thought as Rogiletti studied her. Finally, he cleared his throat to bring her back.

"Why don't you show me out, and I'll get to work on this," he said. "With any luck, the manufacturer will still be making the cases and I'll be able to pick up a set for my sister."

Aleecia gave him a faint smile. Any question of him doubting her story would shortly be removed. It was simply a matter of him lining up the information and coming back to get her.

She walked him to the front door and opened it for him. He stopped when he got to the porch.

"I'll probably have a few more questions, so I'll have to stop by again. Until this whole thing is straightened out, I think it would be best if you didn't take a trip of any kind. I'd have to answer to my boss about why you left."

"Is this the proverbial 'don't leave town' speech?"

"Something like that," he said, nodding his head. "I know you trust Dan, but I've got to tell you that you need to be careful if he contacts you. If he does get hold of you, call me," he said as he slipped another card into her hand. He flashed her his warm smile. "And listen, if things do work out, I know this great little restaurant. Best Tai food around. Maybe we can check it out."

"I'd like that," Aleecia said, wondering if he'd said it just to put her mind at ease.

Merle turned and headed for his car, and she watched him go. When his car began to move, she backed inside and closed and locked the door, letting her forehead bang against it with a small thud.

17

Five Thousand Dollars

Aleecia's mind was racing. If Rogiletti was right, Dan could have been one of the people killed in the fire. Even if he wasn't right, Dan was involved and it would now look to most people as if she was, too. Even worse was the probability that the police would think she was involved in the murder of Tom Howard.

Her first impulse was to call Rogiletti back to the house and tell him everything. Tell him about the phone call, the boat sale, Dan's visit, and the luggage, everything. She could claim fear as the motivation for her withholding the information and ask for his forgiveness and protection. But her knowledge of Dan's character made her reject Rogiletti's theory once again.

This was Danny. The same Danny who had given her money to save her house when things were tight. The Danny who bought her a ticket and flew her to Florida to see her mother when she was sick. The same man she had confided in and who had confided in her. She'd spent so much time with him, she could almost always accurately predict how he would respond to any situation. Danny may have some flaws, but he was no killer. Was her trust in him so shallow, and her loyalty so limited, that she should turn on him without any proof of his guilt? Absolutely not.

She contemplated calling her sister but was unsure how to explain things without sounding like she was exaggerating or overreacting. It was time to talk with an attorney.

She did an Internet search and brought up a list of area law firms. It took hours to decide on one, as she studied and researched each firm. When she finally settled on one and called, she spoke with a receptionist who took her name and contact information and assured her an attorney would call her back within a few hours.

Aleecia went back down the hall and dressed, superstition suggesting to her that this was a day to wear her lucky jeans and T-shirt. When she returned to the living room, she was startled by the clank of the mailbox lid on her front porch. "Settle down, girl," she said quietly in an effort to calm herself. "Bad guys don't come in the mail. Not everybody's out to get you." She decided to try and lose herself in a few tasks because, if nothing else, she did have her house to clean. She picked up a few things, tossed them on the glass topped coffee table, then sat down on her sofa and cried.

When she calmed down enough to stop crying, she began to think about places where she could go to try and relax. The park, maybe, or a movie might help. She was still sitting there when her phone chimed to alert her to a new incoming text. The number was unrecognizable, but the few words in the message got her attention: *Watch the mail.*

Aleecia's head swung around to look at the front door.

"What fresh hell is this?" she asked aloud. After crossing the room, she looked through the peephole to check the front porch. It was empty. She opened the door slowly. When she looked around at her neighbors' homes, she noticed a man in a suit a few doors down, apparently trying to show her neighbor something they were not interested in. A salesman, perhaps.

She opened the lid to her mailbox and stood on her toes to peek inside. Along with a few business envelopes and junk mail there was a small tan shipping envelope. She took it all into the house and looked at the unusual item. She didn't need to check the return address to know who it was from; she instantly recognized the handwriting as Danny's.

She looked at the return anyway, wondering from where it had been sent, but he had listed his home address as the return address. She also noticed it was sent express overnight from her local post office.

When she opened it, several $100 bills fluttered to the floor. When she looked inside, she saw a lot more. There was also a letter, which she pulled out and read.

Leecie,

I know—a letter, what's up with that? The truth is I thought this would be the best way to get this to you without it being intercepted or tracked. I wish I was writing with good news, but that's not the case. They are determined, make no mistake about that.

I am so sorry this has happened to you, but I doubt I could have changed it. I need to tell you everything. It was wrong for me to not take you with me when I had the chance. Please hear me now and know I mean everything I say. You may hate me in the short-term, but once you learn the truth, you'll understand this is not my fault. We are not the first to suffer this fate, and we won't be the last. Aleecia, you are in serious danger. You need to run, Leecie. Run for your life!

I'm sure you noticed the $5,000 I have included. It's so you can get in your car right now and drive away. Buy a new phone with a new number and call me at the number I've listed at the bottom.

Please, please do not stay home! Please do not go back to work! Please just go! Once I hear from you, we can make plans to meet up. Take the money, memorize my new phone number, and then burn this letter.

Come to me Leecie, and we can work this out. I think I can save you, Leecie, and we can make it through this together, but you need to come to me. Please just get up and do it right now!

I love you,

Danny

A-N-D

810-555-7384

She read the letter twice and cried some more. Now, she was scared. Maybe Rogiletti was right, and Dan was into something bad. He was involved with some bad people, and there was little doubt that Dan was also scared. Run for her life? Was she really in danger? Was he being serious or overreacting? Either way, it was time to go to the police. She would call Rogiletti and confess everything. Show him the letter and ask for his forgiveness, advice, and protection.

She picked up her phone and dialed the number from the front of the card Rogiletti had given her. It was his personal extension, and the line rang at his desk. After several rings, she was transferred to voice mail.

"Hello, Detective Rogiletti. You must be out. This is Aleecia Donnelly. I just received a letter from Dan Knocks. I think you should stop by my house. There are several things we need to talk about. Could you please come by as soon as you can?"

She thought about saying more, but what could she tell him? There would be plenty of time for that when he showed up, so she hung up.

She read the letter again, looking for answers and pausing on the words *Home is not safe*. That was what Dan had said when he left her house. She had thought he was embellishing, but now she realized he may have really believed it, and that maybe she should too. After all, Alex, Megan, and Howard were dead. But the idea that someone was coming was crazy, wasn't it? If this was about the money, though, it might not be.

She began pacing the room. After a few minutes, she shook her head and thought maybe she should rent a nearby hotel room and hang out until she could talk with somebody. Maybe waiting to talk to the attorney first *was* the best path.

She went to the spare room and got out her overnight bag. As she packed a few things, she decided she would use some of the money Dan had sent to rent a hotel room and hide out. After all, she had earned it. Just as she finished packing, there was a soft knock on her front door.

18

Green Eyes and Black Shoes

Struck by Dan's words, Aleecia froze for a few seconds. But then she remembered what she had told Rogiletti earlier that day.

"Most dangerous men don't use the bell," she whispered to herself. "Or knock, I suppose."

She slowly went to the door and looked through the peephole. It was the salesman she had seen at her neighbors. Except it wasn't a salesman. He looked tentative as he kept glancing at the houses around hers. First one way, and then the other. This made her a bit nervous, until she realized why he might be acting this way. In his hands, held close to his chest, were pamphlets with the words *Watch Tower* across the front.

"Just what I need," she whispered.

She opened the door slowly to the smile of a man with short blond hair cut close to his head, which was supported on a set of shoulders wide enough to make Aleecia think he could be wearing shoulder pads. He seemed too thick for a man of his height. Brick-shaped is how Aleecia would describe him, and just a little creepy. Dressed in black slacks, sport jacket, and a gray shirt, the man looked like a shadow come to life.

"Can I help you?" she asked.

"Thank you for your time," he said quietly. "Have you ever thought about what happens when we die?"

"Haven't we all?"

He grinned. "Good question," he said with a slight chuckle. "I think we all have, but you're one of the lucky ones."

"Oh, why is that?"

"Because you're about to find out."

Their eyes locked for a split second, but it was long enough that Aleecia realized two things. First, they were the darkest green eyes she had ever seen, and they were also the determined eyes of a man on a mission.

"Run," she heard herself say, although her hips were already turning for the back door. As she sprinted through the room, the adrenaline kicked in and her mind went into hyper mode, absorbing every detail. From behind her, she heard the distinct sound of the door closing; she knew Green Eyes hadn't left and was instead in pursuit.

She ran down the hall and into her laundry room, hoping her familiarity with the house would be her salvation. It should take Green Eyes a few seconds to navigate her route . . . maybe enough time for her to undo the lock and get out the back door. If not, it would be a cruel irony that her security mechanism would also be her demise.

She raced to the door and reached out with both hands, one to twist the lock and the other to twist the knob. Despite her panic, her moves were precise. The lock released, the latch slid back, and the door swung open with her pull. Even if she couldn't get away, she could scream. Maybe, just maybe, that scream would be enough to convince Green Eyes the gig was up and the neighbors, AKA witnesses, had been called.

As she slowed to allow the door to swing past her body, she risked a glance over her shoulder. Green Eyes was still coming, but he was just now reaching the doorway and was four or five steps behind. There seemed to be no urgency to his movement.

He's giving up, she thought, her fast reaction and ability to get to the door was responsible for taking the wind out of his sails. She turned back toward the back porch, already sucking in the air that would be a scream when she reversed the flow. Ready to break into a sprint, she dropped her head.

Black shoes was all her mind could collect before a yellow light flashed and a hot wave of pain flared through the left side of her head from a blow that seemingly came out of thin air.

Her head reversed directions, but her feet took another step forward before trying desperately to catch up. They shuffled and scooted backward until her heels struck the floor too soon. She fell backward, but, instead of landing on the floor, two strong arms slid beneath her armpits and caught her in mid-fall.

She tried to pull her feet under her, but the arms, which now ended with hands that cupped both of her breast, jerked her back toward the living room. Green Eyes had gotten her, after all, and was dragging her backward so fast her legs couldn't catch up; she wasn't sure they were still trying.

Her eyes took in the shape of a second man coming down the hall after them. He was dressed the same way as Green Eyes and appeared to be pointing a gold ink pen at her. Green Eyes lifted and tossed her over the back of the couch, her body twisting as her legs swung around and her upper body bending awkwardly as her face dragged across the front of Green Eye's shirt. Her mind registered the smell of his cologne: *old musk, just like Granddad used to wear.* The ceiling and the floor changed places twice, but her senses fortunately stayed online just enough to perceive that she had to grab something to keep herself from flying past the seat of the sofa and crashing through her glass coffee table. She groped and snatched at one of the cushions as it traveled beneath her. Her fingers locked onto the seat cushion sitting on the left side of the sofa.

She bounced and twisted yet took the cushion with her. Her left hip hit the coffee table, shattering it into tiny pieces. Either by accident, or as a subconscious act, she flipped the cushion out in front of her and landed on it, chest down, holding on as she slid to a stop. Sliding across the shards of glass held captive in the soft yarn hoops of the carpet, some embedding into her elbows and knees, she found most of herself protected by the cushion.

She came to rest half on, half off the cushion with several small cuts and bruises and a general disorientation from the blow to her head and twirling flight over the sofa.

It only took a few seconds for her mind to cut through some of the haze, but by then Green Eyes was standing over her, and his buddy, Mr.

Black Shoes, was headed for the door. From somewhere through the mist clouding Aleecia's thoughts, she heard the deadbolt clack into the catch.

Being the gentleman he was, Green Eyes kicked the frame of the table aside and helped Aleecia off the floor by grabbing a handful of her hair and lifting until she cooperated. He flung her so that she sat down hard on the center of the couch; she was grateful that at least the cushion was still there.

She looked up at Green Eyes wondering what it would be: robbery, rape, or murder? Possibly rape, not likely robbery, and probably murder. One thing was clear, however, these boys were too smooth to be rookies. These boys had done this before.

Mr. Black Shoes came up from behind her and slipped one hand under her chin, lifting and tilting her head back so she was forced to look up into his eyes. He pulled a half-chewed toothpick from between his lips and grinned.

"Hello, love," he said with an accent Aleecia accepted as Australian. "Now we can do this easy, but if you decide to go rough you won't get to enjoy our company. Just give us what we want, and we'll all kick back with a couple of coldies, yeah?"

"What do you want?" Aleecia asked through closed teeth, as Black Shoes wasn't letting go of her chin.

"We want the stone your buddy from across the road gave you."

"What shtone?" She was genuinely confused, half expecting the answer to be the money. But, a stone? Dan had left her no stone.

"It won't do you any good to play dumb with us, love. I can find out without your cooperation, but it won't be pleasant, and it will hurt quite a bit. So, let's go round that, shall we?"

"I want to help, but I don't know what you're talking about." Her nose was now starting to run, which didn't help the whole speech thing.

"We think it's here, love. We know Danny Boy came to see you and borrowed your luggage. He's a clever bloke, that one. How he got six of us in that fire was one smart trick. But that's enough small talk, so I'll give you one last go. Where's the stone."

"He never gave me a shtone."

"Right. Then I reckon we'll just have to take it." At this, Black Shoes nodded to Green Eyes, who stepped forward and straddled her closed knees as he reached into his pocket.

Here it comes, Aleecia thought. *A gun or a knife, but either way it doesn't matter. By morning I'll be a statistic, and Merle Rogiletti will have another file.*

But instead of a gun or a knife, Green Eyes produced a gray box that resembled an oversized flip phone. Plugged into it was a funky set of headphones. Green Eyes sat down on her lap, pinned her feet to the floor, and leaned forward to put the headphones over her head. Aleecia reached up to stop him, but Black Shoes grabbed her wrist and held her at bay.

"This here is a duplicator," Black Shoes said. "It takes a copy of your memories, so we can have a look at them. It's a fun little toy, but it does hurt like a major bugger. You should feel lucky though, love. We can only use it every so often, and it's only just now charged and ready to go. The things we've had to do over the past few days have been really ugly. You get to give that lot a miss."

Green Eyes slipped the two small, padded disks on either side of her head, but instead of putting the pods over her ears he left them setting on both temples.

Black Shoes looked to Green Eyes and nodded, then lifted Aleecia's chin even higher to get her attention.

"Goodnight, love," he said.

When Green Eyes pushed a button on the gray box, the result was a stabbing bright light behind Aleecia's eyes. Like the flash of a camera that wouldn't quit, pain exploded through Aleecia's brain. It was five times worse than any punch Black Shoes could deal out, her head snapping forward once and then back hard, her mouth and eyes opening wide. Every muscle in her body stiffened and locked rigid. She tried to scream, but no sound came. In fact, she barely had time to make out the grin on Black Shoe's face before her eyes stopped working.

19

Goodbye, Love

Aleecia awoke drenched and lying in the fetal position on the couch. Her eyes were swollen and her cheeks were stained with depleted tears. The front of her shirt was wet with what smelled like a combination of sweat and drool. Her soaked jeans and the cushion, and the salty stench of urine in the air, made her reasonably sure she had wet herself.

Thanks to the dim light, it took several moments for her eyes to focus. The blinds were closed, and only a few lights were on. When she reached up and touched her throbbing temples, her hands seemed to move in slow motion. She thought about trying to sit up, but that wasn't going to happen just yet.

Her living room had clearly been ransacked. She hoped the intruders had found what they were looking for and were long gone, but when she heard something break in the bedroom, she knew they were still there. She had no idea what they had managed to do to her, but she felt lucky to have lived through it. If she was going to keep on living, though, she'd have to get out.

She flexed her toes, trying to determine if things were getting better, and listened to the sounds of her belongings being smashed and thrown about in the other room. She tried to look at the bedroom door, hoping to see if they were watching her. Maybe, in her feeble condition, she wasn't a threat and they considered it unnecessary to keep a close eye on her.

It took three tries to sit up, but when she did manage it, her head started to clear a little. She looked toward the bedroom. She couldn't see them, but their shadows suggested they were on the opposite side of the room near the bathroom. *Good*, she thought. They wouldn't be able to see her without crossing the room. If they were busy, it might give her enough time to get out. She looked at the front door, wanting to get up and run to it the way she had done before, but when she tried, her legs failed her, and she fell off the sofa and crashed noisily onto the debris that used to be her end table. She glanced back at the bedroom door to see Green Eyes looking back at her. His arm reached around the corner and came back holding the sleeve of Black Shoes, who turned to see her.

"Well, well, look who's finally awake. Did you enjoy your nap, love? Kind of like waking up after a three-day binge, isn't it?" he said while walking to her, nonchalantly stepping over the mess he had help create. Casually, as if he were an old friend or a roommate who had come back for something forgotten, he sat on the arm of her sofa.

"What'd you do to me?" she asked.

"We had a look in your memories, and you know what we found?"

"A look at my memories?" she asked, rubbing her temples.

Black Shoes took the half-chewed toothpick out of his mouth and flicked it at Aleecia. It landed, cool and wet, on her bare forearm.

"Don't worry yourself. You won't understand what we did, you're blind to the truth. Just like everybody else on this rock. But it doesn't matter now, does it? We've learned you weren't lying to us, and you have no idea your friend left you the stone. That's bad for you, love. See, if you really don't have a clue where the stone is, you're no good to us."

No good to us. Even in her disoriented state, she knew exactly what that meant. She had seen them, couldn't give them what they wanted, and now it was time to kill her. She tried to get up and flee, but her legs just weren't up to the task. She did manage to get to her feet, but when she tried to move, they collapsed beneath her and she crashed back to the floor. She extended her arms to protect her head, but they were of little use and her forehead bounced off the carpet. Luckily, she had landed in one of the few spaces not covered with junk.

She rolled to her back, and Black Shoes walked to her head and knelt on her hair, holding her in place with a knee on either side of her head. Again, she watched Green Eyes reach into his pocket. Again, he surprised her by not bringing out a gun or a knife but instead a black stick, like a small magician's wand, but with two small points on one end. *A taser*, she thought. *They're going to electrocute me.*

"So, what will it be, love?" Black Shoes said as he grabbed her wrist and pulled her hands over her head to his chest, where he held them tightly. "A brain aneurysm, or a stroke, perhaps? That is one of our favorites. You should feel lucky we don't use the spontaneous combustion thing anymore. That was just too messy."

Aleecia looked up at him. "Please don't," was all she was able to say.

"Let's just keep it simple and go with a heart attack," he said with a smile.

Black Shoes nodded at Green Eyes, who again straddled her thighs, this time pinning her completely to the floor. He reached down and pushed her shirt up, so it stopped just below her breast, and held the wand out for her to see. He twisted a small knob on the end as if he were choosing a setting.

"Goodbye, love," Black Shoes said. Green Eyes touched the left side of her ribs with the points extruding from the wand.

The electric shock she expected didn't come. Instead, she started to sweat, as a pain began to form on the left side of her back. The sweat increased as the pain swelled to the front of her chest and took her breath away. She tried to clutch at her chest, but Black Shoes was still holding her wrists. The next pain came and this time an uncontrollable moan erupted from her throat.

Black Shoes released her wrists and stepped away, allowing her some movement. Her hands instinctively went to her chest and clawed at the left side of her shirt and the breast beneath it. Green Eyes withdrew the wand, and he too stepped away. She rolled to her side and tried to get her knees under her, but the pain was immense. She only wobbled and fell back against the side of the sofa. When she managed to sit up right with her legs out in front of her, Aleecia was gasping for breath that her chest could not pull in.

This isn't right, she thought. *I can't be having a heart attack. That's impossible.* Her conviction left as the next wave of pain caused her vision to fade, darkening around the edges and beginning to tunnel.

She rolled to her side and looked at the front door. So close, yet . . .

The door was the last thing her eyes would see clearly before her heart stopped beating. The final wave of pain came in a burst of heat that flooded her whole torso. As she lost all feeling in her arms and legs, her sight blurred and, if she hadn't already been looking at the door, she would have never seen it break open against the wall. Her mind collected these last bits of information in slow-pausing segments that she wasn't sure if she was seeing or merely imagining.

Four figures rushed through the opening where the door had stood an instant before and pointed to the center of the room. Bright sunlight flooded through the doorway, clouding Aleecia's weakened eyes and submerging the new figures in a soft white aura.

Angels, she thought. After all, isn't that the way things are supposed to end?

Two of her angels moved to the front of Aleecia's face. Her mind had just enough time to register the faces of men before her eyes ceased to function and she gulped at the air one last time, failing to take any in as the darkness of death overtook her.

20

Thanks to the Renegades

Aleecia's mind came back to her in a jerky slow motion, as if she was watching a movie when someone kept pushing the pause button every few seconds. The images were of her life, but in fast-forward time. A scene from when she was two and crying for her mom—stop. A scene from when she was five and broke her arm—stop. A scene when she was in third grade and won a spelling bee—stop.

The images paraded through her mind like short clips a video editor might have selected for the recycle bin. Scenes of her first training bra, her first kiss, her sixteenth birthday, her first lay. They marched on until they ended with the struggle in her living room and the white light just before the darkness. She heard, or at least thought she heard, an audible click. A small wave of pain baked in her chest, and she gasped in a deep breath. When her eyes opened, it took a few seconds to focus. When they did, she found herself looking into the face of an unfamiliar woman. Long, soft red hair framed a friendly freckled face and a warm smile.

"Right on time," the Southern-accented woman said. "Give or take an hour, and the figures are right on the money."

Aleecia couldn't answer. It seemed her mind had come back to her, but her muscle control was still out to lunch. Trying to gauge her situation, she looked around the room. She was apparently nude under a heavy sheet. She fought to remember what had gotten her to this place, but the memories came back slowly as if they were emerging from a foggy night. When the pieces gradually fell into place, she remembered the fight with Green Eyes and Black Shoes and a tiny but clear image of the angels as they came through the door just before the mental lights went out.

She looked around, expecting to discover a hospital room. If this was a hospital room, it was cleverly disguised as a motel room. Knotty pine paneling covered the walls. A single light fixture sat tight against the white ceiling. The only suggestion of medical care was an IV stuck into the back of her left hand and a heart monitor that announced its presence with an unmistakable beeping.

She licked her parched lips and tried to swallow. Her throat was dry, like it hadn't been used for days. It occurred to her it was possible it hadn't been. She pushed air across her vocal cords to see if they'd work.

"Drink?" came out in nothing more than a whisper.

The woman smiled and produced a plastic cup with a protruding straw. Aleecia drew in the cool water and let it trickle down the back of her throat before swallowing. It was heaven-sent. She took two more swallows before turning her head away.

"Wher . . . Where am I?" Her voice was still weak but this time a little louder.

"Someplace safe. For now, anyway." The accent was more defined now, *Tennessee or Kentucky*, Aleecia thought.

"Who are you?"

"My name's Breanne Coombs."

"What happened?"

"That's kind of a long story. I can't tell you all of it now, but the short version is you were attacked."

"I remember, Green Eyes and Black Shoes."

"I beg your pardon?"

Aleecia shook her head slightly. "Never mind. Did they catch the men who attacked me?"

"They weren't arrested, if that's what you're asking."

"Why not?"

"That's not the way it works, sweetie. It's either escape or death."

"I don't understand."

"I know you don't, and the answers will come soon enough. But right now, you need to rest and allow that heart to catch up with the rest of your body."

"My heart," she paused as the memory came back. "Those men touched me with something and made me think I was having a heart attack."

"Don't just think you did, honey, they gave you the real thing. A bad one at that, damaged beyond repair. In fact, you were clinically dead by the time we got to you. If we hadn't gotten you on a portable pump so quickly, you'd be long gone by now."

Aleecia looked around again for medical equipment. The puzzled look on her face asked the question for her.

"The heart pump is only a temporary thing," Breanne said. "It only takes about sixty hours to grow a new heart, thanks to the Renegades."

"Renegades? New heart?"

"That's right, hon. The Renegades know all about stem cells and can grow almost any organ, so now you're growing a new heart," an excited Breanne explained. "One even better than the one you had when you were killed," Breanne said with a smile wide enough to make Aleecia think her cheeks might split.

"When I was what?"

Breanne shook her head. "Never mind for now. That new heart ain't near strong enough yet. You need more rest, or the pain will come back, and you'll feel weak all over again. We can't have that." The smile faded. "We're going to need you ready to move again, soon, I suspect, and we're going to need you as strong as possible, so stay still and take it easy. Try to go back to sleep."

"No," Aleecia said as firmly as she could. "I want some answers."

"In time, darlin', I promise. But right now, you need some rest. Now that the heart's pumpin the way it should, we can give you something to help you relax. You'll need to stay calm and still." Breanne picked up a hypodermic from the table next to the bed and poked it into the branch of the IV tube. Almost instantly, Aleecia felt sleepy.

"Wait," Aleecia said, as she struggled in vain to sit up.

"Shh," Breanne said, raking her fingers through Aleecia's hair. "Don't worry. We've been looking after you for the past few days. We're not going to let anything happen to you now."

"Days?" Aleecia asked quietly, but she couldn't stay awake long enough to get an answer.

21

No Secrets

Aleecia's first reaction was to get up and run when she noticed Black Shoes standing in the doorway. When she did try to move, however, her muscles didn't respond. It was as if she had no control over her own body. He grinned and flung a half-chewed toothpick at her, which landed in her lap. She tried to scream but nothing came out.

From the corner of her vision, Green Eyes approached and stood beside her bed holding a small silver box. He looked to Black Shoes, who turned slowly and shut the door. The lock sounded with a very audible click.

It was the clicking sound that pulled Aleecia from the nightmare she was having and into a sitting position before struggling with the bed sheets to get her feet to the floor.

"Whoa, girl," she heard a woman say. Then there were hands on her, holding her back, keeping her on the bed. "Calm down, Aleecia, it's all right, you're safe."

Aleecia looked up into the face of a woman she didn't recognize. When she pulled away, the woman let go and allowed her to retreat and scramble to the other side of the bed, causing her to expose her breast before she could gather the sheet back in front of her.

"You're okay, Aleecia. Nobody here is going to hurt you. They don't know where you are."

"Who are you, and what are you doing to me?" a not yet fully awake Aleecia demanded.

"Take it easy, Aleecia. I know you're scared, but there's no need to panic. If you just calm down, I'll fill you in on a few things."

Aleecia's senses began to return, and she felt her nerves step down a notch. She realized she was now fully awake, and her brain was firing on all cylinders. In fact, she remembered everything. The fight in her home, the woman with the red hair, the new heart story, and the tubes in her hand. She looked at her hand to find the tube gone, and just a small bandage left in its place. She also realized she felt physically strong once again. Strong enough to put up a fight if she needed to. She looked hard at the woman in front of her.

"Who are you?"

"My name's Tami. Me and my husband, Cavan, who is out getting breakfast, are here to help get you ready to move."

"Move? To where? No, nuh-uh, I'm not going anywhere until I get some answers. I want to know who you are and what's going on. And where are my clothes?"

Tami smiled and held her palms out as a sign of surrender, then walked to the small closet across the room. She opened the door and stepped aside. Inside it was clothing Aleecia mistook for her own. Tami lifted a small brown suitcase from a table, laid it before Aleecia, and sprang the clasp. Inside it were the underclothes Aleecia wore every day. Except, they weren't Aleecia's. They looked mostly the same, but small differences gave away the fact that they were brand-new and not from her dresser. The resemblance was quite remarkable.

"These aren't mine," Aleecia said.

"No, they're not, and yes, they are. The Bound trashed yours and we can't get them back. But we did go shopping and tried to get as close as we could to the things you remember."

Aleecia thought back. The memories of what had happened were not a distant dream, but were now clear and uninterrupted. She determined that the term "Bound" was Tami's name for the guys who had tried to kill her, and Tami must be with the people who had saved her.

"Why?" The word crept from her thoughts.

"Why did we buy the clothes? To try and help you feel more at home, if it's possible. Most people have a hard time adapting to the new life. We've discovered the little things make a big difference. Breanne's good at finding the things you had before. I remember when Cavan and I first hooked up with the Crew. I had such a hard time believing the truth, it took me six weeks to become a part of the team. I thought about running away so many times. You're thinking the same thing, I'm guessing. The question that stopped me, and the one you need to ask yourself, is where to go?"

"I have lots of places to go, and the police top the list."

"That's what everybody says. God knows it's what I said. But I soon realized every place I had once considered safe was now unsafe. There was no place left to go but with the Crew. You'll eventually figure that out, too."

"Right," Aleecia said as she delved into the suitcase and pulled out a bra and panties. "I think I've heard enough of the mysterious talk. I want straight answers, and I feel strong enough to get them."

"I know."

"You know what?" she said as she slid into some underclothes.

"I know you want answers, and I know you're stronger now. It was planned this way. You should be back to full strength by tomorrow. Actually, you'll be a little stronger than you were. That new heart will increase your energy."

Aleecia turned and looked at the mysterious woman. "Again, with the new-heart story, that's impossible and we both know it. Now tell me what happened, who those people in my house were, and who you are," Aleecia demanded as she crossed to the closet. She had to pause when she got there, as some of her favorite outfits were present. Only, they were new versions of her older clothes.

"I could tell you, but I doubt you'd believe me."

"Try me."

"Okay," Tami said. "The truth is you're one of us now, and there's not a whole lot you can do about it. In time, you will know all we do. For now, just consider us a strange family. We are people who have lost everything we held important. Now we band together to save others like us, or now, like you. Targets is what we are, but Aleecia, you're the biggest target to come along in a long while. We're so lucky we got to you in time."

"Why am I a big target?" Aleecia asked while pulling on a pair of perfectly fitting jeans.

"You have one of the lost stones."

"I don't know what you're talking about. The guys who tried to kill me said the same thing, but I don't have any stone."

"You'll do better if you stop with the denial. Those guys didn't try to kill you. They *did* kill you, and we brought you back. And you do have the stone, you just don't know it."

"Whatever."

"Don't just blow this off, Aleecia. We know Dan left that stone with you, we intercepted some of his memories. They tell us he left the stone with you and we need to find it before they do."

"Dan's memories . . . *right*. And who are they again, the Clowns?"

"The Bound, and you need to take this seriously."

"Okay," Aleecia said as she pulled a T-shirt over her head. "Seriously, I don't have any stone."

Tami paused and let Aleecia put on a pair of socks before she said anything else.

"It's a shame about Danny, poor guy. He had no idea what he was getting into when he found the stone. He did quite well for not having any help. He tried to tell you what was happening, but he just didn't know how. He knew you'd be in denial, just like you are now. But now Dan is missing, probably dead, and you still won't listen to anybody. If you keep going like this, you're also as good as dead. Like Dan tried to tell you, nowhere is safe."

The mention of Dan being dead hit home. After seeing the picture Rogiletti had shown her, Aleecia thought it possible, maybe even probable, but to hear it spoken grabbed her.

"What do you know about Danny?" Aleecia asked, as she put on a pair of shoes that were a dead ringer for the ones she'd left in her closet at home.

"I know we could have used his help. He did a good job at hiding the stone, which is not an easy thing to do. He was smart and caught on fast.

But he was a little too smart and hid too well. It was only by accident that the Bound found him. In the short time he had the stone, we started to see him as a hero. The way he outsmarted them is incredible. Took out six of them with the fire."

Aleecia stopped in her tracks. "The fire? A hero?"

"You bet. Our heroes come from very different places."

"I don't know what you're talking about." It was a true statement, but it lacked the fight.

"I know you don't, but you will. Until then, I'm asking you to trust us."

"I'm sorry, I can't. I just want to get back . . ." Aleecia stopped.

"Home?" Tami said. "But you can't go there now, can you? Last time you were home, the Bound broke in and killed you."

The truth struck Aleecia's sense of reality like a blow to the face. She hesitated and looked at the floor, trying to decide what to do.

"I think I'm going to call my sister and take some time to think things over."

Aleecia crossed slowly to the door, wondering if the woman would try to stop her or if the door was locked. Before she could reach the knob, the door opened and a man holding a plastic bag entered. Aleecia caught the open door and held it. When she and the man looked at each other, Aleecia thought there was something familiar about him.

"Oh, good, you're up and dressed. I brought breakfast," he said with a warm smile.

Aleecia stared at him for a few seconds and then it came to her and her mouth dropped open. "You . . . you were one of the Angels."

Both Tammi and the man stopped to look at her.

Aleecia closed her mouth and shook her head. "No, sorry, I mean you were one of the guys in my house the other night when I was attacked."

His smile spread. "Yeah, that's good. I wasn't sure if you were still conscious enough when we got there to remember that clearly. The Bound are brutal," he said as he walked past and left the door open. "Sorry it took us so long to get there, but we did get there, which is the important thing," he said, putting the bags down on the little table.

"You saved my life," she said quietly.

"I had help," he said as he walked over and kissed Tami. "This is your husband?"

Tami nodded. "This is my husband, Cavan." Cavan gave a wave as if his hand was a tambourine. "Cavan," Tami said. "Aleecia was just on her way out."

"Really, to where?" he asked Aleecia.

"My sister's, I suppose."

"Bad idea. The guys who visited you are probably watching her now."

"Watching her for what? She's not involved in any of this."

"She is now. You know her, and the Bound are looking for you," Cavan said while taking the food out of the bags. "You need to accept the idea that the people you know will be safer if you don't make contact with them." She stared at him blankly. He stopped to face her. "The Bound were after Dan, he contacted you, they came after you. See the pattern?" he paused, but when Aleecia didn't answer he turned back to the table. "Would you like breakfast? It's eggs Benedict, your favorite."

"How would you know my favorite?"

Cavan walked slowly to her, removed her hand from the door and closed it, and folded his hands in front of him. "Let me try to explain something to you, Aleecia Donnelly," he said, his tone soft but stable. "Your memories were taken from you and put on the record. We've intercepted and seen them," he said, motioning to his wife. "We've seen and, to a certain extent, experienced everything you have. That's the way it is with the Crew. It's the way it must be. No secrets. It must be complete candor. That leads to trust. Whether you want to believe it or not, you have no secrets here."

Aleecia put one hand on her hip and rolled her eyes, so Cavan continued.

"Shall I prove it?"

"Oh, please."

"Okay, remember Halloween when you were ten? Your Uncle Doug frightened you and your siblings so badly, he made your sister cry." Aleecia didn't answer, but her expression suggested that she did remember, and quite well. "You were happy your sister started crying, weren't you?"

Aleecia's mind went numb from a combination of fear and confusion. "No," she lied. "She was only eight." Aleecia glanced at Tami, who seemed to have found something more interesting on the ceiling to look at.

"Right." Cavan nodded. "She was only eight. But when she started crying it shifted everybody's attention off you, and nobody noticed you had wet yourself. Not a lot, but enough. Not that I blame you. The fear you remember is enough to scare anybody. Woah!" he said this last bit with a stiff shake of the head.

Aleecia was stunned. "How did you . . . I never shared that with anybody."

"I know. Just like the time when you were thirteen, and you sat at the kitchen table doing your homework and you discovered that if you leaned back and set that thick math book in your lap, in just the right position, you could masturbate without anybody knowing." Aleecia's chin began to fall. "Stop me when you've heard enough," Cavan said. "You felt so guilty when you told your mother your brother broke the window that you cried yourself to sleep. Or the time you and Randy Whitaker went for a walk and ended up behind the corner store and you—"

"Stop it! Just stop it!" Aleecia screamed at him. "That's enough," she said as she started to cry. Her defenses had failed, and the turmoil of the past few days crashed over her like a wave consuming the beach.

Tami came over and put a protective arm around her, helping her to the chair.

Aleecia sat with her face in her hands, trying to pool her strength yet falling to the confusion that gripped her. These strangers had gotten inside her soul and looked at things they had no right to look at. She felt . . . molested.

"I know it's hard," Tami said. "I hate it when it comes to this part. I remember when we finally had to surrender our memories. I was so angry and shocked and embarrassed. But it's kind of unavoidable."

"I was downright pissed off for a long time," Cavan said. "But take heart, there is nothing in your memory that shocks any of us. We have seen a lot, and I mean *a lot*, worse. We've all decided you're a good person, Aleecia. We hope you'll join us."

Stopping on occasion and then falling back to the emotions which pulled at her, Aleecia cried. Not from embarrassment but from the thought that somehow the things these people were telling her, regardless of how incredible or insane they sounded, might be true. The uneventful life she'd worked hard to build was gone, and she had done nothing to bring it on. She hadn't volunteered for anything and she had kept her head down, and yet she was now, as Tami put it, the biggest target to come along in a long while. Now her family, friends, and coworkers might be in danger because of it. It was all too incredibly ridiculous to be true. But something beyond her comprehension was happening; of that there was no mistake.

When the crying did stop and she was able to find herself again, Aleecia was grateful for Tami's empathy.

"What happens now?" she asked.

"It's up to you," Tami said. "We're not the Bound. We won't force you to do anything, but what options do you have? You can't go home. You could take it on the run, but all your resources and contacts are compromised. The Bound know where you lived, worked, shopped, banked, the people you knew and hung out with, even what gas you used to buy. The Bound are hunting you, and they will find you again. They will visit each place and person you can think of, and it will happen faster than you think."

"Or," Cavan began.

"Or," Aleecia broke in, "I could buy into this whole mess you're trying to hand me."

"We're not trying to hand you anything but the truth," Cavan said. He moved one of the chairs in front of Aleecia and sat so he could look her in the eyes. "I know what you're hearing makes no sense to you, but consider this. We saved your life. You know that. You remember that. When you first saw me today you told me I was an angel. I'm not, but I am someone who personally laid my life on the line to save you. All I ask in return is that you trust us now. Just for a little while longer."

Aleecia slowly nodded.

"Good," Cavan said. "Are you hungry?"

Aleecia shook her head no.

"Then I suggest we get ready to move. We've been here more than a week, and it's time we got going."

"More than a week?" Aleecia almost shouted.

"Yep," Cavan said. "And if you need proof, remember there were pieces of glass embedded in your elbows and knees from the broken table and a bump on your head when you hit the floor. Consider the fact that those wounds are mostly healed, and it's somewhat obvious."

Aleecia looked at her elbows, remembering the slide across the carpet and glass, but those cuts had been tended to and they were healing nicely. The only explanation was that these people had cleaned and cared for those wounds, and Aleecia considered this another reason why these people deserved some trust.

Tami helped pack the rest of Aleecia's things in the small brown suitcase, a major contrast to the dragonfly luggage. As Cavan and Tami finished eating a cooling breakfast, they heard a knock on the door. Aleecia jumped and moved slightly away from the entrance.

"Relax, kiddo," Cavan said. "The Bound don't knock."

"Yes, they do!" Aleecia said sharply.

Cavan put his hand over his heart as to say, *Sorry, you're right, they did for you* before he opened the door and a couple walked in. Aleecia recognized them. The woman was Breanne, the redhead who had stayed with her while she . . . grew her new heart. Aleecia didn't know the man's name, but he was with Cavan on the night of the big fight. Breanne walked over and gave Aleecia a hug.

"Hi, honey. It's so good to see you up and about. How are you feeling?"

Aleecia shrugged.

"She's having a hard time digesting the truth," Cavan said.

"I'll bet you are, Hon. The truth is hard to grab hold of at first."

"You," Aleecia said, pointing at the man, and almost referring to him as her second angel. "You were with Cavan the night I was attacked."

"Yes, I was, Aleecia. My name is David Mills."

"I think I . . . I should . . . you helped save my life?"

David gave a haphazard salute. "Just doin' my job, ma'am," he said with a slight slur as if repeating the line from an old spaghetti Western. "And actually, there were six of us."

Aleecia caught the fact that something unarticulated passed between the others in the room.

"Who are the other four?"

"We'll get to that later," David said.

Aleecia looked down at the floor. "Still, I think I should at least thank them."

"You might want to save your thanks, until you find out exactly what you're in for." David turned to Tami. "Are we ready to go?"

Tami nodded, and the group gathered Aleecia's things and left for the parking lot. Waiting outside was a dark-blue Lincoln Town Car.

"Nice ride," Aleecia said. "I remember my uncle owned one of these when I was a kid."

"And your father borrowed it and took you on a weekend trip," Cavan said. "We know. That's why we brought this car."

Aleecia stopped walking and glared at Cavan. Tami swatted her husband on the arm. "Will you stop that? Let the poor girl get used to the idea before you spill her life story."

"I was just trying to make her feel more relaxed."

"Well, you're failing miserably, you dolt," Tami said, slipping an arm around Aleecia's shoulder. "Don't worry about it, Aleecia. When we get the chance, I'll let you check out his memory clip. Then he won't say another thing about it."

As they walked to the car, Aleecia asked, "Do all of you have a memory record?"

"We do," Tami assured her.

"Does it always hurt the way it did when they took mine?"

"Not nearly. The Renegades showed us how to get them with some discomfort, but not much pain. The Bound use the old method because they don't know how to get them any other way."

David slid in behind the wheel and Breanne sat shotgun as Cavan and Tami got into the back seat. Aleecia thought for sure they were going to put her in the middle, gangster style, but Tami surprised her by slipping into the center seat. Aleecia looked around; she was standing in a hotel parking lot. A loud scream and a quick run and she could get the police here. She thought of running as fast as she could, and almost did, but what to do was still a question she didn't have an answer for. Instead, she got in the car, shut the door, and began her mystery ride.

22

The Move

"**W**here are we headed?" Aleecia asked.

"Canada."

"Canada? Wait, I can't go to Canada. I heard you need a passport, or a REAL ID driver's license and I've never had one, sorry."

Tami retrieved her bag, fumbled in it for a few seconds, and pulled out something that she handed to Aleecia, who wasn't too surprised to see her own face looking back at her, even if the name on the REAL ID driver's license wasn't hers.

"Now you're asking me to cross the border with a fake ID. This deal is getting worse by the minute."

"Aleecia," Cavan said as he leaned forward to look past Tami. "Let's review this. You've got a group of people out there who have more than likely killed a friend of yours. They've killed you once, and are now probably going to kill you on sight. You have no home and you have no job because you never reported back after your vacation. Your family and friends are off limits because the Bound are likely watching most of them, and unless I'm mistaken the police probably have a warrant out for your arrest. And let's not forget about the bigger problems you don't even know about yet. Now, I ask you, how important is your fake ID?"

Aleecia sat quietly for a few minutes and, after some thought, asked, "Why Canada?"

"The weather's cold. The Reti don't like the cold," David said.

"The Reti? Oh good, somebody new. Who the hell is Reti?"

Breanne turned to look at her. "Soon, honey. I promise."

They drove for hours, only stopping for long enough to refill the tank, empty the bladder, and grab a quick snack. Aleecia had plenty of time to think—and discreetly eye the people she was traveling with. They knew things about her that nobody else did. Things she had never shared with anyone. Things impossible for anyone to know, and they claimed they got this information from her own memories and there was no other place for them to get some of that information. If they could capture memories, could they also plant memories? Could the memories of what happened to her have been manufactured? This seemed more of a probability than the story they wanted her to believe, but if this was the case, why not just install the scenario they wanted her to believe and that she would simply accept as fact?

On more than one occasion, Aleecia thought about what she still considered escape. *Just wait until the next stop and make a run for it,* she planned. The feeling was strongest when they reached the border. Just a scream for help would get the customs officials involved. One nagging detail kept her from acting—these people saved her life. They wanted her alive and safe, and there were others out there who wanted her dead. It was these thoughts that kept Aleecia quiet.

Her tension, curiosity, and frustration grew as they turned off the main roads, followed a few side roads, and eventually turned onto a back road that took them to a rustic cabin. Large and weathered, the cabin looked as if it had been abandoned years ago.

When the Lincoln pulled up and parked behind an SUV, the luxury car produced the appearance of an aristocrat who was lost in the wilderness. Aleecia tensed up when she saw more people emerge from the cabin.

"Pop the trunk," Tami instructed as she got out. The chilly Canadian air filled the car and Aleecia felt her skin turn to goose flesh. Tami returned from the trunk and leaned in through the door and handed Aleecia a jacket just like the one she had left in her closet at home.

A man stepped to Aleecia's door and extended his hand. When Aleecia took it, he helped her out of the Lincoln.

"Aleecia Donnelly, I presume."

"Don't tell me, you're Doctor Livingston."

"No, but I've been called worse. My name is Niles Jority. For lack of a better title, I guess I'm captain of this little outfit."

"Are you the guy who sent these people to get me?"

"We all agreed to try and save you."

"Because you think I have some stone."

Niles nodded.

"I hope you're the guy who's going to give me a few more answers."

"As a matter of fact, I am. Why don't you come on in out of the chill, and I'll help fill you in?"

Niles led Aleecia to the door and the others followed. The rustic look of the cabin's exterior did nothing to suggest what was inside. They entered a foyer that held a large closet, but although Niles hung up his jacket Aleecia elected to keep hers. He led her through an open room with ample space to entertain an extensive family with a large field-stone fireplace that dominated the room. A large mantel stood out from the stonework, looking like the brim of a strange hat. On the mantle sat a large frame, but instead of housing a portrait it contained a large poster with the words, *With us is entrusted the human race.*

A kitchen with modern amenities sat through a door at the far end, and this was where Niles led her. He sat down at the table, as if it were time for tea.

He motioned and Aleecia sat in the chair opposite him.

"Okay," she said. "Now we're all here in this cabin in the middle of nowhere, I think I deserve some answers."

"You do, and you're about to get some. But you need to brace yourself for some strange experiences. I once gave someone the answers, and they went to Looneyville and never came back."

Aleecia folded her arms and waited. David handed Niles a clear plastic tube with a transparent black stone inside.

Aleecia eyed the stone. "Is that what this is all about?"

"Not entirely. This, believe it or not, is just the beginning." Niles held the tube out in front of her, so she could get a good look at the stone inside. "This is a Narration Stone. It's smaller than a Perception Stone. A Perception Stone is what Dan left with you."

"I keep telling people, Dan never left any stone with me."

"We believe he did, and we need to find out how. But first, you need some history lessons so the rest will make sense."

"History lessons?"

Niles responded by moving to the seat next to Aleecia and holding his right hand out flat. With his left thumb, he flipped the lid covering the end of the tube and dumped the stone into his palm. He handed the tube back to David and reached out, taking Aleecia gently by the wrist.

"I'm going to put this stone between our palms. All I want you to do is close your fingers around my hand."

"What kind of game is this?"

"A life-changing one."

Aleecia smirked and stretched out her fingers. Niles rotated his hand and let the stone roll into Aleecia's palm, before closing his fingers around her hand.

The answers came.

Aleecia's mind went completely dark for a few seconds, as though someone had shut off all the lights. The session began with a small flicker as if an old real-to-real film projector was starting and images followed. They were images of people Aleecia didn't know and of places she had never been. She felt uncomfortable, but it wasn't the images bothering her, it was the emotions she was feeling. A sense of dread strong enough to make her want to let go had come over her. When she tried to open her fingers and pull her hand away, Niles tightened his grip.

"Don't panic, this is normal. You're not alone. I'm here with you," she heard him say. But it would be more accurate to say she *felt* Niles say, as if he was part of her now or at least somehow connected. "The emotions you're going to experience may feel odd because they are being transferred to you through the stone. These emotions are part of the record and you will feel some of the emotions present within the narrators at the time they were collected." This would have freaked Aleecia out even more, if not for his words being accompanied by a feeling of peace and calm that counterbalanced the fear. This, too, she sensed as coming from Niles. When she refolded her fingers around his hand, the lesson continued.

23

One Huge Experiment

A skinny woman appeared in front of Aleecia and she felt a wave of anxiety and fear came over her which produced a slight shiver that coursed through her body. But to Aleecia this emotion did feel odd as if it was prearranged. Her first impulse was to back away, but nothing happened. It was as she was having an out of body experience, and she could witness the events unfold, but unable to interact because she was not part of the actual occurrence. Aleecia felt like a ghost.

There were several seconds of silence, while Aleecia took the time to examine the preoccupied-looking woman. She seemed old, pale, weak and drained of energy, and there was a strangeness to her slim form that Aleecia couldn't quite describe. When the woman finally directed her attention forward, she began speaking.

"Stone narrative by Chrysanthe. Hello to whoever might access this. I am the official historian aboard city-ship three, or as we refer to it, *Olimbia*."

At this, the woman gave a celebratory fist pump, but Aleecia felt no enthusiasm, even when she realized the woman was floating as if weightless.

"It is my responsibility to keep these journals and record our story. I am not sure who might use these so I have decided to make use of a reflective surface so you may see me. I have decided to include some history to help you better understand who we are. We are the Luren of Atlantis, and we have progressed, by trial and error, through a Stone Age, a Metal Age, an Industrial Age, a Technological Age, an Inter-Exploration Age, and the current Age of Survival. No one knows whether there will be another age. If there is one, we might refer to it as the Age of Adjustment.

Our culture has changed and is now difficult to explain. We work, play, and worship, and to the extreme these days, we die. Until recently we worked in factories, offices, outdoors, and in the mines, and we vacationed at the beach, in the wilderness, or within lavishly illuminated cities of entertainment. We studied in academies and focused on intelligence, but we also feigned wisdom, we polluted nature, struggled to clean it, and killed in an attempt to obtain peace. We allowed our petty differences to divide us for a long time, and it took our possible extinction to bring us together." She gave a sarcastic grin. "Stupid," Chrysanthe muttered softly. Through the stone, Aleecia experienced the woman's regret.

"Our big problems began when an astrologer noticed a strange light at the edge of a distant planet. This light turned out to be a large comet, with our calculations suggesting it was on a collision course with Atlantis. So, we studied the comet, and made plans, and we waited, and worried. When the comet instead passed close to a neighboring planet the course was altered just enough that we were spared. The comet passed so near to us that it affected the tides and put on an extraordinary light show that streaked the sky by day and illuminated the night with brilliant colors." The woman tilted her eyes upward and nodded slowly. "It was amazing." Aleecia's own mouth opened as she experienced Chrysanthe's awe.

"I had never imagined some of those colors," the woman continued. "I am no poet, but it was so beautiful, and it inspired me to feel thankful that I was alive to see it." Chrysanthe paused and grinned. "We had a planet wide party that lasted for days, and, for a short time, life continued as usual. But with our attention so focused on our demise, we put little thought into where the comet might go, which turned out to be toward our sun. The impact caused huge solar flares carrying electrically charged atoms and the atoms struck our planet. When they did, there was a second light show in the form of the Aurora Borealis and the Auroras Austral. Sightings were reported almost to the Equator."

Sorrow suddenly clutched Aleecia's heart.

"It turns out that the comet did not really miss us. In the ensuing days, some people reported headaches and a feeling of lightheadedness, or disorientation. These appeared to be the harshest effects and we once again believed the worst could be over. But this time, the real damage was far greater."

"The electrical ions recharged the magnetic properties of the planetary poles, rendering them stronger. Unfortunately, they were also reversed so magnetic north became magnetic south. This alone caused no great difficulty for us, but the suffering of what we considered lower life forms sealed our fate.

"For example, birds, dependent on their magnetic instinct, flew north instead of south. In the first two years alone, we lost hundreds of bird species. We tried to help but also learned this was not our only problem. The oceans' suffered greater losses and the consequences were more severe. Spawning fish and turtles trying to return to nesting grounds did not reproduce. In fact, any land or sea creature that lived by territorial boundaries lost their home, wandered aimlessly and when rivals met, confusion and instinct took over and they fought to the death."

The woman began physically drifting away until she reached out and pulled herself forward. Aleecia also experienced the sensation that Chrysanthe was mentally switching gears. "Our plants suffered just as badly. Most of us did not recognize the plant's susceptibility to magnetism of the planet, but within a year most plants did not seed and began to die off. To compound the problem, insects, reproduction partners of the plants, suffered in the same way as the birds. Once an insect left the nest, it became lost. With little food for the young, insect numbers plummeted and that caused staggering consequences. Seventy percent of the plants that provide food are dependent on flying insects for pollination and considering that one out of our every three bites of food depended on these plants, the loss of the insects crippled our food supply and it quickly became evident that the entire ecological system had to be remade.

"This finally forced all luren to put our differences aside, as we joined in a common struggle for survival. We looked for ways to combine our knowledge and information; and while some worked to save animals, others worked on plant life, and yet others on sea life."

The woman stopped for a moment and wrung her hands. "We made some great strides, we really did, and we prolonged the life of the planet, but ultimately we couldn't prevent its demise. Not only did the loss of plant life result in major food shortage, but because the byproduct of plant life is oxygen, the atmosphere was changing and becoming contaminated. Without animals to fertilize, or insects to pollinate, restoring the plants became an impossible task."

The woman sighed slowly, heavily.

"It became apparent that our only option was to abandon the surface and start over. We were left with no choice but to rush to develop the technology to build these huge orbiting cities from which we will try to rebuild our planet."

Chrysanthe faded and after a moment of darkness a man emerged

with the appearance of someone who had not eaten properly or slept well in months. His projected feelings suggested he had no more to give, and Aleecia sensed his emotions being devoid of compassion.

"Stone narrative by Stefein, onboard city-ship *Babel One*. Hello, from *Babel One*, called that because it was the first city-ship built. I am here to pick up where Chrysanthe left off, she died of one of the new viruses. There seems to be new ones coming every 30 turns of the horologe. The term 'horologe' still feels odd when I use it, but with no day and night it is the only way we can track time. Up here we see four sunrises between meals, so we stopped using surface terms and track time by the turn of the horologe.

I have not been down to the surface in more than a hundred turns and we have removed just about everyone we can provide for from the planet. The air on the surface is mostly noxious now and I feel bad for the people, including my brothers, who were selected to stay behind. They are doomed to suffer until they die. It may sound heartless, but resource capabilities dictated a selection process and the weak and uneducated were left behind. We had to look to our strength and intellect as sources of salvation. The city-ships could not even accommodate half of us, but the species continues to exist and that is the goal. I ask that you forgive me for sounding cold-hearted, it is not that I do not grieve for those who were lost, it is just that I have seen so much death that I have developed emotional calluses. If I took the time I need to grieve, I would be no use and they would send me back down."

He turned to look at something and when he looked front again, he huffed.

"We continuously face new problems, and everything we try seems to fail. I am afraid we may never regain balance and we might be up here forever."

There was a dark pause before the same man appeared again, this time accompanied by a sense of dread and anxiety that caused Aleecia to fold her free arm across her body.

"Stone narrative by Stefein. It is over now, and most projects have been abandoned. The oceans have become so toxic that every storm further poisons the planet. It is an unstoppable cycle, one that is beyond repair. We have abandoned any hope of migrating back to the surface, because without the oceans there can be no foreseeable expectation of improving the situation. We have lost our planet and our new home are these ships and we will live out our existence here."

He looked to the side and knocked his knuckles together five or six times. Aleecia perceived his sorrow.

"I do not think our existence will be that long. The viruses have forced us into small groups called pods, and there is no physical contact with other pods. We believe living this way is our only hope of preventing the viruses from taking us all.

Again, he faced forward.

"I have now been in space for over six hundred turns, and my body is changing. My legs are weakening, my joints ache and I am having an increasing number of headaches. I cannot imagine doing this much longer, and truth be told, I am okay with that."

Aleecia saw another black pause and she felt Niles say, "The blank spots you're experiencing are a result of the passage of time and are breaks in the timeline. We're being moved forward and only seeing pertinent narratives."

Another woman with thin hair, big eyes, and pale skin appeared.

"Stone narrative by Marei, onboard city-ship *Delfy*. Hello to any who may view these reports. I am picking up this task where Stefein has left off. He volunteered for a surface mission and disappeared. I am to make these records now and I do not know why. I doubt there will be anyone left to see them, but the counsel insisted that I persevere. I wish they would find someone else, because I am already struggling to keep up, but we do as we are asked.

We continue to orbit Atlantis because there is no other option. Our formerly beautiful blue planet is now red, and the readings indicate that no life remains. Our new plan is to develop probes that we will send out in search of a new planet. The city-ships were not designed to move away from Atlantis, so I am not sure what we would do if we did find a better planet, I suppose we have to try something."

She looked off into the distance and Aleecia felt overwhelmed as Marei rolled a red stone between her fingers. "I will make another entry when I can."

Break

"Stone narrative by Marei." This time, Marei seemed older and frailer and Aleecia felt ill. "I know it has been a few thousand turns since I had anything encouraging to say, but it looks like the first probe is ready to be sent out. The plan is to launch a new one every 100 turns. This is a challenge because we can only harvest some of the material we need from the planet, and descending is so dangerous we lose about thirty percent of those who try.

"I do not think it will ever amount to much, but I suppose it will keep us busy. It has also been suggested that we begin to procreate. There was a mandatory stop on births because we could not feed extra mouths. Now if we do not start increasing our numbers there will be no mouths to feed. Yet we do not know if it will help. The synthesized food is hard on the body and no one knows whether infants will be able to tolerate it. I know I do not want to eat any more. It hurts when I do."

Break

"Stone narrative by Tomoshki, onboard city-ship *Tewatikwanon*. Hello, fellow Atlanteans, or whoever you may be." Aleecia was stunned. This being looked different from the others that had come before. The eyes were three times the size of her own and black in color, and fuzz covered the unusually large head that sat atop a thin frame. The extremities were also thin and the skin extremely pale; the creature looked unhealthy. Aleecia's reaction would have been more negative if she didn't experience a feeling of great delight and happiness that made her smile.

"I have been instructed to restart these records because we have incredible news to share. After more than three hundred thousand turns the incredible grace of our forebears has blessed us with new hope. After thirty generations of worship, our ancestors have answered our prayers! We received a message! One of the very first probes has transmitted data that suggest there might be hope for a planet of similar size to Atlantis. I am not sure what we can do about it because the city-ships were not designed to leave orbit, but I have faith that our ancestors and heroes of our history will bless us with the wisdom to overcome."

Break

"Stone narrative by Tomoshki."

When Tomoshki appeared, Aleecia smiled brightly at the joy she perceived on several levels.

"We received more information from the probe sent out so long ago. The data we received indicate that the planet will need a lot of work if we are to live there, but it might be possible. The counsel is in session to determine what we should do, but the party has already begun. Thanks be to our ancestors for looking out for us. And, on a personal note, my son was born ten turns ago. He is beautiful, and like most infants his eyes are bigger than mine and they should serve him well."

Break

"Stone narrative by Tomoshki."

Tomoshki appeared looking somewhat older and weakened, and Aleecia realized his projected joy was less intense but still there.

"The plans are laid for our cities to be equipped with solar sails. If our calculations are correct, these sails will provide us enough power to break out of orbit and chart a course for the new planet. This will be a hope-filled journey, but no one knows whether it will be successful. The whole endeavor is one huge experiment, so the project has been given a name; Experimental Atlantis: Relocation Trek of Hope, and the new planet will be called Earth."

Break

"Stone narrative by Tomoshki."

Excitement filled Aleecia, as she realized she was starting to like this guy, his presence filled her with welcoming sensations that gave her a sense of happiness that some people refer to as the warm, fuzzy feeling.

"It has begun! The sails are a success, and we are moving! I never thought I would see the day when we no longer looked down on Atlantis. Our ancestors have blessed us with the knowledge to overcome and we will move across the vast emptiness to our promised land. I know I will not live long enough to see Earth, but we are on the move and Earth is our destination. I am so proud that one day I will be able to tell my great grandchildren that I was here the day the city-ships moved for the first time."

Break

"Stone narrative by Katrinea, onboard city-ship *Mesapetama*."

The creature in front of Aleecia looked like Tomoshki but there wasn't any physical suggestions of gender. Nevertheless, Aleecia perceived that she was female and full of aggravation and hurt. In fact, Aleecia frowned as tears formed in her own eyes.

"My name is Katrinea, and I have been given this task by way of an accident. The *Tewatikwanon* was struck by asteroids as we moved through our solar system and Tomoshki and his family were killed. We do not yet know if we can save the city, but we are trying to evacuate as many as we can to other cities. It is a hard time for us, but we will succeed if we stay faithful to our ancestors. We are presently forming a line with the other city-ships and preparing for a slingshot maneuver around our last planet. This will increase our speed fourfold."

Break

"Stone narrative by Katrinea."

Sadness and loss flooded into Aleecia as tears now ran down her cheeks.

"We lost the *Tewatikwanon*. There was no repair we could make to include her in the journey, and we had to leave her behind. Only half of the inhabitants were transferred. The others had to stay with the city and do the best to endure. Several friends are still onboard *Tewatikwanon* and I know I will never hear from them again. I fear that staying with the city will bring them only misery and death."

Katrinea wiped tears from her eyes.

Break

"Stone narrative by Katrinea."

Aleecia's shoulders slumped and exhaustion flowed through her.

"The slingshot maneuver was a success, and we are moving at a much increased pace, but it will still take millions of turns to arrive. There is some hope that we will develop faster ships which can take small teams ahead and begin terraforming Earth."

Break

"Stone narrative by Katrinea. The first advance team left for Earth."

Katrinea reported with a feeling of loss, accomplishment, and pride and Aleecia put her free hand over her heart.

"They will travel to Earth well ahead of the cities and begin terraforming operations. The data tells us that Earth is covered in ice, so they will place immense solar reflectors in orbit to reflect the sun and heat up the planet. If they are successful, the ice will melt, rivers and oceans will form, the water will evaporate, and weather patterns will begin to develop. They have taken one of the stones, so we will be able to communicate and track their progress. We celebrated their sacrifice with a heroes' party because we will never see them again and they have determined the fate of their families. Even with their incredible rate of speed, it will take them 60,000 turns to arrive and it will be their descendants who will finish their mission. Other advanced teams will follow these heroes and we will revere them all."

Break

"Stone narrative by Surimgi, onboard city-ship *Babel One*. I hope this is coming through okay. We are passing through an anomaly that is interfering with the stones."

Any emotion that was transferred to Aleecia was more distant and unsubstantial. Surimgi was much shorter and had larger eyes than the preceding narrators, and her complexion was clay colored.

"I am here with great news. We received a message from Advance Team One saying they have reached Earth, and everything is progressing according to plan. Advance Team Two will leave soon with the generational goal of placing solar-powered machines on the soil. These machines will create carbon monoxide that will hang heavily in the air and create a warming blanket around the planet to form a workable atmosphere for growing plants. Once sufficient soil becomes available, bacteria will be introduced for germination."

Break

"Stone narrative by Dominico, onboard city-ship *Delfy*, saying hello to you."

This individual's physical appearance was vastly different from that of the previous narrators. He possessed no hair and had large, almond-shaped black eyes that were supported by a head three times the size of the first narrators, and his arms were twice as long and half as thick as theirs. Dominco's emotions passed through the stone and Aleecia felt his great pride and happiness and she sat taller in her chair.

"I am a teacher for the young and I use these records to educate and help them understand where they came from and how to determine their purpose. I have requested this tradition because we are living in remarkable times. We received word that Advance Team Two has arrived at Earth. Team One is absent, as expected, and assumed deceased. We knew the equipment would eventually fail them and they would crash to Earth, but they are the first luren to touch our new home and will join our ancestors to be celebrated and worshiped in perpetuity.

Break

"Stone narrative by Dominico. Team Three has departed, and the celebration lasted eight turns. These new heroes will have the honor of introducing our first seeds. The carbon-heavy atmosphere and bacteria-rich soil should provide a perfect environment to support plant life. If the seeds take root lush green plants will grow and produce oxygen. The heavy carbon should trap the oxygen near the surface, and a new oxygen atmosphere will develop. Once this occurs, insects for pollination will be introduced. How exciting it is for my students to know that someday their descendants will stand on Earth and breathe the new air created from plants that last grew on Atlantis! They call it 'Atlantis Air,' and I think the term will stick."

Break

"Stone narrative by Mionici, onboard city-ship *Babel One*."

The only way Aleecia could describe the feeling being transferred to her was to call it 'hope.'

"Our engineers have developed a ship that will travel faster and last much longer for Team Four. Their goal is to introduce huge creatures created by our geneticist; enormous creatures that are a result of the DNA combined from different animals. When the time is right, the DNA will be cultivated in eggs and that is how the creatures will reproduce. These creatures will roam Earth and help spread seeds and fertilize our promised land."

Break

"Stone narrative by Homstom, onboard city-ship *Olimbia*."

Happiness and relief flowed into Aleecia.

"The descendants of Team Four are still alive and well, and in orbit around Earth. They report that the terraforming plan is moving forward. However, two of our previous phases are now obsolete. The first is that the solar reflectors are problematic because the carbon in the atmosphere has raised the temperature of the earth and it could become harmful if it continues to increase. Second, the enormous creatures are no longer needed. To eradicate both, Team Five will be sent to harness a nearby asteroid and send it on a collision course with Earth. This will exterminate the huge creatures and readjust Earth's orbit releasing the reflectors."

Break

"Stone narrative by Povantol, onboard the city-ship *Mesapetama*."Emotion coming from this man was almost nonexistent, and Aleecia got the sense that he believed he was performing a mundane task and was just going through the motions of something that needed to be done.

"Team Five reports that they have reached Earth and have located Team Four. For the first time we have greatly increased our number around Earth."

Break

"Stone narrative by Povantol. The asteroid impact was more severe than anticipated but we did obtain the desired results. Earth is now in a stable orbit and maintaining an appropriate temperature. Everything is going according to plan and we are moving to the next phase."

Break

Aleecia suddenly felt excitement, pride, and joy, and she wanted to rise from her chair and do her happy dance.

"Stone narrative by Narieo onboard the city-ship *Olimbia*. "If there is anyone not celebrating, shame on them. Team Six will depart in two turns and be the mission that represents our finest accomplishments thus far. Our engineers designed an improved ship with advanced propulsion systems, which will shorten the journey. But more importantly, the system will supply an increased amount of artificial gravity so the team can get acclimated to Earth's gravity. Our greatest scientists are included in Team Six, as they will reincorporate strands of DNA preserved from our divine ancestors into the team members to reverse the effects of living in space for so long. When they reach Earth, they should look very much like the luren of old. This is critical, because they are equipped to send people to the surface who can survive on Earth. With much happening on this mission, it was determined that this ship will be our ark, so the team will also take a copy of the DNA nucleuses of many animals and fish to begin rebuilding the wildlife.

"It is incredible to think that we have done the impossible. We have taken an uninhabitable planet and turned it into one we can live on. All praise to our ancestors, and may they grant those in Teams Four, Five, and Six happy and healthy lives on Earth."

Break

"Stone narrative by Jakiog, onboard the city-ship *Mesapetama*."

Aleecia received the feelings of great pride, hope, happiness, and a little hung over.

"We are celebrating because we have received word that not only are we halfway to Earth, but Team Six has reported through the stones that they are alive and living well on Earth. They will now start introducing the animals. Due to this team's success, it was decided that they deserve a name. Therefore, Team Six will go down in history as team Adamnoah, named for the designers of the city-ships and for those who began it all."

Break

The narration continued with information and emotion that stirred Aleecia's own reactions and pulled her in different ways. By now the beings all looked alike: huge black almond shaped eyes; small mouth; overly big hairless head; a compact body with limbs that were thin and long; and gray-colored skin.

"Stone narrative by Heneli, onboard city-ship *Babel One*. The reports from Team Ananokey show us that the descendants of previous teams have devolved into a very primitive culture. They tell us that much knowledge has been lost, and Team Ananokey spends a lot of time teaching them things we expected them to already understand."

Break

"Stone narrative by Belanca, onboard city-ship *Delfy*. We received a stone transmission from Team Ra. They tell us that the descendants, whom we have dubbed Earthlings, are surviving in their primitive cultures, and the team will try to educate them about our identity. They will also show Earthlings how to use sound waves to move stone and supervise with their building of monuments to our ancestors."

Break

"Stone narrative by Larimose onboard the city-ship *Olimbia*. We received a stone transmission from Team Vishnu. The landing was hard, but this was overcome and there was a safe landing. The education of the Earthlings continues, but they alter and confuse previous information. Vishnu tells us that members of Teams Ananokey and Ra are considered gods by the Earthlings, which is helpful because honoring our ancestors and heroes is culturally correct. I feel badly for them, for they are our cousins and descendants of our exalted ancestors, but they do not know their place is beside us. Vishnu also reports a concern saying that the Earthlings are not counting their population and they will flood the area with offspring until the population cannot be supported. This mistake we suffered on Atlantis and we hope to save the Earthlings from the same dire consequence."

Break

"Stone narrative by Petor, onboard the city-ship *Mesapetama*. Team Jupiter has left for Earth, and Team Zeus will soon follow. We hope the Earthlings will remember what the previous teams have taught them and that they are respecting our planet. There is much debate as to what rights they have and how we should best assimilate the cultures."

Break

"Stone narrative by Zankilus, onboard city-ship *Babel One*. The twin team led by the two brothers Romulas and Reamious has left for Earth to establish a culture and teach the inhabitants some techniques that will help them live better. They will also remind them of their responsibilities, especially toward the ancestors. We are getting close to Earth. A few more generations will see the city-ships above our promised land, and we will take our place and rule this new planet with wisdom."

Break

"Stone narrative by Sempronius Asellio, Roman citizen and historian from Earth."

Aleecia's mouth sprang open in surprise; this narrator was completely human.

"I hope this works as I'm new to it, but the goddess Concordia is aiding me with the stone. I am happy to say that the construction of the new cities is moving forward with haste and are laid out in grids as we were shown, mostly thanks to the new concrete. We can now travel between cities using the roads the gods have shown us how to build. The technique of building the arches, is allowing the aqueducts to bring fresh water into the cities. Water is also stored in the concrete reservoirs. Most citizens have hot and cold water in their homes and the dirty water is moving out of the cities by way of the sewers. None of this would have been possible without an understanding of mathematics and numbers. Praise be to all the gods who have helped us."

Break

Aleecia had been accepting the myriad emotions and sensations melding with her senses, but now an onslaught of reports barraged her causing her to clench her fist in rage, long for peace, stomp her feet, sob, and curse.

"Stone narrative by Richaiousus, onboard city-ship *Delfy*. There is talk that the Earthlings are harming the planet, but we are not going to intervene. For countless generations, my family dedicated their lives to building a home for us, and I will not give up on their dreams and traditions because some of our ancestors left their descendants there to take our world! We have created Earth. It is ours, and I will fight to protect it!"

Break

"Stone narrative by Franth, onboard city-ship *Babel One*. The counsel has decreed that all visitations to Earth will stop until the city-ships arrive. There are so many earthlings now that plans to assimilate them into our culture will be immensely complex. Some are blaming our ancestors for allowing this to happen, but they are wrong. Our ancestors are the reason we are still here, and we owe all that we are to them and I pray they will show me the path."

Break

"Stone narrative by Adathor, onboard city-ship *Mesapetama*. My ancestor is a hero. Her Earth mission with team Ra was a success and helped prepare Earth for us. We learned about her in our early lessons and in our prayer meetings. She is to be worshiped and revered. To hear some say that what she did failed and my distant relatives are intruders is incredibly hurtful to me."

Break

"Stone narrative by Georgeian, onboard city-ship *Delfy*. We are here! At long last we have arrived near Earth and have taken orbits around the fourth, fifth, and six planets in the system. It has been determined that the inhabitants of Earth do not respect or understand our ways. Although they are unimportant to us, what we should do with them is a lingering question. We cannot simply destroy Earth. That is sacrilege."

Break

"Stone narrative by Aeristont onboard city-ship *Olimbia*. The Earthlings are destroying our planet. Fortunately, our recent abduction missions and studies have proven useful as we have developed a new virus which should eliminate most of the Earthling trespassers. Then we can begin to take our place on the surface."

Break

"Stone narrative by Fadornia, onboard city-ship *Mesapetama*. Someone has gone down to Earth and provided a vaccine to the Earthlings. As a result, the council has rendered the decision that anyone caught helping Earthlings are to be considered a traitor to our cause and therefore tried for treason. If found guilty they will be launched into space."

Break

Stone narrative by Nalkiny, onboard city-ship *Delfy*. My son is a traitor! He has admitted to giving information to an Earthling called Marie Curie, who is a descendant of Menrva. He insists that Earthlings have the same rights as any of us and should not be harmed. I am heart broken, and I must endure my son's execution when he is discharged through the traitor's airlock."

Break

"Stone narrative by Spartadea, onboard city-ship *Babel One*. Soon we will have enough data to overcome the biological difficulties we have developed from being in space so long. This information should help us adapt to surface living. Making these biological adjustments could render the study of Earthlings obsolete, then all of them should be eliminated."

Break

Aleecia realized this break was different and darker than the others and was followed by a soft light when Niles released her hand. The images stopped and Aleecia came back to the present as quickly and as easily as closing a book or pushing stop on a screen. Although the transition was smooth, she was woozy. She didn't think that holding the stone had caused the feeling and it was instead because everything she had taken for fact was indeed fallacy. When your sense of reality leaps off the deep end, it takes a few minutes for your mind to catch up.

She suddenly felt sick to her stomach. Although she felt wobbly, she discovered her legs still worked well enough to get her to the sink in the kitchen. It was a fight to keep her gorge down until she reached it, but when she did, she vomited.

24

Vaccinations, Cures, the Atomic Bomb

Aleecia's retching lasted a long time, and just when she thought it had passed, another revelation of what the world was really like came to the forefront and caused the retching to start over. Breanne was at her side throughout most of the process, holding a cool wet rag on the back of her neck and waiting for the condition to abate.

Aleecia's mind raced to catch up with the new reality. People and professions that she had respected a short time ago, doctors, teachers, and lawyers were bungling their way through life without any idea as to the reality of living. The truth was she thought this has been true for the lawyers for a long time, but now she viewed the rest of those respected people as children in need of schooling.

Finally, with nothing in her stomach and the shock gone from her mind, Aleecia was able to stand straight. With Breanne's help, she made it to the kitchen table and sat heavily in one of the chairs.

When she looked up at the people watching her, she saw them for who and what they were: warriors. She felt a little sick all over again, but the muscles in her abdomen were too weak and sore for her to vomit.

"This is real," she said as a statement and not a question.

"Yes," Niles said while placing the tube with the stone in it on the table. "And if you doubt it, consider you just received a history lesson from a stone." He waved his hand as if saying hello or, more accurately, goodbye, and some of the team—that's the way Aleecia viewed them now, as a team—went back to doing whatever they had been doing.

Niles, David, Cavan, and Tami filled the rest of the chairs around the table as Breanne brought over a pot of coffee and cups.

"Okay," Aleecia said, finally finding her voice, "I know what I saw, and I somehow feel it's all true, but tell me, person to person, who and what are we?"

Niles smiled. "Okay, but only the *Reader's Digest* version. Our race, humankind, began on a different planet. The name I'm sure you're familiar with—Atlantis. When their sun was struck by a comet, they were forced to leave their planet and build a new one. After the planet could sustain life, a few of the earlier settlers landed to start anew. When their technology failed, they devolved into what we now think of as early man. Over time, they populated Earth and re-evolved to what we are today.

"The Atlantean city-ships arrived and we were, in mass numbers, living on their planet. Most of them still see us as a possession or as intruders because they had existed first and, after all, they terraformed this planet. They decided we needed to be eliminated, so they could lay claim, and this is the fight we are engaged in now."

"And the guys who attacked me?"

"The Bound? Technically they are called Retis' Bound. They work for the Reti."

"And Reti is?"

"The Atlanteans. The term "luren" is equivalent to our human, and Atlanteans and Reti, refer to the same species, just like you are both human and an Earthling."

"I understand Atlanteans if they're from Atlantis, but why do we call them Reti?"

"Reti is a nickname taken from the scientific name Zeta Reticuli because Atlantis is located within a star system in the Reticulum constellation. You're probably more familiar with the Reti as the gray aliens made famous by the area 51 crash. I'm sure you've seen renderings of what abductees call the Grays?"

"Those are the people I just saw, but I always thought that to be a joke."

Niles chuckled. "Most people do, but those are images of the Reti and are fairly accurate. I'm sure you noticed the physical changes in the people making the journals, so you saw the evolution from beings a lot like us to what they look like today. Generations of living in weightless conditions did several things to the body. Without gravity, the legs grew long and thin. The arms took over the job of body transportation, and constant reaching and stretching to get from one hand hold to the next caused the arms to grow long and nimble. Lack of light caused the eyes to grow large. But the term "Gray" comes from the pigment of the skin. Without the elements to contend with, there was no need for hair and the pigment of the skin changed from various colors, like we have," he said laying his arm against hers, "to gray."

"So, all those people who claim they were abducted really were?"

"Most of them. They were taken for examination and returned to Earth for different reasons. Some are sending data back to the Reti without knowing it, and some were released for biological warfare."

"What do you mean biological warfare?"

"The Reti want the planet, so they need to find a way to eliminate us without destroying the earth. An effective way to do this is with disease or virus. The Black Plague, Cholera, Polio, Cancer, AIDS, the Bird Flu, SARS, and more recently COVID-19 are attempts by the Reti to do away with us."

Her mouth slightly agape, Aleecia looked at him. "You mean all those diseases are a creation of the Reti?"

"Yes, and they seem to like sexually transmitted diseases and the idea of breeding ourselves out of existence. That way, they don't worry about harming the planet."

After a few moments of silence, Aleecia rubbed her face and asked, "So we're out here on our own? Just us, this little band of ordinary people, trying to find a way to save the entire human race? That's discouraging."

Niles grinned. "It would be, but we're not alone," he said. "Together we are called the Crew, and there are thousands of us, some who have big strings to pull. We have our resources, and we do receive help. There are several Reti who believe we are all Atlanteans because we have the same ancestors. When it comes right down to genealogical heritage, they're right. Our ancestors are one and the same. Because of this, some believe we are born with the same rights as all Atlanteans. The Reti who aid us are labeled rebels or renegades and are considered traitors to Atlantis. The penalty for treason is death, so making the decision to help us isn't taken lightly. But, still, we receive help."

"Help in what way?"

"Vaccinations, cures . . . the atomic bomb."

Aleecia's eyes opened wide. "The atomic bomb?"

"Well, sure, Renegades gave us nukes as a threat. The last great act of defiance. If the Reti try to destroy us, we destroy the planet. But of course, nobody really understood it that way, apart from Shopenhimer, Einstein, and the others in their circle."

"Wait," Aleecia said putting up a hand. "You're telling me Albert Einstein was a member of the Crew?"

"He sure was. Don't you think the theory of relativity is a little advanced for a patent clerk?"

Aleecia nodded her head and chortled sarcastically. "So, all of our greatest human achievements were given to us by rebellious Reti?"

"Most of them. The great philosophers like Aristotle, Plato, and Socrates were taught by Atlanteans trying to advance the culture. Most of the great inventors, such as Archimedes, Cai Lun, Leonardo da Vinci, Marie Curie, and Tesla were shown ideas or theories by Atlanteans for the same reasons. Some advancement we achieved on our own, and some by conspiracy. The Area 51 crash was a Reti ship sabotaged by the Renegades. It crashed in the dessert and we recovered it; the technological advances in the fifties, sixties, and seventies were a result of our reverse engineering the technology. Fiber optics, the silicon chip, laser technology, even Velcro were just some of the things we were able to salvage."

"So, the government knows?"

Niles shook his head. "Only a select few know the entire truth. We tried several times over the decades to educate people, but each time it ended poorly. Like back in the sixties when we were able to gain a meeting with President Kennedy. He appointed a committee to check into our story and initiated the space race to establish contact with the Reti and meet them on their own turf. He was our greatest hope before he went for a limo ride in Dallas, Texas and they killed him."

Aleecia's chin dropped. "You're telling me Kennedy was killed by the Reti?"

"No, it was ordered by the Reti, but the Bound pulled off the assassination. The Warren Commission is a crock, I can assure you of that. The Crew involved back then felt responsible for the death of the president, and it was the last time we tried going to the government. But there was one other time when it happened as an accident. John Kennedy left copies of the evidence, which was eventually discovered by his brother Robert. He asked the wrong questions and a Bound found out and gunned him down too."

Aleecia was saddened and shook her head. "So, nothing good came from their deaths?"

"I wouldn't say nothing good, as Kennedy did give us our best and biggest weapon: NASA."

"The National Aeronautics and Space Administration?"

"Actually, it's Neutralization and Subjugation of Atlanteans. But we couldn't just come out and call it that, now could we?"

Aleecia sat dumbfounded as Niles continued.

"Consider the things NASA has done. Along with its other attributes, think of the Hubble Telescope, and now the James Webb Space Telescope as huge spy satellites, much like their smaller counterparts.

Aleecia pointed at the ceiling and made a circle with her finger. "You mean our spy satellites?"

"Sure, we've been using them for decades. Everybody accepts the idea that we spy on each other, yet nobody considers that the cameras can be pointed away from the earth as well as toward it. The lunar missions were an attempt to see if we could build a defense on the lunar surface. The explosion on board Apollo 13 was no accident., it was sabotage by the

Bound. The Mars Rovers are sent to see if we can find a way to defend from a farther distance. And I'm still shocked nobody asked the real question about the Voyager program."

"The Voyager program?"

"Yes, the probes that were sent out in the seventies specifically to contact other life forms and ask for help. Everybody kind of smiles or smirks when they hear talk of the SETI program, the Search for Extra Terrestrial Intelligence. The thought of scientists sitting and listening to the signals coming from space and hoping to hear from an alien race makes people grin, but they never stop to ask what specifically they're listening for . . . They're listening for an answer to our call for help."

Aleecia shifted in her chair. "So why don't all the presidents know?"

"We try to tell them all, unofficially. Some do their own research and work for a solution, others ignore it. Most recently President Trump created Space Force, yet nobody asked why. It seems so logical, but nobody gets it. The Navy defends our interests at sea, the Army on the ground, and the Air Force in the sky. What do you suppose Space Force defends?"

Aleecia took some time to digest some the information, then she asked a question that had never existed in her thinking. Until now, it would have been as ridiculous as asking, how high can your pig fly?

"These stones, what exactly are they and how do they work?"

"The easiest way to think about them is to consider the Narration Stones, like this one," Niles said, holding up the tube and allowing Aleecia to look at the stone once again. "Think of this as a radio receiver. The one Dan found is bigger, because it's a Perception Stone. It's not only a receiver, but a transmitter as well. Or, the Narration Stone tells a story, while the Perception Stone perceives and records human senses and creates the story.

"When the human body experiences something through the senses, the experience is relayed to the brain through electrical impulses. Those impulses can be recorded and duplicated by the properties in the stones. Crystals are great for storing data. In fact, our technology is just starting to catch up. Do an Internet search for 5D optical data storage and you'll see what I mean. The Narration Stone can relay anything ever picked up by a Perception Stone to the brain just by touch. The Perception Stone Dan found can gather information and also send it. The Perception Stones can capture the information and pass it on to whoever is holding either kind of stone.

"When you hold any of the stones with a specific question in mind, the stones will relay to your mind the information you seek. Holding one with a sense of wonder can allow the information to flow unchecked into the psyche. In the hands of an inexperienced person, the Perception Stones can push so much experience into the brain that it will overload the neural net and cause pain, blackouts and, if exposed too long, death."

Aleecia cautiously poked at the tube with her finger. "How long is too long?"

Niles shrugged. "It depends on the person. Dan inadvertently activated a Perception Stone twice. The fact that he lived through it is something special. He must have been in a position to disconnect from the stone, even if he was unconscious."

"How many stones are there?"

"The Narration Stones, these small ones," Niles said nodding at the stone in the tube, "are more common and number in the dozens. I'm not sure exactly how many there are. The Perception Stones are a much bigger deal. There are twelve, and each one works in combination with, strengthens, and gives more attributes to the others. That's what the Reti are after. If they can gather all twelve stones, they will be able to harness all the knowledge collected since the time the stones were created. With so much knowledge, getting rid of us Earthlings will be much easier."

"Where did the stones come from, and why not just destroy them?

"The Reti made them. They accidentally stumbled on the ability when they were researching their home planet in their attempt to save it. Destroying the stone is a last resort option. The stones could give us access to an incredible amount of information, and we don't want to lose that. Consider that the Reti helped develop Rome, you saw the narration. When Rome fell that technology was lost and it took us two thousand years to get it back. Imagine what we could lose or gain through the stones."

Aleecia folded her arms across her chest. "If the stones are so important, how did one get lost so that Dan could find it?"

"Some of the earlier Reti expeditions brought a stone with them, so they could communicate with the fleet. Back then, we were all one big team. One of the early ones came with the Annunaki, believed by our ancestors to be immortal gods that came to Earth during the ancient Sumerian times in Mesopotamia around 4,000 BCE. Vishnu, and Zeus each had their own, as did Ra and the Atlanteans who helped build the megalithic structures."

"Megalithic structures? You mean like the Egyptian pyramids?"

Niles nodded. "That's the first one people think of, but the pyramids were constructed between many others. Megalithic structures exist all over the globe: Göbekli Tepe, Stonehenge, Puma Punku, Teotihuacan, and the Angkor Wat Temple, to name just a few. Over so much time and distance, some of the Perception Stones were lost.

"The Atlanteans who arrived throughout time were stranded here, when they came it was a one-way trip. Some tried to duplicate the stones with the minerals they found here on Earth, but they couldn't find the same properties. As a result, the ones they built had to be much bigger. They tried to explain to Earthlings how they worked and, as a visual aid, made them in the shape of skulls, hence the famous crystal skulls. The skulls and the crystals they made contained some of the same properties as the Atlantis stones, and they were able to capture some of the same attributes. But they don't work nearly well enough. The crystal skulls are slow and sending and receiving information takes a long time and isn't always reliable. It's kind of like comparing the 1800 snail mail to IM or texting."

Aleecia drew a deep breath and sighed. "You say there are twelve Perception Stones. How many stones are still missing?"

"Four, including the one Dan found. We have three, and the Reti have the other five. With each new stone they recover, the Reti find new information and weaknesses, which allows them to develop a new weapon or disease. It's impossible for me to know or explain how they combine and use the information a new stone brings to them, it's beyond our knowledge. But it always ends in catastrophe for us. Our best estimate is that at least twenty million lives will be lost, if the Reti get to this one first."

A

25

Bodies in Your Living Room

Aleecia sat quietly for a few minutes as she ran the number through her head. "Twenty million lives are at stake?"

"All depending on us," Niles said with a sour grin. "Granted, it's just a guess,

but our experiences have made us pretty good at guessing."

"And what's my part in all of this?"

"It's up to you," David said. "Like it or not, you're involved now that you know the truth, but where you go and what you do from here is your choice."

"But my choices are limited, aren't they?"

"I'm afraid you have only a few, but our hope is you'll join us," Niles said.

"Join you? What, I'm just supposed to give up everything I knew before I met you?"

"Aleecia," Niles said shaking his head. "Those things have already been taken from you, just as they were taken from us. Your past life is in the past. If you try to go back to your old life, I'm afraid it will be a very short life."

Aleecia put her hands over her face.

David touched her sleeve. "I know it's hard to accept, I speak from experience, but the truth is it all comes down to a single choice. You work with us and you will have a chance to live long enough to see your next birthday, or you won't. It's really that simple."

"Oh, excuse me, but I don't see any of this as simple, and I don't see how I can help."

"This part, you're not going to like," Niles said. "We need to take you back home and continue looking for the stone."

Aleecia's expression hardened and she pointed at David. "You just dragged me away from there and now you want to take me back?"

"We have to go back. Your home is the last place the stone could have been. It's our best and only lead. Wherever the stone is now, the trail picks up at your place."

"But the Bound already turned the place inside out. If it was there, they would have found it."

Niles shook his head. "They might have, but I don't think they did."

"Why not?"

"Because they like to brag. If they'd found the stone, they would've let the Reti know and they would have made sure we picked up on it."

Aleecia tapped the tabletop with her finger. "So why bring me all the way up here, if you were just going to take me back home?"

"A few reasons. First, it gives us some time to allow things to cool down. The police are looking for you, and they're bound to be watching your house."

"You're worried about getting caught by the police? That seems small now."

"I know in the scheme of things the local police seem like a small concern, but what good would it do us to be arrested? We'd never get a chance to look for the stone. We can't afford a confrontation with them. But budget restraints and manpower will only have them doing spot checks in a week. Then we'll have a better chance of getting in and out without getting caught."

Aleecia nodded. "Okay, it makes a little sense, but why would the police be so interested in me? I don't think they'd stake out my house just because I lied about my luggage, even if they are still looking for Dan."

There was a pause and again something passed through the group that resulted in Breanne leaving the table.

"There's more to it, isn't there?"

"There is."

"I get the feeling I don't want to know what you're about to tell me."

Niles looked at the others before allowing his eyes to rest back on Aleecia. "What's the last thing you remember seeing the night you were attacked?"

Aleecia thought back. "Four of you busting through the front door."

"That's right, four of us came in the front and two others came in through the back. You've already met Cavan and David, but you have yet to meet Derick Gates or Ramiro Lopez."

"I look forward to meeting them, but that's four, so what about the other two?"

"Jammie Holmes and Glen Stover. You'll never meet them, Aleecia. They never left your house. The police aren't looking for you because of your luggage or because you helped with Dan's boat sale, they have bigger questions for you now. Like why they found two bodies in your living room."

Aleecia sat stunned. She had never considered the fact that some of them didn't make it out. The thought of how close she came to dying hit home.

"What about the Bound?" she finally asked. "If they haven't found the stone, won't they still be looking?"

"We're sure they are."

"Isn't there a chance we're going to run into each other?"

"I'll be surprised if we don't."

"Oh, sorry," Aleecia said facing her palms outward. "But the last time I ran into these guys they tried to . . . okay, they *did* kill me. I'm not interested in meeting them again."

"None of us are, but our best chance for finding the stone is to have you with us. The slightest thing could make a big difference, and since you were Dan's girlfriend and he . . ."

"I wasn't his girlfriend," Aleecia said, cutting him off.

"Close enough," Cavan replied, waggling his eyebrows at her.

Aleecia rolled her eyes toward the ceiling.

"Regardless," Niles said, "you're our closest link to Dan. If there's anyone who might be able to figure out what he did with the stone, it would be you."

26

Mind Games

Everett Koltz stood naked to the world. With his feet tied together, he stood on a wooden plank three feet off the ground. His hands were not only tied behind his back, but also around a tall wooden post. Around him, nearly waist-high, were stacks of small tree limbs tied together with simple white string. The crowd standing around, watching, remained mostly silent.

An executioner appeared dressed in a black hooded robe that hung to within an inch of the ground. A cheer went up from the spectators as the man in black stopped near a lighted torch, gripped it in one gloved hand, and raised it to the sky.

Mid-evil is what ran through Koltz's mind, but the thought was forced away by fear—not the feeling of being afraid, but real, primitive fear. A sweat broke out on his skin, despite the cool night air.

"Wait! You can't do this to us!" he screamed as he looked to his right. Standing on a plank of wood, bound to a pole, and surrounded by bundles of twigs tied with simple white string was his eleven-year-old son, Tony. A thin piece of faded red cloth tied around his head and covering his eyes was the only garment present.

"Daddy, I'm scared! What's happening?" Tony cried while trying to cross his legs to maintain a little pride.

"It's okay, son," Koltz said, trying to control the terror leaking out in his voice.

"Daddy?" This voice came from the left, and Koltz looked to see his fifteen-year-old daughter, Courtney, staked in the same way as Tony. Courtney's breasts were partly hidden beneath her long brown hair, but the brush stopped mid-thigh, steeling away any remaining dignity. The same faded red cloth covered her eyes.

The executioner walked slowly toward Koltz, the crowd parting to let him through. When he reached the condemned, he stopped in front of Koltz.

"You have been found guilty of treason by your superiors, and have been sentenced to death by burning," he said in a dark voice that Koltz associated with demons.

"You can't do this to us, there are laws!" he screamed.

"It has been decided," the executioner responded.

"Fine, kill me, but leave the children alone. They didn't do anything!"

"Guilt by association!" the voice roared back at him. "They are fruit of a tainted tree."

"No!" Koltz screamed, as he fought against the ropes holding him.

"Daddy!" Courtney screamed.

"No, you bastards! No!" he screamed again.

The executioner stepped to his left and stood in front of Tony. "You are the son of the betrayer, and you shall die."

"Dad, I think they're going to burn me!" Tony screamed. "Don't let them kill me, Dad, please!"

"Come back over here, you coward, leave the boy alone!"

The executioner leaned down with the torch and lit the twigs near the ground in front of Tony. Smoke began to roll from the brushwood in front of the boy, and the executioner stood and held the torch in front of his chest as if it were sacred.

"No! No! No!" Koltz screamed as he fought harder against the rope. He could feel the rope cutting into his skin. "Tony! It will be okay, son. It's okay," he said, trying to comfort his son in the last few seconds of his life.

As the smoke rose, it slowly gave way to a yellow flame rising toward Tony's feet.

"Dad! It's hot on my legs! Dad!"

"It's going to be okay, son," Koltz lied as blood ran down his arms from his yanking against the rope until it cut in and touched bone.

"Daddy! What's happening?" Courtney screamed, her chest heaving with panicked breaths.

"It's going to be—" his words were cut off by the sudden shriek from Tony, one of both pain and horror.

Koltz could see Tony fighting against his bonds and the bubbling and welting of his skin as his small body tried in a vain attempt to protect itself against the burning.

Tony's screams came louder and more intense as the flames grew and licked up his body to his waist—screams that entered through his father's ears, but which he felt throughout his whole body.

The executioner slowly turned and walked in front of Koltz, who spat at him.

"You pussy! Bring that shit to me!"

The executioner walked past as if he didn't notice and stopped in front of Courtney. "You are the daughter of the betrayer, and you shall die."

"No! You get away from me!" Courtney screamed "Daddy, help us! Why won't you help us?"

On the other side of Koltz, Tony's screams started to fade as the flames now encircled his head. Koltz could smell his son's flesh burning, like pork left on the grill too long.

The executioner bent and lit the brushwood in front of Courtney. As Tony's screams ceased, Koltz looked to see his son's hair burning, his eyes melting, and his tongue, like dry leather, poking in and out of a lipless mouth no longer making noise.

A horrifying scream came from the left of Koltz as the flames grew around Courtney. Koltz's own screaming matched his daughter's, as he closed his eyes tight and fought against the ropes.

When he opened his eyes, however, there was nothing there. His hearing preceded his vision, and he was struggling to loosen himself from the restraints around his wrists.

"Hold his head down," said a voice in the darkness. "I've seen them bash in the back of their own head from thrashing when they come out of it."

Mary Reyes grabbed Koltz's head and held it down on the gurney. Everett was aware of pressure on his head, but he continued to fight to get loose. "Get away from us, you son of a bitch!"

"Easy, Koltz, it was all in your head," Doc said while preparing a needle. Koltz pulled at the restraints as Doc jammed the needle into his leg and waited until the thrashing stopped.

Koltz slid from anger and terror into drug-induced comfort.

"How long was he in contact with the Reti?" Doc asked.

"I'm not sure. He was found up in his room, lying on the floor, with a Narration Stone near his hand. We heard a thump and went to check, finding him out cold."

"He couldn't have been in contact long. It will be interesting to hear what they did to him. I usually don't have much of a chance to talk to the people who get searched. Most of them are gone by the time I get there."

"I'm surprised they didn't just kill him," Mary said, releasing Everett's head.

"There are fates worse than death, and the Reti come up with new ones on a regular basis. Death is a release, after they're done with you. Maybe they decided they still need him, and finding the stone is too important to kill him off now. Besides, Zack and John are getting close. They did kill two Crew members. That counts for something."

"How long before he comes back?"

"Who knows, I've seen people bounce back in a matter of hours and some never bounce. The longer they stay out, the harder it is to come back. But he was only out for a few hours at most, so I'm betting he'll be back before long. The thing is, if he does come out of this, we may not have the same Koltz we had before."

"Meaning?"

"Some of my patients don't come back quite the same. I'm usually not real concerned about this, because in our situation people come and go, and what difference does a little personality change make? But Koltz is in a position of authority, and if he comes back a few watts short of a lit bulb, we could all die. I want the rest of you to keep an eye on what he's doing. If there's any sign of him acting a pickle short of a picnic, I want to know."

"And what exactly should we look for?"

"It's hard to say, anything out of the ordinary."

"Oh, sure, Doc! Look around, does anything look ordinary?"

Doc shrugged.

"Oh, come on, Doc. You have to give me more than a shrug. How about some helpful words of advice here?"

"What do you want me to say, Mary? The only thing ordinary around here is the notion that it's better to be feared than admired." He nodded to his patient. "Koltz told me that and it has served me well. In this situation he might see the opportunity to do some daffy shit just to hone the edge of uncertainty and heighten any reluctance to challenge his authority. I don't envy the people who are going to have to be around him when he comes to." Doc shook his finger at Mary. "So, nobody tells him he's under medical surveillance. I don't need him pissed off at me."

27

Just Not in the Budget

Merle Rogiletti was having a rough day that was only about to get worse. The report on his desk confirmed what he already knew. None of the profiles matched, and John Doe numbers One and Two remained a mystery. Nothing in the data banks, social media, or commercial data could help figure out who they were. They must have been living off the grid, and it was like they didn't really exist, which must mean they must be professionals with a good-sized backing. The only thing he knew about them for certain is they were found in Donnelly's busted-up living room. The pressure on him to find Aleecia Donnelly and Daniel Knocks was building. Since the resort in Puerto Rico, there were now twelve bodies he could tie to that couple. They had things to answer for. Questions he tried to answer in his own head.

He picked up a letter he'd found in Donnelly's house when they found those guys' bodies and, what do you know, it was from Knocks.

"Man, what an ass she made out of me," he muttered.

"Talking to yourself now, Merle?" The question came from Rogiletti's captain, Bob Portanget, who had come in and sat in the chair opposite his desk. "You look like a man with a problem."

"I guess I should, I've got one."

Portanget looked at the letter in Rogiletti's hand. "The Donnelly woman?"

Rogiletti nodded.

"Any new leads?"

"None, disappeared into the great beyond. I suppose she's somewhere with Knocks," Rogiletti said shaking his head. "I just can't believe I missed the mark on this girl so badly." He tossed the letter down on his desk. "She played me for a fool. She told me about the letter, so I'd go over there and find those bodies. Her message was just her way of getting the last laugh. 'Hey, detective, come over here and see what I have.' She purposely led me over there to prove she'd outsmarted me."

"Just goes to show, you can never tell." Portanget said supportively.

"So I've heard, but to be off by this much stings a little. I mean, except for the luggage, every question I asked her seemed to be met with an honest answer."

"She lied about that too, did she?"

Rogiletti nodded. "I was pretty sure it was her luggage in the fire, but she had me doubting what I'd find until I spoke with the manufacturer. She's good at this sort of thing, I'll give her that much."

"The best ones are the hardest to recognize," Portanget said. "She and Knocks have been living here for years and never raised suspicion until now."

"They picked a hell of a way to raise suspicion."

"Something went wrong, and it fell apart for them in a hurry."

"I'd like to know what and with who, hell, I'd like to know something. Right now, we have next to nothing."

"What do we have?" Portanget asked with the tone more captain than friend.

"Little more than questions and theories."

"Let's hear it."

"My theory is when things went bad for Knocks in Puerto Rico, he had his coworkers murdered. One was his cousin and might have been somehow involved. Knocks called Donnelly and told her they had to leave. She sold the boat, took the cash, and had Howard killed, I don't know by whom yet, but it wasn't by the two guys we found in her living room. Those two could have been the ones coordinating the slayings, or they could have been the ones she sent over to start the fire."

"The first rule of assassination, assassinate the assassin."

"I suppose."

"Any luck identifying the bodies?"

"No, so far they're just John Doe Five and John Doe Six. And that's something else that's wacky here, I can't even find out the identities of the people in the fire. DNA records can't match anybody recovered. The John and Jane Does are piling up, and I was hoping one of them would be the toothpick guy."

Portanget raised an eyebrow. "The toothpick guy?"

"The unidentified DNA found on the toothpicks in the hotel rooms in Puerto Rico and in Howard's face match samples we found in Donnelly's house. That sicko is apparently working with Donnelly and is still out there shoving toothpicks into people."

Portanget nodded, and Rogiletti watched him knowing there was more.

"I haven't told you anything you didn't already know or couldn't read in my reports. So, captain, why are you really here?"

"The bean counters are screaming. We can't afford to keep watching the houses twenty-four-seven."

"Their homes and any sentimental belongings are the only connection I have to them."

"I know, but I have to scale back. It's just not in the budget."

"Not in the budget? Donnelly and Knocks are connected to twelve dead people, and you're talking budget?"

"I know it's shitty, and I don't like the idea any better than you do, but I don't have a say in some of these things."

Rogiletti shook his head assertively. "I think it would be a mistake, Bob. She left in a hurry and didn't get a chance to take anything with her. Most women tend to come back for sentimental things."

"I know, but she sold that boat for two hundred and twenty-five thousand. With that much money, they could start over. The odds of her coming back are growing slimmer by the day."

Rogiletti started to object but Portanget cut him off. "I know it's not what you wanted, but I can't justify the cost of sitting and watching a house I doubt we'll get anything from. I'm afraid we'll have to cut back to sporadic drive-bys."

"Drive-bys won't find Aleecia Donnelly or Daniel Knocks."

"Maybe you're right, but I don't think sitting in front of the house is going to help us much either. We'll keep posting on social media, and we are already running profiles on TV. I think that might be our best chance now."

"I think you're wrong. I have a gut feeling she's coming back."

"You may be right, Merle. After all, she did leave one loose end I can think of."

"What would that be?"

"You. Have you stopped to consider that she left the message about the letter hoping to get you there, so she could have you eliminated too?"

Rogiletti sat looking at his boss with the blank expression of a man who had just been informed the sandwich he'd eaten for lunch wasn't his.

"I didn't think so. I have to cut back on the stakeout, but I want you to stay on this. I want one of those two sitting right here," he said, tapping the arms of the chair he was sitting in. "So, do what you need to do, and find another way to track them down. Bring them in and impress me, Merle. Just watch your ass."

28

Engineered Disasters

Aleecia awoke from her fourth restless night of tossing and turning, a common scenario for newcomers. She looked at the clock; it was just after five. She got up and, for the first time since she arrived, needed to get dressed. She felt so insecure, she had taken to sleeping in her clothes. Thinking this might have supported the nighttime aerobics, she had decided to see if changing into nightclothes would help. It did, but not much.

She walked across to the closet in the room given to her and dressed before making her way to the kitchen. There, she found herself alone and wasn't sure what to do about it. In the morning, she usually waited until she had heard movement before venturing out of her room. She decided to make coffee and find something for breakfast. The coffee was easy because all she needed sat on the counter beside the coffee maker, though breakfast would take a little more looking for. She opened one of the cupboards and found it loaded with food; cans of soup and crackers, cookies and other snacks filled the shelves. She moved to the next cupboard, which was also full. As she moved down the line, she found some filled with food and others with cooking essentials.

When she found breakfast cereal, she brought it to the table. In the refrigerator—which was full, of course—she retrieved the milk. Aleecia had half-finished her bowl of Cheerios by the time David Mills walked in.

"Good morning," he said, his eyelids flying at half-mast.

"Morning," Aleecia said, noticing his grogginess. "There's coffee," she said, pointing.

"Oh, good," he mumbled as he made his way to the pot. "You make this?" Aleecia nodded. "Thank you," he said as he took his cup to the table and sat across from her.

After he had a couple of sips, Aleecia broke the silence.

"Where does the money come from?"

"I'm sorry?" David asked, still trying to pull himself online.

"The money we use. This stuff can't be free," she said, pointing around the room and then to her clothes. "How do you cover expenses?"

"You'd be surprised," David said. "We have some very wealthy members who transfer funds in various ways. One even claims to have an extensive gambling habit. Her feigned losses make their way to us. We also have other sources, including government funding."

"Niles said no one in the government knows."

"Most don't, but there are some who manage to funnel funds from other places."

"How?"

"They bleed monies off different budgets and reroute supplies from other projects." He smiled. "You don't really think they spend three hundred dollars on a wrench or a thousand dollars for a toilet seat, do you?"

After some thought, Aleecia shook her head. "No, I guess not." David grinned and took another sip of his coffee. Aleecia watched him for a few seconds before asking her next question. "How many of you are there, really?"

"You mean Crew members?" he asked, to which Aleecia nodded. "There are thousands of us worldwide, but our numbers change every day. We have safe houses set up in different states and countries, but it's hard to stay anywhere for long."

"And you all communicate through those stones?

"Not a chance," David said, making a sour face. "The stones can be dangerous to read. The experiences the stones send to the mind are real, and the brain and body react accordingly."

"You mean if the stone passed an experience of someone running, my pulse and breathing would quicken?"

"Exactly." David held up his hands and wiggled his fingers. "If the stone tells you you're holding something too hot, the mind and body react and your fingers blister in defense."

"If the stones are so dangerous, how are they used?"

"In a trained hand, messages, or experiences, can be sent and received with no physical effect. The Reti can read the experiences of anyone with a stone almost instantly with no more effect than, say, reading about those experiences in a book. But they can also send visions or experiences on demand, and an untrained holder can do little to stop it. They can also probe memories. If they don't like what they find, they punish people by planting thoughts or suggestions. The experiences are so real the targeted person has no choice but to believe them to be genuine. The results can be devastating, even to the point of death."

Aleecia nodded. "And that puts us at risk, because anyone holding a stone would be open to the Reti."

"Very good," David said. "But only to a certain point. Every time a stone is used, it leaves a fingerprint, kind of like how an email or digital photo contains metadata. But to find a specific experience, you'd have to know what you're looking for. It makes them safe for limited use. But the stones are a communication device of the mind, and the Reti has a way of programming how the stones work. We humans have yet to achieve this trick, but the Renegades have told us we will in time. Some of the stones we have were altered or reprogrammed by the Renegades to block out most of the attributes of the stones the Reti possess, that's how we can uses them if we need to. It's kind of like listening in on a two-way radio. They can't detect us listening in on their communications, but we also can't monitor all of their channels."

Aleecia had a few more bites of breakfast allowing David more coffee before she went on. "Niles said some of the stones are unaccounted for. Does anyone know where they are?"

David shrugged. "Not really. We have our suspicions, theories, and stories, but most of the time it's old information and the stone isn't where it was said to be. Sometimes the stories are real and we get lucky. Like the one aboard the *Titanic*."

"The *Titanic* had a stone on it? That's rotten luck, an accident put a stone on the bottom of the Atlantic."

David smirked slightly. "Aleecia, stop relying on what you think you know, there was no accident. The Titanic was intentionally run into the iceberg. The Crew had a stone, and the Bound were outnumbered five to one. They couldn't get it back, so the Reti ordered the ship slowed until reinforcements arrived. The Bound got to the wheelhouse, hijacked the ship, and rammed the ice in the hope of slowing it down. Remember, most people thought the ship was unsinkable. But it wasn't, and it took the stone to the bottom."

"You've got to be kidding. The Bound would do that?"

"They'll do just about anything the Reti tell them to do. You must understand that most Bound are held hostage by missing loved ones. The Reti take the ones they love and holds their fate over the Bound. Unlike us, the Bound must always have someone in contact with a stone, so the Reti can contact them whenever they wish. They search the recent memories of the person holding the stone and show them images of either how their loved ones are doing well and living happily, provided that Bound is doing a good job, or, if the Reti are unhappy with them, reveal visions of their loved ones suffering in some horrific way. Living with the idea that your spouse or children could suffer or die because you don't do what the Reti order is a huge motivator, and they will do almost anything."

"Like sink the *Titanic*?"

"Yes, and much worse. Most disasters that you might be familiar with were engineered, including the Hindenburg, the Great Chicago Fire, the 1952 Great Smog of London, Chernobyl in Russia, the Minamata Disease in Japan, the Bhopal Disaster in India, 9/11, and they have started just about every major war you can recall."

Aleecia sat stunned for several minutes, while David sipped at his coffee and moved to make some toast. Finally, a question formed in her mind.

"If they go to such lengths to get a stone, how do we keep the Perception Stones we have protected?"

"That's kind of ironic. With all their attention having to go into surviving in space, we have an advantage in one area the Reti doesn't. Almost all Reti equipment is designed for zero gravity, or what's here on Earth. They can look at and visit the earth and study the land, people, plants, and animals, but they can't do much about what's under the water. The oceans are our haven, where our main base is located and where our stones are kept. Reti expertise revolves around the vacuum of space, but they have nothing to withstand the oceans' depths. We got the idea from the Titanic situation. That stone was out of the Retis' reach, so eventually we got it."

"We got it?"

"Yep, that's what the expeditions to the Titanic were about. We went down and retrieved the stone."

Aleecia watched David as he took another sip of coffee and a bite of his toast. "It seems so easy for you. You accept this and talk about it as if it's all just a matter of everyday life."

David grinned. "To me, it is a fact of everyday life, and it will be to you too someday."

She shook her head. "I don't know about that."

David leaned forward a little and looked at her. "Let me see if I can make this a little easier for you. I'm assuming you've heard the tale of Plato's City of Atlantis."

She nodded, "Sure, an island of advanced technology that disappeared into the sea." David just kept looking at Aleecia waiting for her to come up to speed. When she did, she nodded her head in understanding. "It wasn't an island, was it?"

"No," David said smiling at her, "Plato witnessed something, but there are no words in the ancient Greek vocabulary to precisely describe what he observed. There was no way for him to accurately describe a Reti spacecraft sinking into the sea."

Aleecia sat quiet as she mulled things over. After a few minutes she looked back to David.

"So, what's your story, David? How did you become a member of the Crew?"

David set the coffee on the table and gave her a weak smile. "My wife Sally worked for a professor of psychology at LSU. One day, she overheard him talking with another staff member about how the Bound people were real and how we all needed to believe. At first, she thought it was a joke, but a few days later she found half a letter jammed in the shredder. The part she saved provided some details about a double murder in Florida and how it was the work of the Bound people. Sally was convinced the professor was into something bad.

"To calm her fears, we did some online investigating and were surprised to find the news story and how the crime was unsolved. Sally wanted to go to the police because the letter she read answered some of the questions the police were still asking. I talked her out of it because we didn't have any proof and I didn't want to sound like a loony. I mean, how can you go to the police with a story about unknown people who are the Bound people?

"I knew she was probably right, but I was afraid to get involved in something like that," David gave a small chuckle. "That seems so funny, considering where I am now.

"Anyway, she kept snooping around his office and listening to conversations." David paused and stared at his coffee for a few seconds. "I'll spare you the details, but to make a long story short, we discovered more than we'd expected to. Within five days of finding the half-shredded letter, the professor was found beaten and dead from a stroke. Another staff member was missing, and the rumor was he had been abducted by someone. And Sally . . . well, Sally was found dead in her car from an apparent heart attack. I started to raise all kinds of hell about it, because I knew there was something wrong. I got lucky and the Crew found me before the Bound did."

Aleecia choked back the lump forming in her throat. "I'm sorry you had to endure that, and yet I can't imagine your story is unique."

"It's not. Most of us come to the Crew after accidentally learning the truth. We were a lot like you, living ordinary lives until one day it was all taken away and we were thrown into this mess." David leaned forward and looked her in the eyes. "You feel alone, Aleecia, but you're not. You have lost everything dear to you—been there, done that. If there are people in this world who can understand and sympathize with what you're feeling, it's the people of the Crew. This life and one another are all we have. It's hard, I know, but if you just trust us—trust me—you can learn to live with this. I'll show you how, but you must believe in me and do the things I ask. It's the only way we can protect our best asset."

Aleecia blinked back a tear. "You mean the stones?"

"No, the stones are just a tool. A weapon in the war we have to fight, but it's not what we're holding on to."

"What are you holding on to?"

"Hope, Aleecia. We hope one day this will all be over and nobody like you will ever have to come to us again. We hope, one day, even one of us will be able to walk down the street again without fearing for our lives. We hope, one day, we won't ever have to rescue another Aleecia Donnelly. Hope is what we have and is what keeps us going, and we have died and killed to protect it."

29

See If He Does Something Nutty

It had been three days since Everett Koltz watched his children burn, one and a half days since he realized it might have just been a psychological experience the Reti used to punish him for not getting the stone - he and doc had a long talk and Koltz understood all he could do was to choose to believe his children were still alive - and twelve hours since Doc had allowed his body to filter out the drugs. It was now 5:30 in the afternoon, and Koltz was in a room at the Ramada Inn in Aleecia Donnelly's hometown of Troy, Michigan. He felt as good as he thought he could. He was still a little drowsy, but he had slept on the way in from Chicago.

As soon as the drugs allowed him to think clearly again, Koltz decided to bring out one of the bigger guns. In this case, technology. He got himself together and retrieved a briefcase tucked away in his closet. He then had a man named Hank Pelhem drive him to Troy to find Zack and John. Hank wasn't exactly a favorite, but because of his intermediate medical experience, Doc had insisted he go. Koltz also took Mary, since she was more fun on a trip than Hank.

He had tried to reach Zack by phone, but his calls were going unanswered. This was the first time it had happened, and Koltz had to consider Zack and John might be dead. Part of him was hoping they were. He picked up the phone, redialed Zack's number, and waited.

"Park right there," John said, pointing to a spot against the curb eight houses down from Aleecia's. Zack pulled the black Jeep he was driving into the space and shut off the engine.

"Nice spot, straight shot to the door."

"Yeah, this is where the cops have been sitting all week. I figure by sitting here, the common folk will think we're a part of the force and the next guys on watch."

"Good thinking, as long as nobody comes snooping."

"I got this, just in case," John said as he pulled out a badge and fake ID.

Zack took it. "FBI, nice. Even the local blues won't give us any trouble."

"That's what I was thinking," John said, taking back the badge and putting it back in the inside pocket of his sport coat. It was the first time he and Zack had worked together since the fight with the Crew over Aleecia. Working with a dozen other Bound who were also watching Aleecia's house, watching the actions of the police, paying visits to Aleecia's friends and relatives, and looking for the next link kept separating them.

When Zack's cell phone rang, he made no move to answer it. The ring tone told them both who was calling.

"Koltz is pissed," John said.

"I'm sure he is."

"You're not going to answer?"

"Why should I?"

"Well, he is kind of our boss, and the Reti won't be happy. Not afraid they'll order your demise?"

"Not really, if I do get searched by the Reti, they will see we've been bustin' our asses trying to find the stone, and Koltz is more talk than action. Besides, he's more afraid of us than we are of him. Not to mention, ignoring him makes me grin. I can imagine him right now, stomping around and bitching."

Both men chuckled before John said, "I guess he has a right to bitch, if the rumors are true."

"They probably are. If the Reti did get him on a stone, I'm sure they messed with him bad enough. I just don't know why he'd be on the stone. If I were him, I'd stay as far away from them as I could."

"He can't," John said. "It's like he's addicted, and I guess that's possible. He spends a lot of time with the one he has."

"What do you mean?"

"He has a second Narration Stone."

"Really?"

John nodded. "I've seen him with it more times than he knows. He's always scanning it, looking for something."

"Like what?"

John shrugged. "Word of his kids, I'd guess, but he won't admit it."

"He'd be smart not to, he's already playing a dangerous game by reading the stone so much."

"So I've heard."

"You've never tried it, mate?"

"Nope, you?"

"Only once, and it gave me one hell of a headache." Zack smiled, and nodded at a woman as she walked past pushing a stroller. "Why have you never tried it?"

"I was going to once but decided I didn't need to. I didn't see the point. Besides, I figure the less time I spend around those damned things the better."

"And yet here we are trying to find one. Just another thing that goes against my better judgment."

John nodded his understanding and looked back down the street at Aleecia's house and the yellow *Do not cross* police tape across the front door.

The phone stopped ringing as the call went to voicemail, and they sat silent for a few minutes.

"I'm beginning to wonder if you're right in thinking they'll be back," John said.

"They have to, the woman doesn't know anything about the stone, but I still think it's in there somewhere."

"Zack, we took that place apart. If it was there, we would've found it."

"Maybe, but they haven't found it yet. I'm sure of it. Unless they found a clue that we didn't, they have to come back and look some more. When they do, I intend to take one of the Crew and discover where they took the girl. I still think she's the key. I'll catch her or kill her to level the playing field."

"Damn it!" Koltz screamed at his phone. "When I catch up with those bastards, I'm going to kick their asses!" The message flowed through the door and down the hall of the Ramada Inn. "If they think they can just ignore me, they've got shit for brains!"

"No offense, boss," Mary said as carefully as she could, "but if you keep screaming, the manager will be here in a short. That's not what you want."

"Fuck the manager! I can deal with them!"

"And the local police? Boss, it'll be a short trip if the local PD shows up, and you still won't find Zack."

Koltz looked as if he was going to shout some more, but instead he lit a cigarette and ran his fingers roughly through his hair.

"Well, with any luck," he said more quietly, "they're already dead. Any idea how to get to the house?" The voice was softer, but the anger was still there.

"Yeah," Mary said. "I looked it up. We're only fifteen minutes away."

"Good, let's go see if we can find those two. And if they're not dead, they'll need a good excuse to stay that way!"

Koltz picked up his briefcase and headed toward the door. Mary got up to follow, but Pelhem pulled her aside.

"You think he's okay?" he asked quietly.

Mary shrugged. "Is Batman a Reti? Who knows? Doc said he would probably go through a period of babbling, or doing daffy shit, but unless he does something really nutty, I say we just go with it."

"Oh, great. The guy's carrying enough technology to bring half the country to a screeching halt, and we have to wait and see if he does something nutty."

Again, Mary shrugged. "You could tell him you're worried about his mental state if you want, but I suggest you take his gun before you do."

30

Bait and Switch

Niles sent eleven of them, in separate vehicles. Two matching Kia Sorentos, painted a neutral tan color, would carry the search team. A green Ford Focus would serve as the dump car, and a modified silver Honda Civic as the bait car. David Mills, Sam Dayton, an electrician from Montréal, Canada, Derick Gates, the college football player from Ohio, and Debbra Sorensen, the dentist, rode in the lead Kia. Cavan, Tami, Breanne, Aleecia, and Brian Crawford, a former cowhand from Texas, rode in the second.

Wayne Fulton, a factory worker from Maine, drove the bait car, while Ramiro Lopez from Orzaba, Mexico, drove the dump car.

When they got within five miles of Aleecia's house, Cavan's cell rang. When he answered it, he put the call on speaker.

"Aleecia, this is David, can you hear me?"

"Yes."

"Okay, I'm going to start several blocks away from your house and use the GPS to guide us in using a square spiral pattern. But, this is your neighborhood, so you have to make sure were on course and look for anything that might be signs of cops or Bound. Got it?"

"I think so," she said. "There's a stoplight up the road, we should make a right there."

"That's good, Aleecia. I'll keep this connection open, and the rest of you need to keep a sharp eye for anything suspicious."

Aleecia guided them in and when they were two blocks from the house, David stopped and used a two-way radio to reach the other cars.

"Okay, bait team, you're up. The rest of us are going to park here and wait for your word. Aleecia's house is the third from the corner."

"Copy," said one voice.

"Got it," said a second.

"Okay, gentlemen, let's see whose watching."

The two cars came from the back of the line and headed for the house. Ramiro led in the Focus and Wayne followed in the Civic. One street before Aleecia's, Wayne peeled off and stopped in front of the house belonging to the neighbor that shared Aleecia's back fence. Ramiro, trying to act as normal as possible, drove down Aleecia's street while searching the cars. He spotted two men sitting in a black Jeep down the block.

"We have sitters," he said into the radio.

"Be careful and be fast," David responded. "Wayne, did you copy?"

"I did, and I'm in position."

"I copy," Ramiro said, and drove to the end of the street. There, he stopped and said a small prayer before spinning the car around and heading back toward Aleecia's house.

Zack watched the Focus as it came back, and nudged John who was in the process of eating a sandwich.

Ramiro drove along normally until he got to Aleecia's house, then drove up onto the front lawn. Not bothering to shut off the ignition, he simply jammed the car into park, got out, and sprinted to the front door. He slowed only slightly when he reached what was left of the door and hit it with his shoulder. The door, only a door in the sense that it was on the front opening of the house, came loose from its feeble hold on the frame and Ramiro burst into the room. After tripping on the rubble that once composed Aleecia's possessions, he crashed onto what was once her entertainment center.

The sight of the brake lights on Ramiro's Ford kicked John into action; he shoved open the door of the Jeep and hit the pavement running at the same time as Ramiro did. He raced to the front door and threw himself against the side of the opening, pulling the Eradicator from his pocket and peeking inside as he jammed a tiny communication speaker in his ear.

"You with me, mate?" he heard Zack ask.

"Five by five," he said quietly into his cuff before sticking his head into the opening of the doorway for a better look. Ramiro had scrambled up from the floor, fought his way to the back door, and was now struggling to get the back door open.

"I don't see him," John said.

"Just remember to shoot first and ask questions later," Zack said.

John heard the noise coming from the back of the house and moved toward it. Ramiro got the door opened just as John rounded the corner. The yellow ball of light from the Eradicator hit the wall just behind Ramiro as he lurched through the doorway. John scrambled over the mess he'd helped create.

"He's out the back door and heading for the fence," John said into his cuff as he climbed over the wreckage.

Zack's voice came through John's earpiece. "I'm going around to the next block."

John, after coming out the door to see that Ramiro had reached the back fence, leveled the Eradicator and fired. The shot reached the fence just as Ramiro leaped, the energy dissipating when it struck the fence and causing a bulge in the wire mesh. Ramiro ran a zigzag pattern to get behind a tree, then waited for a few seconds before darting for the cover of a small aluminum shed standing at the back end of the driveway. A hollow *boom* let Ramiro know another shot had found the shed. He risked a glance back at the man chasing him. John was in the process of jumping the fence, so Ramiro broke cover and sprinted toward the street.

Zack turned the corner as Ramiro raced down the driveway. He hit the brakes and came to a stop in the street directly in front of Wayne. He jumped from the Jeep, pulled his 9mm, and waited for Ramiro to come down the driveway. When he spotted Zack, Ramiro froze in surprise and fear. Zack pulled the trigger, not because he was ready to shoot, but because he was startled by the sound of squealing tires. The shot came through the silencer of Zack's 9mm with a soft *pop*, the bullet missing Ramiro by an inch and embedding in a neighbor's tree. Zack spun to face the noise but was lifted off his feet by the Civic bashing into his hip. He traveled over the hood and fell off the other side, landing hard on the concrete; his head bounced off the pavement and he lost his grip on his gun which skidded to the other side of the street. Wayne swerved, trying to get the tires to run over some part of the man in the street, but he only managed to run over Zack's pant leg.

Wayne slowed as Ramiro sprinted toward the car and dove for the window but making it inside only as far as his chest. When he started to fall back, Wayne grabbed his shirt and pulled. Ramiro got a grip on the headrest of the passenger seat and pulled himself in just as John stepped from between the houses, aimed the Eradicator, and pushed the button. The yellow ball caught the Civic's back corner, dented the bumper, shattered the light cover, and broke the bulb beneath.

Zack got to his feet and staggered toward the Jeep. John got there at the same time, looked at his partner, and realized he was a little off his game.

"Maybe you should let me drive," John said. The two switched places and picked up the chase.

"We're on our way out and have a black Jeep in tow," Wayne said into his radio.

"Copy, Wayne," David said. "Take them out as far as you can."

"You got it, and good hunting."

"Okay gang, here we go," David said into his phone. The two Kias moved together, and soon they were staring out the window at the yellow police tape hanging on the sides of Aleecia's front entrance. At the sight, Aleecia shrank in her seat.

Breanne touched her on the hand. "You okay?"

"I guess I'll have to be."

"Okay, gang," David's voice sounded through the speakerphone. "We have to be fast. I'd be surprised if someone hasn't already called the local cops. Tami and Debbra will stay with the rides and be our drivers. I figure we got about four minutes before local PD shows up. Breanne, I want you to stand guard at the door. Keep time and an eye out for anybody coming by. Shout out the time every thirty seconds. As soon as four minutes are up, we go. Everybody else, take a room and see what you can turn up."

They parked on the street in front of the house, got out, and ran to the door.

31

A Piece of Wrapped Hard Candy

As soon as they were through the front door, the Crew separated in all directions. Breanne took her place by the front door to stand watch and keep time. Aleecia looked around at the remains of her life. It was obvious someone had done more searching, because everything she owned was in shambles. The Crew wasn't any more cautious with her things than the Bound had been. As Aleecia sifted through the things she used to consider important, the sound of ripping and breaking was echoing off what was left of the walls.

"One!" Breanne shouted from the door opening.

It seemed to Aleecia there was nothing left unsearched. Places she wouldn't think of searching had been probed. The wall under the sink was open. The refrigerator was lying on its side. The light fixtures were broken and pulled away from the walls and ceiling. Even the dishwasher had been pulled out. Aleecia heard what she was sure was the sound of what was left of the porcelain toilet breaking in the main bathroom.

"One and thirty!"

Aleecia stood and watched as the Crew flung, tossed, and broke. Not that there was much left to begin with. It looked as though the Bound had done a thorough job. The refuse of her home was knee-deep in the center of the room. Pieces of the furniture created a dangerous trash heap that grabbed at ankles, like hands from a grave.

"Two!" Breanne shouted.

Aleecia wandered into the remains of her bedroom and looked around. She didn't have a clue of what she'd expected to find, but when she saw her mother's ring, she bent down and picked it up then shoved it in her pocket. She suddenly wanted to grab anything she could, then she remembered the earrings her grandmother had given her on her sixteenth birthday and began to look for them.

She walked with a purpose now, kicking things out of her way as she looked. Her drifting led her past the bathroom, where she noticed the remains of her jewelry box. She walked, stepping over pieces of her nightstand, into the bathroom where the water poured from the line feeding the toilet. She picked up a section of the jewelry box, which still held a small drawer. She turned the box over and found it empty.

"Two and thirty!"

She dropped the drawer back to the tiled floor, watching it bounce to a stop near what was left of the toilet, when she caught a shimmer in the water. One of the earrings! She bent down to pick it up, closing her fingers around it, when something tugged at the back of her mind. There, on the edge of the baseboard, just under where a section of wall had been crushed in, was a small smudge too level to be random. She bent closer and felt her heart double in beats. There, she discovered the symbol she had seen on the card Dan had given her. It was the same symbol he had left on the picture of them at his cousin's wedding. With what Aleecia guessed was eyeliner, *A-N-D* was written on the baseboard. The letters were so small she never would have noticed them if she hadn't bent down to gather the earrings. It took her a few seconds to react.

"Three!"

She peered into the hole that had been made in the wall above it, but the broken drywall had caved in and was covering anything beneath it. When she reached in and moved aside pieces of the wall, she saw a cardboard tube and it took her a few seconds to realize it was the tube that used to be inside a roll of toilet paper. It had been twisted on the ends to hold something in the center and the whole thing looked like a piece of wrapped hard candy.

"David!" she shouted.

David came around the corner and knew, by the look on Aleecia's face, that she had found something. "Just tell me where it is."

Aleecia simply pointed to the baseboard. David pushed past her, bent down, and stuck his small pry bar behind it. The baseboard moved before he could apply any pressure. When he pulled the board away, the tube rolled out.

A mile away, John was getting frustrated because his Jeep didn't have what he needed to catch up with the Civic. Every time they got closer, the Civic widened the distance.

"I can't catch them," he said.

"I don't think we need to, mate. Go back, they may have been a lure."

John stepped on the brake and wheeled the Jeep around, heading back toward Aleecia's.

When the tube rolled out, David carefully picked it up and untwisted one end while holding the other to make sure nothing fell out. He peered into the tube and the reddish tint told him what it was. He reached into his pocket and retrieved a plastic cup and lid, like a specimen cup you might find at the doctor's office. He removed the lid and, making sure not to touch it, carefully transferred the stone which fell into the cup with a soft knock.

The Perception Stone was his! He held the cup out and showed it to Aleecia, before fastening the lid. Once it was secure, he hugged her with his free hand.

"You've done it!" he said, kissing her forehead.

"Three and thirty!" Breanne shouted.

"We've got it!" David shouted, releasing Aleecia. "Let's get out of here!"

David grabbed Aleecia by the hand and ran for the door. They all met in the living room, with David holding up the stone as if it were a trophy. For a few seconds, everybody simply looked at the cup before reality settled on them.

"Let's make tracks!" David said.

The delay was over, and the Crew wasted no time. David handed the cup to Cavan, gave a quick peek outside and the Crew sprinted to the waiting Sorentos, getting in with the same order and sophistication as a Chinese fire drill. Debbra and Tami wasted no time; as soon as the bodies were in, they hit the gas, the acceleration closing half of the doors.

As soon as David managed an upright position, he swiped his cell screen, touched an icon, and waited for Cavan to answer.

"It's Miller time!" Cavan said when he answered his phone from the back seat of Tami's Sorento. Aleecia could hear the cheer in the background voices.

"Just about," David said. "I want to get back to the cabin before we party too much, but we have a need to celebrate."

High-fives went through the vehicles and hugs soon followed. Cavan held the cup out in front of Aleecia so she could get a good look.

"How does it feel, or has it not hit you yet?" He asked her.

"What's that?" she asked, caught up in the excitement.

"You probably just helped save millions of lives."

For some reason, the statement seemed to take the fun out of it for Aleecia, and her smile began to wane. As Brian took the cup to get a better look.

The Crew was so caught up in the victory that nothing existed outside of their vehicles. The celebration was consuming and contagious, and the traffic passing them could have been a million miles away. Cavan leaned over the front seat and gave his wife a hug from behind, causing her to swerve a little.

This caught the attention of others who weren't as distracted. Zack recognized the man leaning over the seat and hugging the driver in the passing vehicle.

"Damn it! Turn around, that was the Crew. I recognize one of the guys who took the woman."

John watched the matching Sorentos in the mirror. There was no sudden acceleration from the Crew's trucks to indicate they had noticed Zack. John slid the Jeep to the curb to turn around, blocking traffic as he did.

Debbra brought her Sorento to a stop at a traffic light and looked in the mirror at Tami, who waved at her happily.

"Who's got the stone?" David asked over the phone.

"I do," Brian Crawford answered from the back seat of Tami's Sorento.

"Make sure you take care of it," David said to a smiling Brian, who held the cup to the window to get another look at the stone inside.

A horn sounded as a driver expressed his opinion of John's driving abilities, which caught Tami's attention.

"Hey, there's something happening behind us."

Cavan turned and looked over his shoulder to see the black Jeep that was causing the disturbance. He retrieved a small pair of binoculars from under his seat and peered through the glass. He tried to focus on the passengers inside the Jeep but found it impossible until the driver was forced to either stop or hit a school bus. It was then that Cavan got a good look at the driver.

"Oh, shit!" he said as he grabbed the cell phone.

"David!" Cavan could still hear the celebration in the other car.

"Yeah, buddy, what is it?"

"Bound!" Cavan shouted. "Bound, behind us and moving in!"

In unison, every head spun.

"Are you sure?"

"Positive! It's the bastard who killed Glen!"

"Shit! Then go! Go! Go! Go!" David shouted.

Requiring no more incentive, Debbra waited for the next car to pass and stepped on the gas. The tires squawked once and grabbed the road, and the Sorento shot out into the traffic. An oncoming driver, reacting quickly, stomped on the brake pedal to avoid hitting not one but two vehicles that ran the red light.

32

It All Comes Together

Trying to complete a left turn that would take his red Dodge Intrepid past Aleecia Donnelly's house, Merle Rogiletti couldn't believe what he was seeing. Two matching Kia Sorentos were running the traffic lights and nearly causing accidents.

"What are you, a frickin' nut?" he said to the driver of the first Sorento as it drove by. Next, he focused on the driver of the second Sorento. "You're so lucky I'm not in the traffic division anymore, I'd have your butt on a plate," he said as the driver shot past. He was so locked in on the driver that he only got a glimpse of the woman in the back seat, but a glimpse was all it took to make the hairs on the back of his neck stand up. Was it really Donnelly, or was it just wishful thinking? Rogiletti would have to find out.

The drivers in the intersection were still in shock over the Sorentos and had hesitated long enough for Rogiletti to seize the opportunity to complete his left by swinging his Intrepid into the southbound lanes and then quickly into the left lane to track the two Kias.

John looked up at the sound of the horns and noticed the Sorentos accelerating; he knew he'd been spotted. He slammed the Jeep into four-wheel drive and reverse and stepped on the gas. The Jeep lurched backward over the curb and onto the grass alongside a bus. He slammed the shifter into first gear and began his pursuit.

Few people in the area didn't notice the erratic movements of the Jeep. Those who suddenly became aware of a problem included the passengers in a maroon Dodge Durango, where Everett Koltz sat humming the theme to Scooby-Doo.

"There they go," Mary said, pointing.

Koltz snapped to attention and screamed, "Halt, or I'll shoot!" Mary looked carefully at her boss, who turned to her. "Make damned sure you don't lose them. I just found them, and you won't make me look for them again, Mary."

Out of confusion more than anything else, Mary raised an eyebrow at her boss and wheeled the Durango into the left-hand turn lane to pass the traffic in front of her. Horns sounded as the oncoming drivers, including the driver of a red Intrepid who seemed more than just a little upset with Mary's maneuver, swerved to avoid contact.

The Durango kept coming toward Rogiletti, who proceeded to squeeze the steering wheel even tighter than he already was.

"Has everybody lost their minds?" he shouted as he swerved and stepped on the brake, trying to wave off the Durango's driver, who also swerved and was now directly in his path. Rogiletti blew his horn, but the Durango kept coming. The cars were less than a foot apart when both drivers finally came to a stop, making it impossible for the other to move.

"Get the hell out of the way!" Koltz screamed in a high-pitched voice. Hank Pelhem also rolled down the back window and stuck his head out.

"Back up, jackass, and I mean now!"

"You back up!" Rogiletti shouted as he reached inside his sport jacket to get his badge.

As Koltz pulled his 9mm from his side holster and started to get out, Rogiletti managed to free his badge and flash it at the occupants of the Durango.

"Wait, boss," Mary said, grabbing Koltz by the sleeve just before he swung his legs out the door. "He's a cop, and that's about the last thing we need."

Without waiting for Koltz to answer, Mary slipped the Durango into reverse and let the cop swing around and head north in front of them. Koltz slammed his door. Mary quickly followed, trying to keep an eye on both John's Jeep and the cop's Intrepid.

Koltz looked at the mess of traffic in front of him as the chase began to grow. "I can't even tell what the hell is going on," he said as he tossed his pistol onto the dashboard where it banged roughly off the windshield.

"As far as I can tell," Mary said, looking at the gun, "the cop seems to be after Zack and John."

"Well, too bad, I saw them first," Koltz said. "And I'm not going to lose them now. I'm going to use the nanites and kill everything." Koltz picked up the case sitting beside him, sprang the clasps, and opened the lid.

"Are you serious, boss?" Mary asked. "I know we have a better handle on the thing now, but the last time we used it, we knocked out the electricity in the northeastern region of North America."

"Yeah," Koltz said with a grin. "That was so cool." He turned a little to talk to Pelhem. "The blackout of 2003, they called it. We knocked out the lights of millions of people," he said with a chuckle. "It's been toned down now," he said, stroking the case gently, "but it will still knock out everything within three or four miles. Not just the lights, it'll take out all kinds of stuff." Koltz looked at the controls and paused, as if he had heard something strange. He tilted his head and smiled. "It's a red button," he said, as if he had just discovered something special. "Isn't it funny how we humans make every button that we consider important red? I mean, you never see a blue emergency-stop button or a purple launch button. They're always red. I wonder why that is."

With raised eyebrows, Mary looked at Koltz. "You okay, boss?"

"Yeah," Koltz said nonchalantly, and pushed the red button.

The box sent out a radio signal that ran the band of all frequencies within seconds. The radio waves laced with nanites that were programmed to disrupt circuits became invisible assassins to most things electrical.

At first nothing seemed to happen, then the check-engine light in the Durango's dash came on. The engine sputtered twice, then died. Like a stone's ripple in a pond, the circular wave spread out from Koltz's Durango. Anything equipped with a receiver began to die: all vehicles stalled, wireless phones failed, wireless connections failed, and for more than three miles, almost everything electrical stopped working.

"Well, that's it," Mary said, as she shoved the gear shift into park.

"No sense in staying here," Koltz said. He retrieved his gun from the top of the dash and tucked it into his beltline as he opened the door. "We might as well start walking before everybody gets out. Let's go see where Zack and John are."

Merle Rogiletti had picked up the phone and dialed the number to the front desk of the station when his car stalled.

"Oh no, don't do this to me now," he said. He looked in his rearview mirror expecting to see some impatient driver, but instead mental warning red flags went up in his mind when he realized everybody seemed to be having problems. Some people were trying to coast their cars to the curb while others were still coasting down the center of their lane trying to restart their vehicles. Other less-experienced drivers had simply applied the brake and tried to stop. With the engine dead, the power brakes proved to be anything but, and those drivers who were able to bring their car to a stop were rear-ended by those who were not.

Rogiletti witnessed a dozen minor accidents and thought about what he was going to tell dispatch, when he realized he was still holding his phone, yet nothing was happening. When he checked for a signal, he was both surprised and frustrated to find his phone wasn't working at all.

John looked down at the warning lights shining on the Jeep's instrument panel. "What the hell is this all about?" he said as he popped the clutch in an attempt to restart the Jeep.

"It's not just ours," Zack said. "Seems like everybody's got the same problem." John let the Jeep coast to a stop as the cars around him fell dead.

"Let's leave it," Zack said, opening the door and getting out. "I'm guessing Koltz might be around."

John jumped out, not bothering with the keys, and started down the street with Zack.

Everett Koltz spotted Zack and John getting out of the Jeep up the street and shouted, "Don't you dare think you can run from me, Zack! Don't you know who I am? I'm the guy with the technology! I have the dangerous toys! I'm Batman!"

"The engine's dead!" Cavan said into the phone, not realizing the phone had stopped working. In the Sorento in front of them, David Mills was looking around as Debbra ground the starter to no avail.

"Forget it!" David said. "It looks like everybody's got the same glitch. I'll bet it's a Bound thing."

"Now what?" Debbra asked.

"Get out and take it on the run," he said, opening his door. He ran to the other Sorento and motioned to the rest of the Crew, who were already abandoning their ride.

"Let's go," he said as he started to jog down the street. Brian Crawford got out and left the door open for Aleecia, who slid out behind him. Her foot caught the edge of the door frame as she tried to step out and she went down on her knees, giving a small yell as she did. Crawford took her by the hand, pulled her to her feet, and started running.

Merle Rogiletti was standing outside his car, along with several hundred other drivers. He looked at his phone one last time before tossing it onto the driver seat. He had the idea to commandeer a phone from one of the other drivers, but when he looked around to find one, he noticed everyone seemed to be in the same position.

Like an old dock pylon not tall enough to stay above the tide, the confusion was rising around Rogiletti and threatening to sweep him away. As he looked around for something to solve the puzzle, when something tugged at his mind. Someone was running. Not just someone, *many* someones were running. He looked to see what was causing their sprint, but his mind became suddenly aware and attention snapped back to the people running. Aleecia Donnelly was in the lead group. He started down the street after her.

At the head of the Crew, David was looking for a way out of the mess he was in. In the street, people were starting to mill about. He could see the confusion and frustration begin to turn to nervousness and anger. To his left, a fight had erupted between two drivers and shouts were becoming more frequent. Most drivers were staying with their cars, but the people who were on the street or shopping the nearby stores were beginning to gather on the sidewalks. David looked back over his shoulder and spotted two groups of men running in their direction. The two in the front were dressed like the Bound who had murdered Aleecia. There were three people in the second group, and David had no reason to believe they too were anything but Bound as well.

Cavan caught up with him and flipped his head back over his shoulder. "They've got help this time."

"I see that, I think we'd better get off the street. Let's see if we can lose ourselves in the crowd." David motioned for the others to get to the curb and the forming crowd beyond.

Watching from behind, John saw the gestures from David and moved to intercept. There was a crowd of people in the street with their cars and another starting to grow on the sidewalks and by the storefronts. But there was an open divide just past the curb, so John put on some extra speed and beat the Crew to the opening. He pointed the Eradicator down the street and waited.

One of the men, not that gender mattered, stepped into John's sights first. John pushed the button, and the yellow ball of energy flew down the street and struck Brian Crawford on the right side of his back, knocking him off his feet and forcing the breath out of his lungs. Brian tried to stick his hands out in front of him, but he was moving too fast and he landed on his chest, smacking his face on the cement, breaking his nose. and scraping the skin from his right cheek. He slid on the ground and stopped just feet ahead of Aleecia, almost causing her to trip. Aleecia had to sidestep quickly to avoid Crawford. Thinking he had fallen, she stopped and stuck out her hand to help him up.

Instead of taking her hand, Brian grabbed her wrist and shoved the cup with stone into her palm.

"Run, damn it, run," he said weakly.

Aleecia looked at him. "No, get up and come with me," she said, trying to pull him to his feet.

John grinned when he saw the yellow ball of energy slam the man to the ground. He started to trot toward his victim when he spotted the Donnelly woman. He also noticed the man struggling to get to his feet and realized he had made a foolish mistake. He had neglected to raise the power of the Eradicator and the distance had weakened the blow. He paused long enough to adjust the power and looked back just as the man was getting his feet under him, then he pointed the Eradicator at the man and shot. Again, the yellow ball of light flew down the street, nearly striking a woman stepping from her car, and struck Crawford in the back.

This time the blow came hard enough to fracture Crawford's ribs with a loud snap. The momentum compressed his heart, the left chamber exploding under the pressure. His grip on Aleecia's wrist tightened for an instant, and he almost pulled Aleecia to the ground before the grasp broke. When Crawford fell onto his face, he knocked the cup from Aleecia's hand. The cup then proceeded to bounce off Aleecia's leg. She looked down at Crawford, then back up the street at a grinning man.

"Green Eyes," she whispered. Her survival instincts kicked in and she began to run, bending to scoop up the cup as she fled.

Merle Rogiletti was watching Aleecia when a ball of yellow light felled the man beside her.

"What the hell is going on?" he murmured to himself. He looked back up the street at a man dressed in a black suit, who was pointing something too small to be a gun at Aleecia. A second ball of light came from the tip of the thing and flew down the street, striking the man again, this time so hard Rogiletti could see his chest compress to almost half of its depth.

"What the hell?" He instinctively took cover behind a car and watched two men in black run down the street toward the fallen man. Rogiletti started down the street thinking he had somehow just witnessed a murder with a yellow ball of light. He followed them, ducking behind cars, trying to get people to stay put as he went. When the men stopped at the feet of their victim, the taller one moved ahead as the shorter of the two bent to check on the man they had just shot.

Detective Rogiletti pulled his sidearm and moved in.

"Police! Don't move!" he shouted, leveling the barrel of his gun at John.

John hesitated for a second before he recovered. "I'm on the job. I'm a Fed, and I need your help, get over here and help me," he said, turning to face Rogiletti.

"I said don't move!" Rogiletti shouted again. "And drop your . . . that . . . weapon!"

John smiled. "Okay, okay, just relax," he said soothingly. "My ID is in the inside pocket of my jacket. I'm on the job, just chill." Rogiletti stared at him down the barrel of his weapon. "Just relax, officer," John said again. "I'm just going to reach in, slowly, and get my shield." John started to move his right hand.

"No," Rogiletti said. "Use your left hand, and make sure you do it slowly."

"That's good," John said in a comforting voice while slowly moving his left hand inside his pocket. He withdrew his fake ID and held it out to Rogiletti.

"Toss it here." John did as he was told, and Rogiletti caught it and flipped it open. He studied the contents carefully and then folded it shut and lowered his gun.

"Good job," John said. "Now, could you come over here and give me a hand?'

Rogiletti let his arm fall to his side and walked slowly over to John, watching him carefully.

"You're after the Donnelly woman, too," John stated as fact as he stuck out a hand for Rogiletti to shake.

Rogiletti looked at the hand but didn't take it. "Donnelly, yeah," he said.

John nodded. "Us, too. She and her friends are into some heavy shit, but I bet I don't need to tell you that."

"No, I learned that for myself."

"I'll bet you did. This guy," John said, nudging Crawford's foot with his shoe. "We've been looking for this guy for a long time. And that guy," John said, pointing over Rogiletti's shoulder.

When Merle turned to look where John was pointing, he registered the danger too late. John had doubled his fist and focused his energy into a punch that caught Rogiletti squarely on the side of the face and he crumpled to the ground next to Crawford.

"Sweet dreams, bonehead," John said as he massaged his hand, he then reached down and took Rogiletti's gun, rolled Crawford's body over to his back and checked his pockets.

33

The Fight

Everett Koltz arrived at Rogiletti's feet fifteen seconds after John had run up the street and delivered a swift kick to the cop's shin. "Not so tough without your car, are you?"

"Who's the dead guy?" Mary asked.

"Don't know, but I'll bet Zack does. Onward," he said as he headed up the street after his Bound.

David slowed, allowing the Crew to regather and take count. It was only then that he noticed Crawford was missing.

"Where's Brian?" he asked, concern leaking out between breaths.

"They shot him!" Aleecia screamed. "It's the same guy who killed me. He shot him with a light ball." She expected shock or outrage but was stunned when the question was asked by three different members.

"Who has the stone?"

"I do," Aleecia said, holding it up for someone to take. Instead, David pushed her hand away.

"Put it in your pocket and keep it safe. Breanne, you stay with her and protect it with your life."

Breanne nodded and moved beside Aleecia, as David led them through a parking lot to gather at the front door of a Lowe's that, until recently, had been enjoying a rather pleasant day. Then everything electronic seemed to fail at once. First the computers and phones, followed by the lights. Even the automatic backup generator failed to engage. With the exception of a few battery-operated emergency lights, the once well-lit aisles became sinister and mysterious. The store manager decided it was time to close the front door, and he and the employees did a quick and efficient job of gathering the customers and escorting them safely to the exit. Most of the staff was already gathered at the exit when the Crew arrived.

"Sorry, you can't come in here," the manager said. "We're closed because of some kind of electrical problem."

"That's fine, we'll leave, where's the back door?" David said as he pushed past the manager.

"Hey, I said you can't come in here."

"Sorry, no choice," Cavan said, leading the rest of the Crew past the manager and following David into the store.

"I said you need to leave," the manager said, grabbing Breanne's arm as she passed. His grip was broken by Derick, who grabbed him by his wrist and squeezed until Breanne was free.

"We're just going out the back, now let us pass," Derick said.

The manager jerked his arm free and started to put up a fight when he noticed the gun tucked into Derick's belt.

"You got it, mister," the manager said, gathering his employees and taking them out the front door.

Merle Rogiletti awoke face down in the street. The swelling on his cheek was indication enough he was going to have a black eye, and as he rubbed his face he wondered if it might even swell shut. Noting a pain in his shin, he got to his knees and looked around. The so-called Fed was gone, but the guy he shot with the light was still there. Rogiletti checked for a pulse and confirmed what he already knew.

He struggled to his feet to get his bearings. The people chased by the fake Fed were heading north; there was no reason for Merle to think they still weren't. He got his thoughts in order and moved up the street. When he checked his holster and found it empty, he thought about giving up the pursuit. But he owed the would-be-Fed some payback and Aleecia Donnelley could still be near. He started to walk faster, and quickly found himself in a dead run.

David and the rest of the Crew found their way through the maze of a store and reached the back door. When David pushed on it, however, it wouldn't budge.

"Oh, you've got to be kidding."

"What's the matter?" Cavan asked.

"It's locked with an electric lock and touch pad. Back up front," David said. "We have to get out of here."

Zack had followed the Crew to the front of the Lowe's and waited for John to catch up. When John did arrive, Zack was standing behind a minivan and motioned for him to come over.

"Sorry I'm late," John said. "I had a run-in with a cop."

"A cop?" Zack asked with some concern.

"I don't think we need to worry about him. I used the badge, convinced him I was a Fed, and cold-cocked him. I put him to sleep and took his piece."

Zack shrugged. "The Crew went in there," he said, motioning at the store. "They must have done something unfriendly, because everybody seems to be coming out in a hurry."

John pulled the fake badge again and smiled. "I'll see if I can find out what's going on." He started to approach the store when a voice boomed out from behind him.

"Well, look who we have here, where have you two ladies been?" Both Zack and John turned to Koltz, who was walking up. "I thought I'd hear from you guys sooner, I didn't think I'd have to track you down because you'd be too afraid to tell me you can't find the stone or the woman."

"Koltz, it's nice of you to show up," Zack said. "But we don't have time to play right now. We're in the middle of chasing down the woman and some Crew members. Unless there's something else you want us to do?"

"You know where the woman is?" Koltz asked, his thoughts seeming to drift off.

"Inside the store," Zack replied. "We were about to have a look at what they're up to, but if you want to talk about our inefficiencies, we can wait."

"No, no," Koltz said as if he was only partly present.

The other Bound looked at Koltz and at each other, wondering if he was going to continue or just fade into the sunset. They were still waiting on Koltz when Cavan came out the front door, spotted the Bound, and quickly reversed back into the store, taking the rest of the Crew with him.

Koltz shook his head, appearing to come back. "We'll deal with where you two have been later," he said firmly, again in control. "Zack, Mary, you're with me to the front. Pelhem, you take John and cover the back."

Zack and John looked at each other briefly before John grinned and started toward the back of the building.

"Bound out front," Cavan said.

"How many?" David asked.

"I counted five."

As the Crew waited for their instructions, David looked around.

"If we run for it, they'll chase us and pick us off one at a time like they did with Brian. We have the advantage here. The light from the windows will illuminate anyone coming in, while we hide in the shadows. We'll make a stand here. Get some stuff up here to form a line. We'll see if we can put a stop to them when they come in. Derick, go to the back door and see if you can get it open. The rest of us will hold them off here."

"No, you should go to the back," Derick said. "You know you can't shoot straight, and we might end up needing me here."

David considered, then nodded. "Okay. Any other thoughts?" When no one answered, he said, "Let's dig in."

The Crew scrambled to get cover for the coming fight, and David pulled two of them aside.

"Wait, Tami, Deb, we're going to need some wheels sooner or later. You two scoot down the street and see if you can find us a ride. Stay close to the building and make like you're scared customers trying to get out of the way."

"You got it," Debbra said as she tugged at Tami's sleeve. Tami looked toward Cavan before turning to go with Debbra. They didn't bother to look around as they hit the door; instead, they put their heads down and sprinted.

Mary saw them from the street and nudged Zack and Koltz as she pointed. "There go two people, should we chase and find out if they're Crew?"

Koltz looked at the two women running down the street, then back at the Lowe's store. "Let them go. I want the Donnelly woman."

Inside, the Crew set up behind a long counter and formed a picket line.

"Tami, Deb?" Cavan shouted while looking around and staring toward the front door. David grabbed him by the arm. "Woah, buddy, stay put."

"David, Tami's missing, and I can't find Debbra."

"I sent them to find a ride."

"You did what?"

"I sent them to find us a ride, Cavan. We can't do this on foot, sooner or later we're going to need—"

"You sent my wife on a mission with Bound bearing down on us! What the hell were you thinking?"

"I was thinking we're going to need a ride to get the stone to safety, and that's all that matters right now. Everything else comes second, including you being with Tami. Now shut up and get in position." David didn't wait for a reaction. Instead, he turned on his heels and ran for the back door.

Breanne pulled Aleecia aside. "Do you have a gun?" Aleecia shook her head. "Me neither, let's make ourselves scarce," Breanne said as she led Aleecia into the shadows.

The three Bound sprinted to the glass doors and peeked inside.

"It looks like they're forming a picket line," Mary said. "We're going to have a hell of a time getting past it alive."

"Not if we rush it together," Koltz said.

Mary looked at Koltz as if she was finally convinced her boss had turned the bend. "Look at them in there. There's no way we're getting past their line without getting shot."

"We can if we work together," Koltz said. "Zack, I'm going right. As soon as they focus on me, you go left." Zack nodded.

"What do you want me to do?" Mary asked. Koltz smiled and nodded to the opposite side of the door. When Mary looked, Koltz whacked her on the back of the head with the butt of his pistol. Mary's legs turned to jelly; if it hadn't been for Koltz catching her under the arms, she would have fallen to the ground. Koltz half carried, half dragged Mary through the glass doors and pushed her inside. He fired two quick shots into the line of crew members before shoving himself away from Mary and to the right of the store.

Return fire from the Crew was fierce. Bullets slammed into Mary's chest and passed through her body, shredding her organs and shattering the glass doors and window behind her. Mary wavered on her feet for a few seconds longer, before she fell to the floor. As soon as Mary hit the ground, the Crew turned their attention to the right to hunt down Koltz.

Zack took this opportunity to run through the opening that used to be the front door and dove for cover behind a display of paint cans stacked pyramid style on the left. He was fast, but not quite fast enough. A bullet found its target on Zack's right arm just below the shoulder. The force of the bullet knocked him off balance and he simultaneously hit the floor and the pile of cans. Support cans for the bottom of the stack shifted and the pyramid began to topple. Zack rolled back and to the left to get around the corner before the paint cans crashed to the floor. He crawled and scooted around the end of the next aisle, then scrambled to his feet and hurried into the shadows.

"Okay, at least two of them are in," Cavan said. "I'm going right to track the first guy. Derick, go left and track the second. Sam, stay here and guard the front, there's two more out there somewhere. If they come in, shoot them."

"Got it," Sam said.

The sound of gunshots did several things. The gunshots caused David, who was struggling with the back door and a small pry bar, to double his efforts. They caused Aleecia to let out a small cry as she and Breanne moved farther into the darkness. They also created a panicked stir in the people on the street, who were now moving away. And they got the attention of Detective Rogiletti, who was near enough the front of the store to recognize the source of the noise.

Everett Koltz ran down an aisle, two aisles away from the Crew, and walked back up the third to the front of the store. He guessed anyone in pursuit would assume he would try to circle around and try to get behind them, so he tiptoed back to the front. He risked a quick peek around the shelves that concealed him and got a glimpse of the line where the Crew was positioned. He could see at least one of them was still there with attention trained on the front door. Koltz stepped back, looked through the stock on the shelf, and waited.

Zack moved quickly through the dim light. He passed through the window dressings and grabbed a set of sheer curtains as he made his way through the store and past the windows and doors on display. He found a small space between the doors in stock and slipped between them. There was just enough room for him to squat down and tend to his wound.

When he opened the curtains and wrapped one around his arm, he noted that the wound wasn't too serious and wouldn't bleed too badly if he could stem the flow. He tied the curtain tightly around the wound and debated what to do next. Koltz had obviously lost it; if they came across each other in the dark, Zack would kill him. John was still out there somewhere with Pelhem, and Zack wondered how long John would put up with it. He knew his partner well enough to know Pelhem was on his own, and John wouldn't hesitate to lose him in the dark or use him as bait.

Between the Crew and Koltz, Zack determined it would be better to shoot first and sort the bodies out later. He decided to stay put and listen for others, as he waited for an opportunity to present itself.

John and Pelhem were trotting along the side of the building near a dumpster when the shooting began. When they looked at each other, John grinned.

"Maybe you should go back up front and see if they need your help," John said.

Pelhem raised an eyebrow. "I don't think that's what Koltz wants," he said hesitantly.

"Well, it's what I want," John said, launching a punch that landed on Pelhem's left shoulder. Pelhem reeled from the blow, regained his balance, and faced John—but it was too late. The Eradicator flashed and Pelhem flew backward against the dumpster, collapsing in a heap. John didn't bother checking for life; he picked Pelhem up, tossed him into the dumpster, closed the lid, and ran for the back doors.

Merle Rogiletti ran to the front of the Lowe's store, threw himself flat against the outside wall, and peered in through the shattered glass frame. Sam was true to his word and didn't hesitate when it came to shooting. He swung the barrel of his gun toward the movement of Rogiletti's head and pulled the trigger. The bullet buried itself into the frame that, until recently, had supported the window and missed Rogiletti by mere inches.

David Mills dropped the pry bar he was working with and picked up a well-used sledgehammer that was leaning in the corner. He lined up a stroke near the door catch and swung. The bolt bent but refused to give up entirely. His second swing was with more effort, and this time the bolt gave way and the door swung open, slamming against the back wall.

Bright sunlight flooded into the dark room before the door slowly swung shut again. He turned and shouted into the isles.

"Back door is open! Let's go, now!"

To Aleecia and Breanne, David's shouting was a welcome invitation and they headed for the sound of his voice as fast as they could.

David turned back toward the door, and noticed the shadow slowly moving across the gap at the bottom of the door. His fight instincts took over and he reacted quickly, slamming his shoulder into the door and pushing with all his strength. The door shot back open and took John by surprise, and he threw up his hands to protect himself. David hit John with the door with enough force to cause him to stumble but, more significantly, it bent his hand back at the wrist and he lost his grip on the Eradicator. The weapon fell from his hand, and bounced on the pavement.

John reacted with a similar reaction and slammed his shoulder into the door to send it back the opposite direction, hoping to hit whoever was on the other side, but David had stepped back and the door slammed against it's frame before swinging open again.

They recognized each other instantly, and it was David who reacted first. He ran out the door directly at John who took a swing at David's left cheek. But David was fast and raised the sledgehammer, using the handle to block the punch. Instead of hitting David, John caught the handle with his forearm. At the same time, David kicked out and caught John hard on the shin. John was caught off guard and stumbled forward. David grabbed the collar of his shirt and yanked. Physics and momentum overcame John's balance and he fell to the asphalt, grabbing at David as he did, grabbing just enough of David's shirt to slow his fall.

David raised the sledgehammer to bring it down on John, but John had anticipated the move and rolled to the side. The hammer missed John's ribs by inches, crushing the handle and clip of Rogiletti's handgun in the pocket of John's sport coat. David raised the hammer and brought it down again, but this time John thrust out his foot when he rolled and kicked David in the knee. David stumbled back to the open door and, to keep himself from falling, grabbed the door frame.

John rolled to his feet and rushed at David, hoping to drive him back through the door. He expected David to retreat, as was custom when John charged people, but David surprised him by charging back and the collision was fierce. John caught David in the chest with a fist that drove him back through the doorway. His heels caught the doorstep, and David fell back into the store, landing on his back and losing his grip on the sledgehammer. David had used the head of the sledgehammer as a battering ram and caught John just at the lower edge of the ribcage, cracking the lower four ribs on his right side, and generating a groan as the air was forced from his lungs as he fell to his back.

John wasn't used to receiving as much as he gave and he was stunned by the blow David had delivered. He rolled to his side, gulping air, and spotting the Eradicator as he did. As John scrambled to retrieve his weapon, David got to his feet and pulled a pistol from his belt line. John scooped up the Eradicator, rolled to his back, and swung the weapon toward the doorway.

David stepped to the door, raised his gun, and pulled the trigger. But, John had pushed the Eradicator's button, and the yellow ball of light caused David to flinch and the bullet went wide, grazing John's left ribs. The ball of energy caught David squarely in the mouth knocking out his front teeth, as his head snapped back with enough force to break the vertebra at the base of his skull with an audible crunch. David fell backward, and lay lifeless on the floor.

34

Koltz and Eastwood

"**P**olice!" Rogiletti screamed through the opening at the front of the store. "Put your weapon down and come out with your hands in the air!" He knew this was probably a waste of time, but he had to do something.

Sam Dayton wasn't buying the police story. When he heard the noise coming from the back of the store, he wished he hadn't been left alone. He stood slightly and took a quick look over his shoulder. When he did, Everett Koltz raised his 9mm. Sam looked back at the front door and moved to his left to get a better angle on the man out front. Koltz smiled, squeezed the trigger, and shot Sam twice in the back. Sam managed to pull his trigger as he fell, but only shot the ceiling. Rogiletti pushed his back against the wall when the new shots rang out, and Koltz slipped back into the shadows.

The fresh shots caused Aleecia and Breanne to quicken their steps toward the back door. The new shots also caused John to run into the shadows and toward the sound of the gunfire. Seconds later and three aisles deeper into the darkness, the three collided in an aisleway intersection.

John's shoulder crashed into the center of Aleecia's chest. She was lifted off her feet and thrown backward into the shelves, and slammed her head on a display of power saws. John's broken ribs threw waves of pain up his side, and he grimaced as he stumbled to the left and may have even fallen, had he not crashed into Breanne. The collision sent her back the way she'd come for several steps before gravity pulled her backside to the floor.

John was able to stay on his feet and swing the Eradicator at Aleecia, who raised her arms in a feeble attempt to ward it off. John recognized her, grinned, and lowered the Eradicator. He then bent to grab Aleecia, and rendered himself vulnerable to Breanne, who had recovered and found a pry bar on display.

When she got to her feet, Breanne focused her strength and, with a grunt of aggression, swung the bar at John's head. Breanne's grunt triggered John's defense reflexes, and he jerked up his arm in opposition. Instead of the bar hitting his head, Breanne's wrist struck his forearm, which caused her to lose her grip, and when the wrench flew past John, grazing his ear and crashing into the shelves behind him, he reacted quickly and countered with a punch that landed on the side of Breanne's face. Although her feet tried to stay under her, the lights in her mind grew dim and she fell back to the floor and blacked out.

John turned his attention back to Aleecia, whose mind was clearing but who was still in no condition to put up a fight. John pulled Aleecia from the floor and tried to stand her up in front of him to gauge her ability to walk. Although Aleecia's mind was groggy, she understood the danger of resistance and the reaction John would have to a scream. Aleecia let herself fall forward and melt at John's feet, landing within arm's length of Breanne. She grabbed Breanne's limp wrist and hung on as John bent and grabbed her ankle and began dragging. John noticed the strange resistance and looked to see what was causing it.

"I bet your strength gives out before mine," he said with a grin, before trudging confidently toward the back.

Merle Rogiletti peeked in the front window and saw a woman lying on the floor just inside. He waited for several seconds, listening. He could hear commotion coming from inside and decided to see if there was anything he could do for the woman. He got down low and crawled and scooted to the woman on the floor. He could tell from her unblinking eyes that she was dead. He then moved toward a man lying not far away with a gun in his hand. Merle rolled to the man, grabbed him by the wrist, took the gun, and pulled him to the counter to get some cover. The man's chest showed two exit wounds near the heart, but Rogiletti checked for a pulse anyway. Unable to detect a heartbeat he quickly tested the pockets and was surprised to find them completely empty. He inspected the 9mm he had confiscated and checked the clip. Finding it still had bullets. He replaced the clip and headed into the shadows.

Derick Gates was frustrated by the fact that he couldn't find the man he was hunting. He suspected he'd shot him when he came through the door, something the blood trail confirmed. But then the blood trail disappeared, and the man was nowhere to be found.

Cavan heard the noises coming from the back, but instead of heading toward them he continued to look for the man who had come in the front door. The shots from the front made him think the man had tried to get back out, only for Sam to shoot him or at least sent him back inside. Cavan started to move to the front when a shadow crossed at the far end of the aisle. He stopped to listen for movement, then quietly moved to a display of shop-vacs and hunched down to listen for any sound that might give away the man's position. When the man spoke, Cavan jumped.

"I know you're around here somewhere. Why don't we just meet in the open and decide who's the better shot?"

To Cavan, the voice sounded like it was coming from one aisle to his left. He began to backtrack but froze when the voice came again.

"You know you don't stand a chance, right? I mean, I'm becoming quite the marksman and I'm having a good day. Did you see the way I capped the guy you left to guard the front? Bang, all gone. One shot. That's me, Mister One Shot."

Cavan moved toward the center of the aisle near some mailboxes as he tried to formulate a plan. "One lucky shot doesn't make you a marksman, Mister One Shot. Besides, I heard more

than one shot."

"Oh, my name's not really One Shot, it's Everett Koltz, and what's yours?"

"Clint Eastwood."

Koltz grinned as he homed in on the voice, quietly moving to the corner to peer around the shelving on the end. "You know, Clint, that's just one of you pansies I've killed today, you missed the others."

Cavan gauged the distance of the voice and slowly and quietly shifted a stack of mailboxes a few inches to the left to create an opening. "I doubt it," he said. "I just don't think you can count, Koltz."

"That's because you're not counting the two women I killed while they were running away," Koltz said as he took a few steps closer.

Cavan froze. "What two women?" he heard himself ask, then cringed when he heard the concern in his voice.

"The two women who tried to run down the street just a few minutes ago," Koltz said as he continued his creep along the end of the aisle.

Cavan balked. "You lie."

"Do I? Then why is there a quiver in your voice?" Koltz asked, letting out a small chuckle.

Cavan issued a short growl born from anger and fear. "Okay, Everett Koltz." His voice was now coming from the pit of his stomach, down where logic and reason cease and sheer passion and instinct rule. "There's no way you're leaving here alive," he said, slipping between the mailboxes and into the adjoining aisle.

Koltz laughed again. "Really, let's find out." He spun around the corner and fired at boxes where he thought Cavan was hiding, killing the mailboxes inside. Realizing he'd been had, he hesitated for only a second before spinning back around the shelving.

Cavan shot twice through the opening between the stock, grazing Koltz's forearm and piercing the loose sleeve of his shirt, yet inflicting little damage. It was the shock of the shot and gravity that hurt Everett Koltz, the graze causing him to step back and catch his heel on the edge of a floor display. When he fell backward, he stuck out his left hand to protect himself from the fall and landed on it awkwardly. His left wrist bent back, and a wave of pain was sent up his arm as the bone snapped. He reacted by clenching both fists and inadvertently squeezing the trigger. The bullet wasn't friendly as it penetrated the tip of Koltz's right shoe and removed the top of his little toe, causing him to howl through gritted teeth. He used a shelf to pull himself to his feet, cradle his wrist, and limp into the darkness.

Aleecia hung on to Breanne with all the strength she could muster, but she could feel her hands losing their grip. John trudged along toward the back door, reaching the small counter near the back when a shot crossed his chest and the bullet tore into a box of nails. He flung Aleecia roughly behind the counter, stepped over her, and took cover. He lifted the Eradicator over the top of the counter and spotted a shadow to his right. The shadow looked somewhat human-shaped, so he took aim and pushed the button. The yellow ball of light smashed into a cardboard cutout of a woman holding gardening tools, breaking it in half. Derick Gates watched from the opposite side of the aisle, firing at the space the yellow ball had come from and jumping to the right as he did.

A split second later, a yellow ball of light flew down the aisle and smashed into a set of Kobolt tools. Derick shot back and threw himself to the floor, just before another ball of light flew over his head and toward the front of the store.

Rogiletti listened and watched the flashes of light coming from the back. He had begun to move in on Koltz and Mr. Eastwood but couldn't quite make out their positions and the chatter and gunfire had stopped. For all he knew, one or both were now dead. He decided he would head for the back and see if he could do any good there. Besides, it could be Eastwood and Koltz. He slinked toward the sound of the fight, which was apparently just getting started, and stuck his head around a corner to see one of the perps involved. He could also make out the outline of a body on the floor. Whether dead or alive, he didn't know, but he knew he needed to put a stop to it. He moved toward the back counter where the yellow lights were coming from and was surprised by a figure rising from the floor to his left.

"Police officer! Put down—" That was as far as he got. Derick Gates spun at the sound of his voice and leveled his gun, hesitating for half a second as he wondered if the man was really a cop. Unfortunately, his years of training kept Rogiletti from offering the same courtesy, and he reacted swiftly and lethally by sending three slugs into the chest of Derick Gates.

A Full Pair of Red Lips

Everett Koltz moved as silently as he could while trying to put a little space between him and Clint Eastwood. He was breathing heavily, and not just because of his physical pain. He was now fighting strange thoughts of burning children that had to be leftover images curtesy of the Reti.

He groaned as he limped, trying to fight the urge to howl out and run at the first person he spotted, but instead of shooting, Koltz had mental images of throwing his gun as a projectile.

His groaning was, however, not internal, and Cavan moved to follow the sounds; perhaps his shot had done more damage than he'd thought. With Tami stuck in his mind, the emotional pain and anger grew. He wanted another shot at Everett Koltz, so he decided to try Koltz's strategy to see if he could get him to crack.

"I know you're hit, Koltz. Why don't you just lay down your gun and we'll see if we can get you fixed up?"

"Yeah, and why would you fix me up?"

"We're always looking for good people to help us out. Why don't you just change sides and fight for the good guys?"

"You know that's impossible, Eastwood, we'd never trust each other," Koltz said while backing away from the voice. He was in no shape to bring the fight to Clint, and he knew it. When he found a door leading to a small storage room off the aisle, he stepped inside and locked the door. If he could only get a few moments to get his head straightened out, he'd be better.

Cavan heard the door open and close and the bolt slip into the catch. He walked silently down the next aisle until he found the door. It was a steel door inside a steel frame, and Cavan knew he had no chance of breaking in without some major tools. Of course, major tools were no more than a few aisles away.

Tami and Debbra ran down the street, dodging confused people who were gathering in small crowds in the growing chaos as they did.

"Try that one," Tami said.

"It won't work, Tam, we need to get out of this area," Debbra said. "Maybe whatever happened is somewhat local and if we move farther out, we'll have a better chance." There was a sudden noise up the street of people yelling, and a blaring car horn. Tammi and Debbra looked at each other, smiled, and ran toward the sound. The sounds grew louder when they entered a large parking lot, and a Honda Civic weaved between several small groups of people and stalled cars. The Civic was being chased by several people, as if the world were ending and the car was their only chance of survival. Debbra pulled a small .22 from her pocket and pointed the handgun at the driver. When the driver got close, however, he smiled and Debbra lowered her gun.

Ramiro waved, as Wayne tried to avoid a man attempting to grab the handle of the car as it passed. The car then came to a screeching halt directly in front of the girls.

"Want a ride?" Wayne screamed. The women wasted no time running to the back doors, which Ramiro unlocked for them just as they arrived. Wayne couldn't afford to spend the time it took for the doors to close, so he stepped on the gas as soon as he was sure the two wouldn't be left behind. The Civic shot forward, the right fender knocking a cursing man to the ground and simultaneously pulling the open door out of reach of anyone else's grasp as it did. The forward motion slammed the doors shut, as the girls struggled to sit upright.

"What the hell's going on?" Ramiro asked as Wayne maneuvered to avoid another crowd.

"We're not sure," Tami said. "We got the stone, but there were Bound on our tails and suddenly everything went dead."

"We've got the stone?" Wayne asked while swerving to the right.

"We did," Tami said. "But when this happened, we took it on the run. The Bound chased us to a Lowe's, where the guys are holding out. David sent us to try and find a ride, and we're so glad to find you."

"Whatever this is, it must have a limit," Ramiro said. "We must have been just out of range when it happened. We tried getting someone with the radio and got no response and we tried calling, but just got an out-of-service message."

"Who has the stone?" Wayne asked.

"The last I knew, it was Aleecia," Debbra replied.

"Then we need to get back and find her, and pray she still has it," Ramiro said.

"Which way?" Wayne asked, stepping on the gas, again swerving to the left around a couple of cars and onto the sidewalk as Tami gave directions.

Trying to find a second way to Everett Koltz, Cavan checked the area. After finding nothing, he went back to the door and, except for a wire-mesh vent just above the door, decided it was the only way in or out of the storage room.

"Hey Koltz, can you hear me?"

"Sure, I can hear you just fine."

Cavan took a step back and moved to the side of the door at the sound of Everett's voice. Not only did it seem that he was standing right against the other side of the door, but there was a tone to Everett's voice that made Cavan cringe. It was the tone of someone who wasn't worried and one who had already given up and had nothing to lose.

"You know there's no other way out?" Cavan asked.

"What's your point?"

"The point is you're trapped and there's no way for you to get out."

Inside the room, Koltz stood with his back to the door and his head grasped between the heels of his hands, his fingers tightly laced through his hair just above his ears.

"Maybe I'm not supposed to get out. Did you ever think of that? Maybe none of us are supposed to get out, Eastwood." Koltz chuckled. "You Crew members are all alike, you go on believing you're in control. You people think you can save the world, but the world is already lost. You people just won't accept it."

"It's not lost yet, Koltz, and as long as there's a chance, we're going to keep fighting."

Cavan waited for an answer. Inside the room, tears were rolling down Everett Koltz's cheeks. He yielded a low groan of defeat and surrendered to the thoughts running through his mind.

"Tell me something, Eastwood," Koltz said, as he wiped his eyes and looked around at the contents of the room. A tub sink stood in the center of the outside wall. As if he was sent there by design, the room was where most of the flammable chemicals were stored. At the back, three rows of shelves housed various powders and liquids that all wore red warning labels.

"Did you lose anybody important to you in this war?"

"I imagine we all have," Cavan said quietly.

"I suppose you're right, I've lost children," Koltz said. "And do you know what's worse?" he asked as he sorted through the labels on the containers.

"No," Cavan answered.

"Losing them over and over again," Koltz said as he took the lid off a gallon of turpentine and poured half of the contents into a flimsy plastic container.

"That's not possible," Cavan said, except he knew that it was.

"Sure it is," Koltz replied as he moved to the sink and retrieved a bottle of dish soap. "I have lost my children five times now, and this last time was the worst. The Reti find new ways to make you pay, you have no idea what it's really like."

Cavan didn't answer and Koltz squirted some of the dish soap into the turpentine then gave it a swirl.

"You Crew members think you have it bad, always on the run and in hiding until it comes to a fight." Koltz tore off part of his shirt and stuffed it into the mouth of the container to soak up the liquid. "You should try living in constant fear. Fear of not only what's happening on the outside, but fear of what they can do to you on the inside."

Koltz reached into his pocket, pulled out a lighter and, without hesitation, lit the soaked cloth at the top of the container. Like magic, a blue flame glowed.

"It's better to die once than to die a dozen times," Koltz said flatly. "I don't want to play anymore."

With all the strength he could muster, he threw the container at the wire mesh.

The container split down the side as it hit above the mesh resulting in an eruption of flames. The turpentine burned hot and the soap caused the flaming fluid to stick to anything it came in contact with. The blazing solution setting fire to boxes and plastics in the aisle outside the door.

If Cavan hadn't been standing to the side of the door, he would have been engulfed, and he jumped further away from the flames, in total shock of what Koltz had just done.

The new glow coming from the other side of the store was of little concern to Rogiletti. He was still concentrating on the man he had just killed when a ball of yellow light struck the shelves next to him with the force of a flying bowling ball. Rogiletti jumped to his left to hide behind the shelves' steel structure when he saw the figure of a man pointing in his direction. Merle jerked up his weapon and fired.

Aleecia's mind still swam in a shallow pool of dusky murk, but she understood she was in serious trouble. Green Eyes was there, hiding behind a counter and shooting it out with someone. One thought came to the front of her mind; when Green Eyes was finished shooting the rest of the Crew, he'd finish her, and this time it wouldn't be something as mysterious as a heart attack or stroke, and Aleecia knew if she didn't do something, she would be one of the people in the next picture Detective Rogiletti pulled up on his phone. The thought kicked her survival instinct into gear and her mind cleared.

She realized if she moved suddenly, she would catch Green Eyes' attention and climb up his priority ladder to catch the bus to the afterlife sooner rather than later. Green Eyes was bent low behind the counter and she thought about pushing him out from behind the cover, so whoever was shooting at him could have a better shot, but if she failed, he'd have her.

Green Eyes moved to within arm's length of her, and when he bent low again, what she saw might have encouraged a grin in other circumstances.

The physical activity had rumpled John's clothes, his dress slacks having dropped down to the bottom of his hips to reveal his plumber crack.

What a pleasant image, Aleecia thought. *This is not what I want running through my mind if I die, and I probably will die, all because of this stupid stone, and I will . . . I will . . .* and the idea came from somewhere deep inside her.

She reached into her pocket and retrieved the plastic cup holding the stone, popping the lid with her thumb and looked back at John, who had no idea she had moved. She reached up, grabbed the back of his belt, and opened the gap at the back of his pants, and dumped the stone down the track.

John whirled and slapped her hand away, then pointed the Eradicator at her face. Aleecia waited for the yellow flash to announce her death, but instead a look of surprise crossed John's face and his eyes shot open. When he stood up, he lost his weapon as he reached for his head.

The Eradicator dropped from his hand and landed on the counter to his right. The look of surprise on John's face was replaced by a look of pain, and finally of shock. He stood still for only a second before his body twisted and a bullet exited the front of his shoulder. His legs refused to work, and his feet tangled before he tripped and fell to the floor, face up, staring dully at the ceiling.

Acting on instinct, Aleecia moved away from him and toward Breanne. She wanted to make sure Breanne was going to be okay, but she also knew she had to get the stone back. She turned back to John, and hesitated and grimaced briefly, before fumbling with John's belt and unbuttoning his pants. She jerked until the pants opened and she could roll John onto his chest to get at the seat of his underwear. She hesitated once again before she gripped the back of his shorts and pulled them past his backside, where her eyes were drawn to a pair of full red lips that were tattooed on his left butt cheek.

Using the cup, Aleecia reached between his thighs and scooped up the stone. She had only fastened the lid and started to get up when a hand grabbed her shoulder from behind and pulled her back. Losing her balance, Aleecia fell on her butt and looked up into the face of Merle Rogiletti.

"Well, well, look who's turned up after all," he said, before glancing from Aleecia's face to John's bare cheeks. "What the hell . . . Stand up and give me whatever you have in your hand," he ordered.

Aleecia stood and looked at the stone in the cup. "You really don't want this," she said.

"Don't give me any crap, hand it over," he said, reaching for the cup. Aleecia pictured him dumping the stone into his hand and she wanted to save him the shock of what was coming but was unsure how. She decided if she could get the stone back from him quickly, he'd live. She surrendered the cup, which Rogiletti took and held up to the faint glow of the emergency lights as he looked at the shadow rolling around inside.

He jumped in shock as a lead slug plunged into his flesh and sent him reeling against the counter that had sheltered John. Aleecia dropped to the floor as Rogiletti bounced off the counter, staggered once, and fell on his chest. The cup was freed from his grip and rolled across the floor. Aleecia scrambled to it, snatched it before it rolled too far, and quickly shoved the stone back into her pocket.

When Rogiletti moaned, Aleecia went to him and rolled him to his back. The chest of his shirt was soaked with a long streak of blood that covered most of the right side. The death and inhumanity she had witnessed over the past week had finally taken its toll. The man lying before her was not a Bound or even a Crew member. He was an ordinary guy whose biggest fault was ignorance to the truth. Aleecia had reached her limit. She dropped down to her knees while clenching her fists, as her mind led her back to a last resort.

"No!" she screamed. "No, it has to stop! No more! Somebody help me! Somebody, please, help me!"

36

A Strange Smoke Monster

Koltz was locked inside, with little chance of him coming out the room without being consumed by the fire, and still Cavan couldn't leave without making sure he would die. He scanned the aisle, found an empty cart, and quickly filled it with anything he thought would burn. Wooden shims, small cardboard boxes, display catalogues, and store fliers were heaped into the cart and topped off by an open container of paint thinner.

He lined up the cart just beyond the flames and pushed it as hard as he could. It rolled through the blaze until it crashed into the steel door and proceeded to overturn. The paint thinner spilled on the combustible stock and floor, flowing into the already burning flames and igniting at once, with new flames running to lick the door.

Cavan heard Aleecia's screams, and knew he had to respond. She had the stone, and it was what they had already lost so much to protect. Cavan took one last look at the door and, convinced the new inferno would keep Koltz from escaping, sprinted toward the sound of the screaming.

Cavan's actions would mean nothing to Everett Koltz, who was standing near the tub sink and reliving part of a nightmare. The canister holding the burning fluid had split when it hit the mesh, but not all the contents made it out. Some had remained in the container and spilled down his side of the door, causing the fire in the storage room to threaten to ignite everything else.

Koltz leaned against the tub sink and waited for death, as the smoke rose to the ceiling and began to roll back down the wall. He thought about shooting himself in the head and ending it all, but for some reason that seemed to him like it would be breaking the rules. Instead, he considered shooting holes in some of the containers to hasten things a bit. If he was going to die, he could at least decide when. It was Koltz's last ounce of control.

He raised his gun and fired round after round at the containers at the far end of the storage room. They jumped and dumped, and their contents spilled to the floor and surged toward the flames. As soon as the chemicals touched the blaze, a flame danced upstream until it reached the punctured containers. The result was a burst of fire and several small explosions. Koltz was knocked off his feet as the far end of the room turned into a growing inferno. He lay on his back and watched the smoke and flames build on the ceiling, finding himself making mental shapes out of the rolling smoke.

"That's a cow, that's a tree, that's a pig in a tutu," he said aloud.

As he watched, he noticed the smoke being pulled to a spot high above the sink; he cocked his head at what he saw. A vent, painted the same color as the wall that he hadn't noticed before. When he crawled to the sink and used it to pull himself to his feet to get a better look, Koltz discovered it wasn't only a vent, but a rather large vent.

"To get rid of the fumes," he said to the smoke. He climbed into the sink and pried at the louvers, which sprang open. The airflow from outside pulled the smoke past Koltz and through the vent. He pulled harder, and one of the louvers slipped toward him. He grabbed a mop next to the sink, put the handle between the slats, and began to pry.

Aleecia was trying to remember anything she was taught about first aid. She had Merle Rogiletti on his back, with his shirt yanked open.

"Somebody help me!" she continued to yell, but she was beginning to understand her mistake, and the scream was only emitted at half volume. The survival and instinct inhabitants living in the back of her mind were throwing up red flags and setting off flares. Somebody had shot Rogiletti, and they would be coming for her.

Rogiletti's open shirt revealed a wound that seemed to run across the entire width of his chest. Aleecia ripped open a bag of new rags she'd found under the counter and attempted to pack the wound to control the bleeding.

Zack slowly walked up to the counter and peered over the side. The Donnelly woman was trying to help the man he had just shot. There was a second woman with red hair, lying not far away, and John was lying on his stomach mooning him. Zack was about to order the Donnelly woman to her feet or grab her by the hair, when he decided that taking her alive wasn't worth the effort. He started to raise his gun to shoot her in the head when he noticed the Eradicator sitting on the counter. Tucking his gun inside his jacket, he reached out, picked up the Eradicator, pointed it at Aleecia's head, and pushed the button.

The bullet from Cavan's gun completely missed Zack, but it still had the interesting effect of smashing the Eradicator just as Zack pushed the button. The result was an outburst of yellow light equivalent to dozens of camera flashes all going off at once. Cavan and Aleecia were temporarily blinded by the sudden burst of bright light, but to Zack's eyes the effect was much worse, as the image of the light ball etched itself onto the lens of his left eye and the energy burned his face. He screamed and clutched at his ineffective eyes and stumbled into the darkness.

It took several seconds for Cavan to regain his sight, but when he did, he hurried over to the counter and found Breanne now moaning and holding the side of her face. He helped her to a sitting position and almost knocked her back down at the sound of a small explosion on the other end of the building. He walked around the end of the counter and found Aleecia kneeling over a man's body.

"Aleecia," he said, pulling her toward him. "We have to go, this whole building is about to go up in flames."

"What about him?" Aleecia asked, pointing down at Rogiletti.

"Who is he?"

"He's a cop who's trying to arrest me."

"I don't think he's going to be a problem anymore," Cavan said.

"I just can't leave him here, he might die."

"We don't have much choice. He's bleeding pretty badly."

"I won't just leave him!" Aleecia screamed. "He may not know what's going on, but he deserves better than to be left for dead!"

"Trust me, it's for the best," Cavan said.

"I can't just leave him!"

"You have to."

"No! I'm not just going to let him die!"

"Aleecia, you don't understand. We can't take people unless the Bound know about them first."

"No! I don't care who knows about him, I can't, I won't, let him die like this!"

"Aleecia, listen to me. If we take him—"

"No! I've listened to more than I've ever wanted to hear!" Aleecia forced the words past the lump forming in her throat. "The only thing I have left is my sense of humanity! I won't give it up by leaving him here to die. I am not leaving without him!"

Cavan started to object but recognized the resolve in Aleecia's eyes and knew there was no sense in arguing. She had made up her mind.

He shook his head and, for an instant, thought about leaving her. He knew it was what he should do, and he would have to explain to Niles why he didn't do exactly that, but in the end he couldn't bring himself to let her go so quickly.

"Where's the stone?"

"In my pocket. If you want it, you'll have to help me."

Cavan shook his head and reached down to help Aleecia get Rogiletti to his feet.

Cavan grabbed Breanne's hand, and pulled up, and steadied her with his other arm. When Rogiletti's head flopped over, he opened his eyes and looked at Cavan. When Cavan looked back, he stopped and almost allowed the cop to fall back to the floor. Instead, he looked away and spoke as he started to drag Merle toward the exit.

"I'm sorry about this, mister, but she doesn't know any better."

They reached the back door, and found David's body. Breanne let out a cry and bent to touch his face. Cavan pulled her back to his side, tugging her toward the exit.

Out of the black smoke rolling through the vent hole on the side of the store, a lump began to form. As if the vent shaft were giving birth to a strange smoke monster, a blackened and soot-covered Everett Koltz pulled his frame out into the sunlight and gasped to take in air. He allowed himself to fall to the pavement, landing on his back and chugging in the air in huge gulps before he spat out black mucus from the back of his throat.

He rolled to his side and, after a few moments of semi-clear breathing, forced his knees under him and got to his feet. Koltz put his back against the brick wall of the store for support and slid sideways down the wall to get clear from the store and the area. He looked both ways. The front of the store and the crowd out front was to his right, while the back lot, with fewer people, was to his left. He decided the fewer people who tried to help him, the fewer people he would have to kill. Witnesses were a messy business.

Keeping his hand on the store for balance, he stumbled and staggered his way to the corner, allowing his mind to clear as he went. It was apparent that Zack and John were dead. Mary had surrendered her life for the benefit of the cause and who knows what became of Pelhem. In the end, it didn't matter. Koltz would have to get a team together and search the charred remains of the store or the charred remains of the entire neighborhood. No fire truck would get down here anytime soon, and it was probable the whole block would go up in smoke. But Koltz's team would search every building if they had to.

He reached the corner of the building where a silver minivan was parked and looked for the best route, when he noticed four people moving away from the store with two helping two others. He recognized them as Crew members and decided to be safe rather than sorry. Pulling his gun from his pants pocket, pointed it at Aleecia, and pulled the trigger, only to blink at the sound of the metallic *click*. He looked at his nine as if it had back-talked him. He pointed again and squeezed the trigger a second time. The same *click* was all he got.

His mind, still not as sharp as it should have been, didn't perceive the approaching sound until it was right behind him. Koltz spun his head just in time to see a Honda Civic bearing down on him.

His ability to react was slowed by the lack of oxygen, and he wasn't sure if he really tried. The Civic slammed into his left hip and threw him against the minivan. Like a rag doll, he bounced off the side of the minivan and back to the Civic. The gap tightened and he found himself pinned between the two vehicles like clay between a sculptor's hands. His right ankle twisted as it hit the ground directly in front of the Civic's front tire and shattered as the car rolled over it. His good arm fractured as it shattered the side window of the minivan, some ribs snapped and things got worse from there. For better or worse, the Civic finally passed and left a broken Everett Koltz to drop to the asphalt with several cuts, bruises, broken bones, and some internal bleeding. When he fell to the ground, he did so to die.

Cavan and Aleecia heard the noise, looked behind them, and saw the car and crumpled body of the soot-covered man. They also noticed Tami hanging out the rear window and waving madly. Cavan froze and a cry of relief escaped his lips.

"Attagirl," he said as tears welled in his eyes. "Attagirl."

The Civic came to a stop at their side. "You guys need a ride?" Tami said as she opened the back door and stepped out to help.

Aleecia pushed Rogiletti to the door, and, with Deb pulling, got him inside and sitting before climbing in after him. Cavan helped Breanne get in so she could sit on Ramiro's lap up front before climbing in the back and pulling Tami onto his lap. The doors barely shut but they were in and moving.

37

Death Should Be a Release

Zack stumbled blindly through the store for nearly three full minutes before he regained any of his sight; when it did start to come back, it was clouded and shaded by the circular shape of a ball. The flames were spreading rapidly and consuming the store. Zack found his way back to where he last saw John and checked for a pulse. John was alive but unresponsive. Zack debated about leaving him, but decided his partner deserved better than being burned alive. He turned to his right and spotted an oversized garden lawn wagon and pulled it through the thickening smoke to the back counter. He hauled Johns frame into the wagon, pulling up John's drawers as he did. He pulled his partner to the back door and out into the back lot. He had a little trouble rolling over David's body, but the oversized wheels helped.

He got outside just in time to see the Civic leaving the back lot in a hurry. Zack easily guessed what it meant. He started to walk away from the building when he heard moaning to his right and he turned his red swollen face to look over his shoulder. When he spotted Koltz, he pulled the wagon over to his boss, and grinned.

"Hey, Koltz, you look all cactus, how are things going, mongrel?"

Koltz looked up at Zack and simply laid his head down on the pavement.

"That's too bad, Mate. Maybe I can help," Zack said and reached inside his jacket and pulled out his gun and pointed it at Koltz.

"Go ahead Zack, shoot me," Koltz said.

Zack put the barrel of his gun against Koltz's lips and thought it over. "I don't think so. There are fates worse than death, and I think you're going to be living one. You told me death should be a release and I don't think I'm authorized to release you. That would be up to the Reti, and we should let them have the final say." Zack tucked away his gun and bent down to pick Koltz up.

"You pussy," Koltz said, trying to get Zack to shoot.

"Now is this any way to treat someone who's trying to help you?" Zack asked as he reached down with his good arm and clamped his hand around the ankle of Koltz's broken leg and began pulling him to the wagon. Koltz screamed twice but then fell silent when he blacked out. Zack half lifted, half drug Koltz to lie on top of John, picked up the handle to the wagon and wandered off into the growing chaos.

38

The Orbit of Life

Forty-eight hours later, Aleecia sat in a chair next to the bed that supported a comatose Merle Rogiletti. His face was swollen and bruised, but his chest wound had been tended to and he would live. Still, she sat with her face in her hands and tears in her eyes.

"That's why Cavan wanted me to leave him?" she asked quietly.

"Exactly," Niles said. "The plain truth is, if he would have died in the fire his family would mourn his loss but carry on. Unfortunately, now they are all at risk."

"And now I'm responsible for endangering all the people he cares about," she said.

Niles reached out and touched her hair. "You can't look at it like that, Aleecia. If you do, you'll go crazy in the first month. You did what you thought was right, but you'll find the things you know as right and wrong will change with knowledge."

"And by saving his life I probably destroyed the lives of the people who were close to him?"

Niles shrugged. "You may have made the Reti and the Bound aware of him, and they will seek out the people he knows if they think there is anything to be gained by paying them a visit. They won't hesitate to hurt them."

Aleecia shook her head slowly. Niles patted her reassuringly. "The fact is, we can sometimes save lives by occasionally giving one up."

"Is that where I am now, giving up lives to save others? I don't think I can make those kinds of decisions."

"It's a tough spot, I know."

Aleecia bowed her head.

Niles lifted her chin. "Let me give you some news which might make it a little easier. The stone you helped us recover is incredibly special. As it turns out, it's no ordinary Perception Stone. It has been modified, we suspect reformed or reprogrammed by a renegade. It is why Dan was not killed when he read the stone, and how he came to know and understand the situation he was in. Apparently, the stone forced into his mind the information he needed to fight and survive. That's why he knew how to do the things he did. If the Reti had gotten this stone, we would never know the possibilities it represents. There is talk that we might be able to get enough information through this stone to alter the others in our possession, and even use them to communicate the way the Reti do. You may have helped us take a huge step in defending ourselves.

"As far as saving Rogiletti, you made a mistake and may have put his family and friends at risk, but you probably helped save millions of others. It's a fair trade."

It took four days before Merle Rogiletti recovered enough to meet with the Crew and three more before he was healthy enough to absorb some knowledge. He now sat in a chair at a dining room table flanked by Aleecia, Niles, Breanne, Cavan, Tami and a few others.

"And now you're going to explain all this?" he asked motioning toward the Crew members and the cabin they were in.

"Sort of," Aleecia said. "Your wounds have healed well enough and we think you can tolerate a history lesson."

"A history lesson," Rogiletti repeated, rolling his eyes to the side out of frustration. "I don't think a history book is going to explain all this."

"No, no it won't," Aleecia said.

Cavan produced a clear tube with a hinged lid that he placed before Rogiletti. "The history books you're used to are full of fairy-tales and lies, so we're going to introduce you to something you're not going to understand or believe."

Niles picked up the tube and flipped open the lid, and dumped the small blackish-red transparent stone into the palm of his hand."

"This," Aleecia told him, "is a Narration Stone." Rogiletti studied the stone that Niles held and looked at Aleecia. "You had a stone in a cup at the store, but it was bigger, this has to do with that," he said flatly.

"Oh, he's good," Tami said and smiled at her husband.

"That's correct," Niles said. "But that one is headed for the bottom of the sea."

Merle let out a loud sigh.

Aleecia took Merle by the wrist and gently pulled his hand over the table. She turned his palm upward and calmly straightened his fingers as she looked him in the eye.

"Now, pay attention. We're going to share something with you. You need to accept and understand this information. It is not something you can dismiss as a good story. After you've heard it, you will still have trouble believing it. After you've been exposed to it, you will question everything you've ever known. The lives of everyone you know depends upon your accepting the truth and throwing away what you've come to believe as fact. Open your mind and you will see the world the way it really is."

Merle raised his eyebrows and locked eyes with Aleecia. "You're so full of lies and delusions."

Niles grinned. "No, Detective. The truth is you are the one filled with lies and delusions." He flipped his hand over Rogiletti's and caught the stone between their palms.

There was a slight pause and black air.

And then the truth spilled into Merle Rogiletti.

The end . . .

of the beginning.

39

Epilogue

H e awoke in a sweat and with a loud groan. Laying still for a few minutes, he allowed himself a chance to consider the dream he'd had, after all it was different. Until now these dreams were about escape and survival; but now, it was time to fight, and just like before, Daniel Knocks knew what he needed to do.

Author's Note

Greetings, and thank you for choosing the *Atlantis* series. I hope you enjoyed this first book as much as I did.

When I began sharing this first story in the series, I was asked by some of my beta readers where the inspiration came from. In case you have the same question, I'll explain it the best I can.

First, I have to tell you that I have a very logical and analytical mind which always looks for facts over fiction, and is in constant conflict with my imagination that I can't seem to slowdown. Now, that seems like it would be a problem, but as it turns out, it's really good for writing logical fiction.

The inspiration for the Atlantis series comes from the questions that we either can't answer or we are too afraid to answer. After all, questioning the past can be scary and the answers can be hard to accept, especially for cultures that are resistant to change. But, as for me, there are so many unexplained scientific gaps in our history of existence, that I just had to start asking those hard questions. When you ask those questions with the goal of finding a logical possibility, you need to look at the tangible evidence left behind by generations and civilizations that came before. Some of these departed civilizations left no clues at all to what happened, and some clues left to us we simply don't understand. But from the clues left behind we must look at all the possibilities and consider the likelihood of what took place.

The logical part of my brain makes coincidences a struggle for me. Not that I don't believe that coincidences happen, but because, it seems to me, that we have a tendency to use it as an excuse for avoiding critical thinking, and they very seldom hold up to the scientific principles.That being said, one of the things that intrigued me most as I researched the information needed for such a story as this, is the fact that ancient megalithic structures exist all over the globe.Structures at Göbekli Tepe, Stonehenge, Puma Punku, Teotihuacan, and Angkor Wat are just a few. Evidence tells us that these structures were built thousands of years ago, but what intrigues me is that they were built using technology we can't replicate or even understand. They were presumably constructed by people who supposedly never communicated with each other and yet the similarities of some of these structures is uncanny. I know some people will stick with the coincidence theory, but my logical mind won't except that, and I have to consider the probability the the information on how to create these colossal structures was shared between these distant cultures.Thus the logical part of my brain infuses the need for a way for someone to pass that information along, and while I was considering that notion, my imagination interrupted with a though of it's own.The two sides agreed to collaborate, and the *Atlantis* series is the result.

Now, if you do your own research, you will find that some of the information included in this story, to be fact. For example, we are now storing digital data on crystal, do a search for 5D storage and you'll see what I mean. And, in 1977, some of the best minds of the time launched the voyager probes with the intent of leaving our solar system. Both probes are now traveling interstellar space. Both probes are carrying information about us with the hope of contacting an alien intelligence. I just hope when discovered that information will not be considered as a menu. But,these are just a few examples included in my Atlantis stories. I think I'll leave the rest for you to research so you can come to your own conclusions.

Now, I know some of you are thinking that the gray aliens might have been used out of convenience, and I'll admit it was nice the way it worked out, but the research I did with NASA specialist, medical doctors, and with people who spent time in space, supported using the data. The timetable I used to travel to, or from, a distant planet located within the constellation of Reticulum is fairly accurate, and the physical body changes that might occur over generations of weightless space travel are arguably correct as well.

Speaking of being arguably correct, I do want to take this opportunity to apologize to the Aussies if I have misused the terms when speaking with Zack. If anyone see a need to correct what I have done, I'd be happy to hear where I went wrong. Well, that's not exactly true, but I'd still rather hear about it than portray myself as a doofus in the next books. Zack will be around in the next book *Atlantis: the Tree*, and I'd like to make him sound as authentic as possible.

Speaking of the next book, I'd like to mention that, at its conception, this was intended to be a one book deal. But the farther it went, the more questions came up and the more I realized I need to fulfill the promises I made to you, and answer those questions. Starting something in the story that raises questions, generates the need to answer those questions, else it would not be fair to you, and I would probably get the hate mail. So questions like, what happens to Dan? What does the research reveal about the stone? What will the Reti do next? And the very important question of what happens to John now that he's been exposed to the same stone as Dan? (That last one is a clue by the way) these questions and more will be answered in the second book, *Atlantis: the Tree*, and then the third book, *Atlantis: the Storm*. I hope you'll enjoy those stories as well.

I look forward to entertaining you with stories for many years to come, and I truly hope something good happens for you as we travel into the unknown future.

Douglas Hoover, Charlevoix, Michigan, June 2024.

About Doug

I could break into the standard blurb like – Douglas Hoover lives in Charlevoix, Michigan – and such, but it always seemed too clinical to me. Instead, I'll just give you a run down on how I got on this path.

I first discovered my passion for writing as a young teen, but a lack of mentoring, and encouragement left those paths distant. I've always written stories as a hobby and those stories became my escape to better places. After a successful battle with cancer, my wonderful wife, Cheryl, asked me to pursue my true passion and begin writing full time. So I put aside my multimedia design business to follow this path.

I was asked once, if I wanted to be a personal kind of author, where people can get to know me, or if I wanted to keep myself at a distance. It really wasn't a choice for me, as I have always been the person to yell 'Everybody in the pool!'. Over all, I like people and enjoy making them smile. For the most part people are fun, and most are ready to smile if just given an excuse to do it. I have never been that aloof kind of a guy. If you'd like to reach out to me, please visit my website at www.dwhoover.com.

Along with the books in Atlantis series there are several other projects in the queue. Visit my website at *dwhoover.com* to learn more.

Part of literary success comes from the help of readers like you. Your thoughts and opinion can drive and lift stories to new heights. If you enjoyed this story, please leave a review.

Acknowledgements

I want to thank all the people who helped this come to fruition. Whether it is from directing software paths or inspiring the creative process, or sharing your wisdom or resources, please know that your help and encouragement is vastly appreciated. Here's a list of few out of the many.

Cheryl Hoover, Erin McKnight, Brandy Thomas, all my beta readers, Damonza, NASA, Dawn Ursula, Michael Kramer, Jennifer Mendenhall, all the great people with UPPAA and IPNE, Joshua Chadd, and many more who know who they are. Thank you so much!

Also by

Along with the next books in Atlantis series, there are several other projects in the queue. Visit Doug's website at *dwhoover.com* to learn more about Doug and upcoming books.

Part of a books and a literary series success come from the help of readers like you. Your thoughts and opinion can drive and lift stories to new heights. If you enjoyed this story, please leave a review, this author would appreciate hearing your thoughts.